MW00852505

The Maine

Attraction

Morgan Gauthier

This is a work of fiction. Names, characters, places, and incidents either are the product of the author's imagination or are used fictitiously. Any resemblance to actual persons, living or dead, events or locales is entirely coincidental.

The Maine Attraction

Copyright © by Morgan Gauthier 2022

All rights reserved. Printed in the United States of America. No part of this book may be used or reproduced in any manner whatsoever without written permission except in the case of brief quotations embodied in critical articles and reviews.

For more information visit www.morgangauthier.com

Library of Congress Control Number:

ISBN (paperback) 978-1-7368282-9-8

ISBN (ebook) 978-1-7368282-8-1

For Bradley. Always.

One

RAMSEY

Being the only daughter and youngest of seven children, raised by a self-made father and Irish Catholic mother, Ramsey Price was not a giggly girl by nature. But walking into her office after lunch and seeing two dozen roses with her name on them, put a smile on her face.

Two years ago, when she accepted her job as an archivist at the *Museum of the American Revolution* and moved in with her favorite brother, Sean, she didn't expect life to get any better. But just three months into her transfer, on one of her early morning jogs, she literally bumped into one of the most handsome men she'd ever laid eyes on.

David Miller was number eight on the *Top 40 Under 40 Professionals to Watch* list. Apart from his success as a lawyer and countless philanthropic endeavors, his blonde hair, sea blue eyes, dashing smile, and how incredible he looked in a tuxedo were some of the things she admired most about him. Every time they went out, she knew she was the most envied woman within a hundred miles. Who wouldn't be jealous she was dating the most eligible bachelor in Philadelphia, who just so happened to look exactly like Ryan Gosling?

But dating David had its ups and downs, just like any other relationship. Was he guilty of canceling dates last minute because he took on a new case? Yes. Had he stood her up more times than she could remember because he was too busy schmoozing with his bosses to climb the corporate ladder? Absolutely. Did he joke that he already had a wife, and her name was "Work"? Unfortunately.

But then, on a random Friday, he sent her two dozen roses with a romantic handwritten note attached, inviting her to join him for dinner. *A dinner she would never forget.* That's what his note said. And Ramsey knew exactly what would make this dinner unforgettable. David Miller was finally going to propose!

Mrs. David Miller. Mrs. Ramsey Miller. Mrs. Ramsey Price-Miller?

She mulled the options over silently. Would her mother freak out if she hyphenated her last name? Hell, her mother would be ecstatic she was getting married, she might not even bat an eye over the idea of keeping her maiden name. And in a few days, when she went back to Maine for Sean's wedding, she wouldn't go alone or empty handed. Ramsey would have a gorgeous man on her arm and an expensive diamond on her left hand.

"Ramsey!"

She jumped in her seat, slamming her knee against her wooden desk.

"Are those from *him*?"

Poppy McGuinness, another archivist, and consequently Ramsey's best friend, stared at her with puppy-dog eyes. Never without a romance novel in her bag, the pint-sized redhead was always on the lookout for Mr. Right. Unfortunately, she'd already dated Mr. Wrong, Mr. Broke, Mr. Unemployed, and Mr. Liar-Liar-Pants-On-Fire. But those failed relationships and past hurts never deterred her from believing one day, she'd find the Romeo to her Juliet. Though, Ramsey had tried to explain multiple times she should be looking for a love story less tragic to emulate.

"What does the note say?" Poppy swooned, her blue eyes watering with happy tears.

Ramsey smiled, though her grin would never be as wide and wondrous as her friend's. She wasn't the type of person to wear her emotions all over her face. Some called it *resting bitch face*, but it was just her neutral expression.

"He wants me to join him for dinner tonight." Ramsey passed the note to Poppy, who brushed her wild curls from her face, and devoured each word David had written.

"At Vino?" Poppy squealed, crinkling the invitation in excitement. "Oh, Ramsey, I'm so sorry, I didn't mean to ruin it."

She waved her hand in the air, "It's not a big deal -"

"Not a big deal? Vino is the most expensive and exclusive restaurant in the city!"

"I meant, you wrinkling the note isn't a big deal." Ramsey took the card and slipped it into her purse.

"Do you think he's going to propose?" Poppy bit her bottom lip, as if that would contain her excitement.

"I don't know." *She hoped so.* "I guess we'll see."

"What else could it be?" Her friend jumped up from her seat and started to pace their library-looking office. "You'll have to wear your nicest dress, and make sure your nails are done, so you can take lots of pictures."

Poppy's energy was infectious. Ramsey nodded with a tight-lipped smile, her normal grin, and flashed her manicured black nails, "Got my nails done three days ago."

"Black?" Poppy crinkled her nose. "Rams. Really? Would pink kill you?"

In fact, pink could very well kill her. She wore black, grey, white, and on occasion, red. But that was when she would go to a Phillies baseball game with her brother. Pink was not her color. Her long, straight, platinum blonde hair and pale skin demanded her to stay away from wearing bright colors. Her eyes, though blue, even looked grey on most days.

Poppy was the exact opposite. If she didn't have on at least three or four different colors at all times, she felt off. Mixing patterns as well as colors was her favorite pastime. And she wouldn't be caught dead without her signature red lipstick and red nail polish. Color was everything to Poppy.

When they would go out for a girls' night, no one thought they knew one another. Poppy was short and bubbly. Ramsey was tall and serious. Poppy was dressed like a rainbow unicorn, and Ramsey looked like a black widow. But somehow, their differences in appearance and personality were what drew the two of them together from the first day they met two years ago. Poppy brought joy into Ramsey's life, and she brought stability to Poppy's.

"He said to be ready by six, I think." Ramsey shoved her hand inside her purse to retrieve the card to doublecheck.

"Seven." Poppy corrected. Of course, she had every detail memorized after reading it once. "I can't believe when you come to work Monday morning, you'll be the future Mrs. Miller! I wonder what kind of engagement ring he bought. You know it must be expensive. Oh, I bet it's the biggest diamond in Philadelphia. You're so lucky. If I didn't love you, I'd hate you, Ramsey Elizabeth Price."

"Using my full government name. You must be serious." She winked at her petite friend.

The redhead's smile disappeared. "What are you going to tell him?"

"What do you mean?"

"Are you going to accept when he proposes?"

Poppy's question would seem odd to anyone but the two of them, but she'd been there every time Ramsey had waited for hours at a restaurant or movie theater for David not to show up. She'd been the one she called whenever he cancelled a vacation last minute or took another work call and they'd missed their reservation. Poppy, although a romantic to the very core of her soul, was very protective of Ramsey and might try to fight David if he failed to show up to his own wedding.

Ramsey paused before answering. *Would she accept if David proposed?*

"I think so," she nodded.

Poppy smiled, back to her perky self. "Your wedding is going to be amazing! If I'm not your Maid of Honor, I'm going to burn the city to the ground. Not really. But you know what I mean."

She rested her hand on Poppy's shoulder. "I'm envisioning black bridesmaids dresses."

Poppy gasped. "Black is bad luck for a wedding, Rams."

Ramsey shrugged. "I'll take my chances." By this time on Monday, she would be ordering business cards with her new name.

Two

Ramsey

Ramsey rushed through the door of her brother's red-brick row house in Society Hill. She had a couple hours to get ready before her date with David. *A dinner she would never forget.* That line kept flashing in her mind and she was almost excited enough to dance. Almost.

When she found out she'd been offered the archivist job, Sean was the first person she called. Since childhood, they'd been inseparable, even going to the same college, two years apart. He was so excited for Ramsey to move to the city, he offered her a room in his row house, and she gratefully accepted, promising she'd find a place of her own as soon as she got settled. But Sean couldn't part ways with her and told her to stay indefinitely. Ramsey was more than happy to pay him rent and spend her free time with him and his fiancé, Cali.

Ramsey slipped into the little black dress David claimed was his favorite when she heard a key unlock the front door. Perfect timing. She shouted down the stairs, thinking it was her brother. "Sean, I need you to zip up my dress! I don't want to be late."

"Rams, it's me," Cali yelled as she took the steps two-by-two up to the second floor. She pushed the bedroom door open, and her jaw dropped. "Girl, you look gorgeous! Where are you going?" She zipped the back of Ramsey's dress and circled around to get a better look.

Cali's perfectly straight smile looked bright against her brown skin. Her brown eyes scanned her up and down. "What's the occasion?"

Ramsey quickly showed her the note and told her about the roses she had left at her office. By the time she was done telling Cali all about David's gesture and Ramsey's suspicion of a proposal coming her way, Cali was squealing and dancing.

"Rams! I am so happy for you!" Cali threw her arms around Ramsey's neck and giggled. "You'll have to call me as soon as he proposes!"

"I will, I promise." Her phone buzzed and when she saw who texted, her stomach dropped. It was David. *Was he cancelling again? Had work pushed her to the back burner once again?*

"What's wrong?" Cali sliced through her thoughts.

Ramsey hesitantly snatched her phone off the bed, entered her passcode, and opened his message. Relief washed over her when she read, *Look outside*. She rushed to the window that overlooked the street and parked outside the house was a limo. David was wearing a custom-tailored suit holding a bottle of champagne and two glasses. His smile nearly knocked her off her feet.

Cali sighed, looking out the window alongside her. "Your engagement ring is probably the size of Texas."

Ramsey kissed Cali on the cheek and grabbed her purse. "I'll call you."

"Sean and I are going to the *Mythical Sea Breeze* tonight. Maybe you and David could meet us for a celebratory drink?"

She loved Cali too much to say no. Even if that meant seeing that troll, Nico Giovanni, on her special night. "Alright, I'll see you later tonight, then."

The limo ride hadn't exactly gone the way Ramsey had anticipated. And sitting through dinner was worse.

She glanced across the table where her beau was jabbering away on yet another late call from the office. Even when he was with her, he wasn't present. To keep from rolling her eyes or sighing to nab his attention, Ramsey slipped her phone out of her Louboutin purse, another gift to beg her forgiveness after he'd forgotten their first anniversary, and touched the screen. A picture of the couple flashed and she smiled. They'd gone to Hawaii on a whim for their first vacation, back when David was spontaneous. She looked so happy in that picture, but he looked distracted. Not even a trek through the Hawaii Volcano National Park could tear him away from responding to his emails.

"Ramsey?" David's blue eyes scanned her face in search of answers, but she wasn't about to give him the satisfaction of knowing how irritated she was. "Honey, are you alright?"

"I'm great." But Ramsey wasn't great. She wanted to scream at him. She wanted to smash the two hundred bottle of champagne he ordered for their *special night* on the floor. She wanted to make a scene worthy to grace the stages of Broadway. But instead, she swallowed her Irish rage and nodded her head, flashing the best smile she could muster.

David grinned and lifted his champagne flute. Ramsey fumbled to grab hers, nearly spilling it all over the white linen tablecloth. "To us," he said, beaming in pride. "Without you, I never would have made partner so soon."

"Is that *all* we're celebrating?" The question slipped out of her mouth as the waiter cleared their plates. Ramsey thought maybe he'd hidden the ring inside the dessert, but after digging through her slice of cake like an archaeologist searching for lost treasure, she came up empty handed.

For a split second, fear shadowed his joyful face. She could see him scrambling through his mental calendar, wondering if he missed another anniversary or birthday, but right when she thought he had something to say, he shook his head and smiled again. "Yes," he said with confidence and that's when she lost her patience.

"So, all of this," Ramsey motioned around the room packed with some of the richest people in Philadelphia, "is to celebrate you making partner?"

"Ye-es?" He glanced around before leaning forward. "Is something wrong? Is there something you want to celebrate?"

Earlier that afternoon, when David sent two dozen roses to her office with an invitation to join him for a *"dinner she would never forget"* she assumed he'd be on bended knee asking her to be the future Mrs. David Miller. Not toasting to more work and more time spent apart.

"I thought you were going to propose to me." Ramsey whispered and when his brow furrowed, she knew she'd made a mistake.

"Propose to you?" David scratched his clean-shaven jaw. "That's crazy. Why would you think I was going to propose to you tonight? We've never even talked about getting married before."

They had talked about marriage before. Well, not really talked, so much as Ramsey mentioning she'd like to get married one day and him nodding while pounding away at his keyboard.

"We've been together for almost two years." *One year, nine months, and twenty-two days, to be precise.* She gripped the steam of her glass so tightly she thought it might shatter. "Why is it crazy for me to think about our future together?"

"I thought we were focusing on our careers?"

Ramsey leaned back in her chair, flipping her long platinum blonde hair behind her. "I have a jewelry box filled with diamond earrings, pearl necklaces, and more watches than I know what to do with, all apologies for you standing me up on dates, or canceling trips last minute." He shifted in his seat, and she knew she should let the issue die, seeing they were in public, but she didn't. She couldn't. "How long do you expect me to wait for you to make me a priority?"

"Ramsey," he didn't make eye contact with her, "I think this is all a bit selfish on your part, don't you think?"

"Selfish?" Now, her blood was boiling.

"This is supposed to be *my* night, and you're ruining it by starting an argument."

"Are you wasting my time?" Ramsey cut him off and crossed her arms over her chest.

"Look," he sighed, "I'm not ready to get married. But that doesn't mean I don't want to marry you one day."

"You're thirty-three, David." She reminded him, playing with her steak knife, which made him visibly uncomfortable. "When do you think you'll be grown up enough to marry me?"

"Maybe by the time I'm forty -"

Ramsey flinched like she'd been slapped. "Forty?" She slammed her hand on the table, rattling the silverware. "You want me to date you for another seven years without any guarantee of marriage?"

"I didn't know it was that important to you."

"I'm a woman, David," Ramsey hissed. "Of course, marriage is important to me."

"You should have said something before, so you didn't have to cause a scene in public," he said through gritted teeth, smiling at a nearby table.

"You haven't even met my parents. Every time we plan a trip to visit them, you end up canceling, and I show up alone. My mother thinks I made you up." She moved her clenched fists off the table and rested them in her lap, dissuading herself from punching him like she would one of her brothers.

"Maybe we can discuss us living together, so you'll calm down a bit." Well, that was definitely the wrong thing to say. "Where are you going?" David asked when she stood up, although he was more focused on smiling at the other patrons, doing his best to mask the fact they were fighting.

"I'm leaving."

"Ramsey -"

"Don't touch me," she wiggled free of his grasp, drawing attention from other diners.

"I'll call you tomorrow, after you've had a chance to calm down."

"Unless you're calling to propose," Ramsey snatched her bag from the table and pulled the hem of her black dress down, so it laid flat against her thighs, "don't call me at all."

"Be reasonable, sweetheart," he followed her toward the exit, still smiling like a pageant queen for the benefit of other people. "We'll give each other a couple of days to cool off and then we can discuss this. I'll finally meet your family next weekend at your brother's wedding. Maybe it'll spark something in me."

Ramsey slammed the restaurant door open and stomped down the front steps toward the busy sidewalk only turning around when he practically shouted her name. "I don't want to see or talk to you. And you can forget about meeting my family at Sean's wedding."

"Ramsey -"

"Let's be honest, David, you'll probably come up with another work-related reason why you have to cancel. I'm done looking like an idiot. And I certainly don't need any more expensive gifts to buy my forgiveness. Enjoy your promotion. Hopefully you don't wake up one day ten years from now wondering why you're still alone."

She didn't stick around for his rebuttal. She turned on her heel and clicked her way down to the *Mythical Sea Breeze* where she knew she could get a much-needed drink.

Three

RAMSEY

Ramsey ripped the creaky, wooden door of the *Mythical Sea Breeze* open, and all eyes darted to her as she marched toward her older brother sitting at the mahogany polished bar. Sean stopped his glass midway to his lips as she smacked her purse on the stool next to her with a huff.

"Well, isn't this a delight." Nico, her brother's college roommate and best friend of ten years, threw a black and white checkered towel over his shoulder and planted his hands on the tabletop directly in front of her. "Queen Elsa decided to leave her castle of ice to drink with us common folk."

Ramsey narrowed her eyes, cocking her head to the side. "Did the trolls not need their king tonight? I was sure there'd be a virgin or two needing to be sacrificed."

Nico smirked, his brown eyes dancing in mischievous delight, "I was just telling your brother I was surprised you cut your trip to Boston short."

"Why?" She winked, "You miss me?"

"What a ridiculous thing to say. No." He cupped his stubbled chin in one of his hands, elbows rooted to the bar. "Boston is close to Salem where your kind were burned. I'm shocked they didn't sniff you out the moment your hooves crossed into Massachusetts."

"Sticks and stone, Nicole. Sticks and stones." Ramsey slapped her hand on the counter, drawing the attention of other patrons. "No, means no, bar keep," she screeched loud enough for the women ogling Nico to her left could overhear. "I told you before and I'll tell you again, I don't want to see what a micro-penis looks like. I just want you to pour me a shot."

The three women grimaced and retreated to a small booth on the other side of the bar to finish their martinis.

Nico squinted at her, his dark brown hair whisking in front of his forehead as he bent to grab a bottle of vodka, Ramsey's least favorite liquor, and poured her a shot. "One shot of orphan tears for the Lady Satan."

Sean shook his head and sipped his Guinness draft. "It's a wonder you two aren't happily married yet, bickering the way you do."

"He wishes," Ramsey drank the shot to spite Nico.

"Every birthday when I blow out my candles." Nico wiggled his eyebrows, blowing a kiss at Ramsey.

She caught the kiss, threw it at the scratched-up wood floor, and stomped on it.

"You know," Sean rested his forearms on the counter motioning for Nico to pour him another beer, "some people think you two might secretly love each other."

"Some people being you and your fiancé I imagine." Ramsey shoved the empty shot glass toward the edge of the bar, but Nico caught it before it could shatter on the floor. He clicked his tongue, wagging a finger at her. "Speaking of Cali. Where is she?"

"She's in the bathroom. She should be back any second." Sean tapped his phone, a picture of him and Cali holding drinks in hollowed out coconuts on the Mexican Riviera popped up. He glanced at the date and time on the screen and squared his shoulders to his sister. "Wait, I thought you were out with David for some special dinner tonight."

Ramsey snatched Sean's freshly poured Guinness and guzzled half the stein before he had a chance to object. Nico poured Sean another and slid it across to him.

Ramsey wiped the froth from her mouth and shook her head. "David told me to get dressed up because we were celebrating something special. I thought tonight would be the night he proposed."

"I take it, he didn't propose?" Sean spied her ringless left hand.

"As soon as our appetizer was delivered to our table, he took my hands in his and said, *Ramsey, I got the promotion.*" She polished off the stein and whipped it down the counter for Nico to snag. "No proposal. All that effort for a stupid promotion."

"Well, that's a big deal for him." Sean attempted to play devil's advocate. He crossed his arms and leaned against the counter.

"Pick me up in a limo big?" Ramsey's left eye twitched and she slammed a hand up to cover it before Nico could make a snotty remark. "We've been together for almost two years. Not one serious conversation about us getting married. I'm not getting any younger."

"Got that right." Nico saluted her with his shot glass and downed its contents.

"Ramsey!" Cali wrapped her arms around Ramsey, a huge grin spreading across her face. "Let me see it! Let me see it!" She lifted Ramsey's left hand and saw it was bare. She turned her hand over to double check. "Did the ring not fit?"

"He didn't propose."

"Oh, Rams!" Cali hugged her again. "I'm sorry!"

"I'm not." Ramsey snorted. "I told him not to speak to me again unless he was proposing. Then I stormed out of the restaurant."

"Ultimatums." Nico cocked his head to the side with a smirk. "Every man's flashing neon sign to propose."

"As fun as all *this* is," Ramsey motioned a lazy hand up and down Nico's lean, muscular, Italian body, "maybe take the night off, Nikita. I'm feeling real Godzilla-like and I'm on a warpath."

Nico leaned over the counter and whispered with a wicked grin, "Let's tango, Lucifer."

"I loathe you," Ramsey whispered back, inching closer to his lips.

Ah, the uncomfortable game. Ramsey couldn't remember exactly when she and Nico started playing but the game was simple. Whoever could make the other one uncomfortable enough to back away would lose. And she wasn't in the habit of losing to the Philadelphia native.

"Oh, no," Nico said in a baby voice. She could smell the liquor on his breath and hated that she enjoyed the scent. "Not my feelings."

"Excuse me!" A middle-aged woman snapped her fingers to grab Nico's attention. "Can I get some service around here?"

Nico winked at Ramsey before turning his laser eye focus to the woman with a hand on her hip. "Well, not with that attitude."

The customer's mouth dropped. "What did you just say?"

"Oh, sorry," he wiped his hands clean before leaning closer to shout each word separately. "I. Said. Not. With. That. Attitude."

Her arms crossed over her chest, her nostrils flaring. "I want to speak to your manager."

"I'll do you one better," Nico clapped his hands. "I'll grab the owner instead."

"Perfect," she licked her lips, looking eager to demand his job.

Nico held his index finger up, signaling her to wait. "One second." He turned in a complete circle, lifted his arms up, and said, "Ta dah!"

"You've got to be kidding me." The customer planted her hands on her hips with a scowl.

"I'm not much of a kidder, Karen." Nico shook his head, pursing his lips. "But if you don't like the service, you are, in fact, free to go."

"I have never -"

Nico waved his hand in the air cutting her off. "Yeah, yeah, yeah. Go on, get. I'm sure there's someone else out there whose night you can ruin."

She huffed and stomped out of the bar, slamming the door on her way out. Snickers from regulars filled the hole in the wall bar as Nico situated himself back in front of Ramsey to continue their game of *whoever-gets-uncomfortable-first-loses*.

Sean cleared his throat. "How are you still in business?"

"I don't know." Nico shrugged and smiled like the Cheshire Cat at Ramsey. "Perhaps it's my charm."

"As charming as food poisoning," Ramsey arched her back to crack it, presenting her chest to Nico.

"Should I be flattered that you think I'd be tempted by that shameless attempt at seduction?" Nico crossed his arms over his chest, leaning his back against the coolers.

"I catch you looking down my shirt all the time, Nicolette." Ramsey stood on her tip toes to stretch over the counter, revealing more cleavage. "Don't get shy on me now. You can look, but you can't touch."

Nico slammed a hand to his cheek in feigned distress. "How will I find the will to continue living?" He let out a low laugh, looking like a mobster dressed head to toe in black. "Someone thinks more highly of themselves than they ought."

"So," Cali interrupted their warped game of flirtation, "what is going to happen between you and David?"

Ramsey puffed out a breath and shrugged. "Honestly, I don't know. He was supposed to meet our family at your wedding next weekend, but I kind of disinvited him. Maybe even broke up with him?" She scratched a nail through her platinum blonde hair, scowling. "I guess I'll deal with him when I get back from Maine."

"Speaking of Maine..." Sean closed his eyes, as if he were bracing himself. "My boss asked me to make a presentation to our board members on Wednesday, so I won't be able to drive you up to Mom and Dad's."

"When are you supposed to drive to Mom and Dad's now?" Ramsey asked with irritation. Having plans changed last minute was high on her list of pet peeves. It's a wonder she had lasted as long as she had dating David.

"If all goes well," Sean raked his fingers through his blonde hair, "Thursday. Possibly, Friday. But I know you promised to help Mom prepare for family coming into town for the wedding, so I've arranged for you to still get to Maine Wednesday night."

Ramsey's dark brown eyebrows furrowed, and she shook her head. "You know I hate flying, Sean."

"I know. That's why I asked Nico to drive you."

Ramsey crinkled her nose highlighting the silver hoop on her left nostril. "Pass."

"Oh, come on." Nico flashed a perfectly straight smile, "You, me, and the open road. What could be more fun?"

"Well, since you've put me on the spot, and this is just off the top of my head," Ramsey began to tick off fingers, "earthquakes, tsunamis, blind dates, papercuts, leprosy – should I go on?"

"Look," Sean pinched the bridge of his nose with a sigh, "Nico was going to be driving to the wedding anyway. This way you can keep your promise to help Mom and don't have to fly."

Ramsey covered half of her face when she turned to face her brother, preventing Nico from seeing her lips moving. "Why does *he* have to come at all?"

"*He* can hear you," Nico snorted in amusement.

"Your point?" Ramsey cocked her head to the side.

"He's my best friend, Ramsey." Sean sipped his beer, fingers entwined with Cali's. "Plus, he's agreed to take our wedding photos." He quickly kissed the side of Cali's head, and she smiled over at him.

Ramsey gave Nico a quick once over as he sat on the back counter where the taps were, swinging his legs back and forth like a child. "What do you know about photography?" She lifted her hands in the shape of a camera, framing him between her fingers. "Click. See, easy."

"Here are your options," Sean continued, flashing a disapproving look at Cali snickering. "One, you fly."

"Pass." Ramsey crossed her arms over her chest.

"Two, you drive with me and Cali Thursday or Friday, and deal with Mom's attitude until Monday." Ramsey rolled her eyes. "Or three, you ride with Nico."

Nico put a hand up, "Just to make sure you heard him correctly, Ice Queen, he said ride *with* Nico. Not *ride* Nico."

"Pig," Ramsey shook her head.

"Save the dirty talk for the road trip, babe," Nico winked.

"Maybe you should fly, Rams." Cali was now the center of attention, and it made her shudder. "What I mean to say is, I can't imagine flying would be worse than you two being stuck in a car for six or seven hours. You two might kill each other."

"Oh, absolutely," Ramsey turned her gaze back to Nico lazily lounging behind the bar and bat her eyelashes at him. "I promise to make it hurt, too."

"Don't make my night, Medusa." Nico blew a kiss her way.

"Fine." Ramsey reluctantly agreed. "I will ride *with* Nicotine here on Wednesday and avoid Mom's self-righteous wrath."

"Alright," Nico bobbed his head. "I'll pick you up at your place say around 10am."

Ramsey shook her head. "You'll have to pick me up from work."

"I don't even know where you work."

"We've known each other for years." Ramsey flicked her wrist, flashing an open palm. "How do you not know what I do?"

Nico shrugged, "Probably because I just don't care."

"I know what you do."

"Stalker much?"

Ramsey dug one of her business cards out of her purse, grateful she hadn't ordered new ones with *Ramsey Miller* printed on them.

"Here." She tossed it toward him. "That's where I work. Don't come inside. Just wait in the car. I'll find you."

Nico barely looked at the card before squinting over at her. "Why don't you give me your number?"

"My work number is on the card. You'd know that if you took a second to look at it."

"Your cell number."

"You'd like that wouldn't you?" Ramsey narrowed her eyes.

"How are we supposed to travel together if we don't have each other's numbers?" Nico threw the card back at Ramsey. "Give me your phone number or you can fly."

"You're just going to use my number for one of your stupid pranks again." Ramsey pointed an accusatory finger at him. "That's why I had to change my number in the first place."

"I don't know what you're talking about. You've never given me your number before." Nico remained tight-lipped, fighting a smile tugging at the corners of his mouth.

"I know it was you, Natasha." Ramsey hissed. "I was getting phone calls and text messages all day, sometimes even at two or three in the morning. People looking for exotic birds."

Sean and Cali looked away, laughing as silently as possible.

"After two months straight of the endless calls and messages, I looked my number up on the internet and up pops a Craigslist ad about me selling parrots, parakeets, and flamingos. *Any kind of exotic bird you want, I can get it to you.*" Ramsey snorted, "I know it was you and that's why you're not getting my new number."

Nico stepped toward the counter and strummed his fingers on the bar. "So, just out of curiosity, are you allergic to fun and games?"

"I had that number since I was fourteen," she growled.

"Well, it sounds to me like whoever this fine prankster was, he or she was just trying to lighten your dreary, dark, boring life."

"*He* could have just called and asked how I was doing." Ramsey grabbed her wallet and slapped her credit card on the counter. "How much do I owe you?"

"It's on the house." He pushed the card back at her.

Ramsey frowned. She knew what he was doing. He felt sorry for her after the night she'd had. And the one thing she didn't need or want from Nico Giovanni was his pity.

When they met her first day of college, she thought they were going to be close friends, but for some reason he kept his distance. He made it a point never to be alone with her and every time she invited him to go out, he'd find an excuse to turn her down. She eventually quit extending a hand to him and started roasting him instead. That's how their friendship, if they could even call it one, had been for years, and that's how she liked it.

If he started to feel sorry for her, he'd hold his punches, and if she were being honest, she looked forward to their tit-for-tat sessions. It let her blow off steam without offending anyone.

She pushed the card back. "If you don't swipe my card -"

"You'll what?" Nico interrupted her with a snort. "You'll huff and puff and try to hurt my feelings?"

Ramsey held his gaze. She never said the word *please* to him. Never. And she wasn't going to beg him to charge her for drinks so she wouldn't feel even worse about herself. She snatched the card and put it back in its spot in her wallet.

"I'll pay for gas on our little road trip." She didn't want to feel like she owed him.

Nico leaned closer and whispered, "Look, Price -"

"Goodnight," Ramsey interrupted him. She gathered her belongings, kissed Sean and Cali, and rushed out of the bar. She didn't think she could stomach any acts or words of kindness, especially from him.

Four

RAMSEY

The first two things Ramsey did upon arriving at work Monday morning after the treacherously long weekend, was pop two ibuprofens in her mouth to silence her splitting headache and toss the roses David had sent her Friday into the trash can at the foot of her desk.

Poppy suggested they could keep the roses since they were so pretty and probably expensive, but Ramsey refused to look at them for one more second. It was either the trash or she'd rip each petal off one-by-one and light them all on fire.

"I'm really sorry, Rams." Poppy looked across her desk at Ramsey. "Are you're sure it's over between you two?"

Ramsey stopped clicking at her keyboard to meet Poppy's caring gaze which made her insides shrivel. She didn't like that pitying look and meant to end the discussion right then and there.

"It's over because I said it was over."

"Right," Poppy bobbed her head, biting her bottom lip as she refocused on the paperwork on her desk.

Ramsey rubbed the heels of her palms over her eyes, knowingly smearing her perfectly applied make-up. "I'm sorry, Pop. It's not your fault. I'm just on edge about a lot of things, not just the David situation."

"Well, you know I'm here if you want to talk."

Rolling her desk chair out from behind her desk, Ramsey slid to the side of Poppy's workspace and leaned back as far as her chair would allow. "You know how I'm supposed to be going to Maine for five days for Sean's wedding?"

"Yeah," Poppy opened her snack drawer and motioned for Ramsey to snag something for their therapy session. Ramsey grabbed a pack of sour gummy worms and the redhead fished out her favored pretzels.

"Sean and Cali were supposed to drive the six and a half hours to Portland in a couple days and take me with them. You know how I feel about flying."

Poppy bobbed her head and crunched another pretzel. "Are they not driving anymore?"

"They are, but not until Thursday or Friday." Ramsey bit through one of the sour worms imagining it was David. "I promised my mother I'd be there Wednesday evening to help her prep for the wedding weekend. If I don't get there when I said I'd be there, there will be hell to pay. And I really don't need to incur my mother's petty wrath when I'm showing up alone. Again."

"So, what are you going to do?"

"Sean arranged for me to get to Portland in time."

"That's great!" Poppy squealed but with the look Ramsey shot her, the bright smile on her face vanished. "It's great, right?"

"Sean asked his best friend, Nico, to drive me."

"And we don't like him?"

"Right," Ramsey bobbed her head as she bit through another piece of candy. She'd never fully explained her hatred for Nico to Poppy before. There was really no need. Poppy would never meet Nico so she could keep her humiliation to herself.

"You could call your mom and explain -"

Ramsey shook her head, her eyes popping. "There's no calling Anne Price and explaining anything. If I don't show up Wednesday, I might as well not show up at all." She sighed and finished her snack, tossing the empty wrapper into the brightly patterned garbage can. Even Poppy's trash had to be pretty. "I'll just suck it up and travel with Nico. It'll be fine."

Rolling her chair back behind her own desk, Ramsey refocused on her email correspondence until Poppy hopped up and skipped toward her.

"Rams, I know we went out a few days ago," Poppy shook in excitement, "but what if we go out for another girls' night tonight? I know of this amazing Italian restaurant, and they have free breadsticks!"

"I don't know, Pop," Ramsey protested but Poppy wasn't one to take no for an answer.

"What do you have planned for tonight?" She popped her round hip to the side, planting her hands on her waist. By the look on her best friend's face, they both knew Ramsey had no plans, so she relented.

"Fine, Pop." Ramsey huffed a small laugh. "We'll go to this restaurant if you really want to."

"Woohoo!" Poppy slithered her arms around Ramsey's neck and squeezed. "It'll be so much fun. You'll see. And there's this really cute bartender."

"Of course there is," Ramsey teased and her friend clicked her tongue.

"Seven tonight?"

Ramsey nodded, secretly thrilled she wouldn't have to be alone the entire night and depressed thinking about the state of her life. "Seven sounds perfect."

Five

RAMSEY

Once a week, normally on Thursday, Ramsey and Poppy would go out for a girls' night. Their outings frequently involved a few drinks and delicious food, and tonight was no different. Deciding on Italian, the best friends found themselves at Poppy's favorite hole-in-the-wall, *Ristorante de Carla*.

Ramsey didn't realize how much she needed to get dressed up in her favorite little black dress and heels and go out for a drink until they sat down at their cozy table for two. The red and white checkered tablecloths, lone candle centerpiece, and the aroma of creamy sauces she would have to run an extra mile to burn off filled her with a comfortable joy.

As always, Poppy had the loudest and brightest colors on and drew a lot of attention. Her best friend didn't seem to mind the countless eyes on her. Poppy could make friends everywhere she went and most of the conversations started with questions about her wardrobe.

Ramsey snickered when the bartender winked at Poppy. She didn't think it was possible for her friend's face to light up any brighter, but the handsome barkeep proved her wrong.

"Maybe you should go talk to him, Pop." Ramsey wiggled her eyebrows playfully, taking a sip of her wine.

"Oh, I couldn't." The redhead shook her head, messing with her bouncy curls. "I wouldn't know what to say."

"You could start by introducing yourself. Maybe tell him you think he's the most gorgeous creature you've ever laid your eyes on."

"Ramsey, you sound just like a man." Poppy clicked her tongue and swatted her white linen napkin at Ramsey.

Blocking the incoming blow with her menu, Ramsey laughed, but before she could respond, their cute waiter swooped in carrying two glasses from the bar. "Two vodka tonics."

"There must be some mistake," Poppy said politely. "We didn't order these."

At first, Ramsey thought the bartender sent them because he was clearly maki ng eyes at Poppy but then their waiter tilted his head toward the far end of the bar and smiled.

"The gentleman at the bar sent them. Said to tell you to enjoy your girls' night."

Ramsey and Poppy both glanced to the man sitting alone at the bar and Ramsey's smile vanished. Nico lounged lazily on his stool, dressed in all black, waiting for his to go order, sipping a beer. He lifted his pint in her direction with a wicked grin.

"Oh, he is yummy," Poppy puffed out a breath, fanning herself with her hand. "I'd eat him for breakfast, lunch, *and* dinner." She waved and he waved back.

"Yuck, Pop." Ramsey hissed, refusing to look Nico's direction. He wasn't about to ruin her night out with his shenanigans.

"Go talk to him," Poppy urged. "He's still smiling at you."

"I'd rather kiss a snake."

Poppy slammed her hand down on the table, barely missing Ramsey's fingers. "Wait, do you know him?" she whispered with a giggle.

"Unfortunately," Ramsey rolled her eyes, placing her elbow on the table and holding her chin. She was going for the aloof look but all she could think about was her mother chastising her for having her elbow on the dinner table. "That's Nico. My brother's best friend."

"THAT'S Nico?" Poppy's mouth hung open.

Ramsey tapped the cold vodka tonic glass and grumbled, "That troll. He knows I hate vodka."

"You don't have to drink it." Clearly, Poppy didn't understand the nature of the game.

"And let him know he's annoyed me? Not a chance." Ramsey turned her attention back to Nico. She held the drink up and smiled. Then she drank the whole thing, maintaining eye contact with him. The buzz was hitting her faster than she'd like to admit. But she and vodka really did not get along.

If Nico Giovanni thought he was going to catch her off guard with one of his childish antics, he had another thing coming. She wasn't one to back down from a challenge, to her mother's dismay, but this was her night out. She wouldn't let him, or anyone else for that matter, ruin her evening.

When she finished the vodka tonic, she flipped the glass upside-down before placing it on the table. He smirked and there was a glint of mischief in his brown eyes. He took a sip of his beer, his gaze glued to hers.

And there it was: the *whoever-breaks-eye-contact-first-loses* game. It pained Ramsey to admit it, but he won far more of these silent contests than she did. Tonight, with a little bit of liquid courage, she would win. She narrowed her eyes and lifted her head higher.

She willed him to look away, for him to be distracted or feel intimidated by her steel grey eyes, but he didn't even blink. He just stared, as if he could see right through to the very core of her. She almost felt naked under his scrutinizing glare and then thought about what it would feel like having him lying on top of her, kissing down her neck-

STOP.

Where did that thought come from? She had no interest in being intimate with Nico. It had to be the three glasses of wine and one quickly downed vodka tonic messing with her better judgment. She shook the unwanted image free but when she refocused on Nico, she saw something spark in his eyes. Did he know what she had just been thinking?

She leaned back in her seat, still silently watching him, but wanting him to see her just as relaxed as he was.

The bartender leaned across the bar and said something to Nico that ripped his attention from her. When he answered the staff member and turned back to Ramsey, he looked defeated. He held his drink up to her in salute as she mouthed, "I win."

"Yeah," Poppy's voice sliced through their stare off, "that wasn't juvenile."

"Juvenile, yes, but I won." Ramsey needed to get something to eat quick before the alcohol really took a toll on her.

"I can't believe you've been hiding that gorgeous man from me," Poppy bit her lower lip staring at Nico. The alcohol was getting to her bubbly friend too.

"Down, girl."

"I would climb him like a tree," Poppy smirked, as if she were having a bunch of naughty thoughts creep into her mind.

"I'm going to throw up. Do we need to get you home to take a cold shower, you horn dog?" Ramsey crinkled her nose in both amusement and disgust. Was it the wine or vodka tonic that was making her wonder what Nico would look like shirtless?

"So, why do you hate him exactly?" Poppy asked. "Cause if he was looking at me the way he's looking at you..." She used her hand to fan herself with an impish smirk.

"It's complicated."

The redhead's eyes widened. "Now, I have to know. Tell me. Tell me. Tell me."

"You're not going to let this go, are you?"

"After seeing the beautiful devil? No. I need to know why you and he aren't together." Poppy puffed her bottom lip, looking like an adorable puppy begging for table scraps. It was nearly impossible to deny her when she made that precious face.

Ramsey folded her arms over her chest. "If I tell you the story, you'll drop it?"

"Absolutely!" Poppy held her hand up as if swearing an oath.

"Fine." Ramsey shifted in her seat to get more comfortable. "It was my first day of college and I got lost on my way to class. I was able to find a campus map in the quad and scanned it for some guidance but couldn't seem to find the building I needed to get to. About to call it quits, I turned around and asked the first person walking by if he could help me. He pointed to the building on the map and gave me some directions, but I was still so confused that he offered to walk me. It was a ten-minute walk and I wished it had been longer. When we got to my classroom, he asked for my number just in case I got lost again. This tall, hot Italian junior from Philly asked for *my* number. Of course I gave it to him, and I thought about him all day like some giggly schoolgirl."

Poppy was holding her chin up, both her elbows digging into the table. "What happened next?"

Ramsey sipped a bit of her wine before continuing. "Later that night, I met up with Sean and his roommate for dinner. His roommate turned out to be the same guy who helped me earlier."

"No!" Poppy burped but waved her hand for Ramsey to keep talking.

"Instead of being excited to see me, he acted like he didn't know me. I was embarrassed but thought maybe he was surprised I was Sean's sister." Ramsey spared a glance toward the bar where Nico was still sipping his beer, but his attention wasn't on her, it was glued to the television watching the Phillie's game. "Through that first semester, I asked if he wanted to hang out, grab a bite to eat, watch a baseball game, catch a movie. Every time, he had a reason to turn me down, but if I hung out with Sean, Nico was there." She looked away from Nico and refocused on Poppy's watery eyes. "Finally, I realized I'd misread his kindness my first day for attraction and was so embarrassed that I stopped reaching out to him."

"Why did you move to Philadelphia then, if you knew he was from here?" Poppy asked after a moment of silence.

"Several reasons." Ramsey stretched her back until it cracked. "I was living in Boston where two of my brothers live. Phineas is a pilot and is never in town and Liam is a doctor with hardly enough time for his wife and child. And I was a couple hours away from my mother who was constantly popping in to see if I was dating anyone yet. It was lonely and claustrophobic at the same time. Sean and I have always been close. He's my favorite brother."

Poppy gasped, "You can't say that, Rams!"

"Everyone in the family knows Sean and I prefer each other's company," Ramsey chuckled. "Our oldest brothers, Connor and Collin, the twins, are still inseparable at thirty-five. Patrick and Liam, the middles, text each other constantly, even if they're in the same room. Phineas is a floater, and he prefers it that way." She pat Poppy's hand reassuringly until the redhead smiled. "Anyway, when I saw the job here open up, I thought it'd be great to get away from my dreary and boring life in Boston and be near Sean again. Plus, I wanted to get to know Cali better. I never thought when I applied that I'd get an interview let alone be offered the position." She smiled remembering her brother's face when she told him the good news. "Sean was so excited I got the job he insisted we go out for drinks to celebrate. I didn't realize until I got there that it was Nico's bar. He didn't look surprised to see me, but then again, he's Sean's best friend so Sean most likely told him I was thinking of moving to Philly for a job."

"What did Nico say when he saw you again?" The waiter came by to refill their glasses of water and put breadsticks in front of them. Poppy immediately snatched a piece and chomped away.

"I said, 'You've aged.' And he responded, 'Like a fine wine.' And it's been like that between us ever since." Ramsey reached for a breadstick but was deterred when her best friend grabbed her hand.

"Does Sean know any of this?"

Ramsey shook her head, "I've never said anything. They've been best friends for ten years. Why ruin that because I had a stupid crush and got rejected? If Nico can act like nothing happened, so can I."

Poppy shoved her hand away and whispered, "He's coming."

"What?

"Nico." She motioned with her eyes to Ramsey's left. "He's coming this way."

"Evening, ladies." Nico's husky voice stilled Ramsey in her seat.

Ramsey composed herself enough to throw him a disinterested look. "Hello, Nicole. I would say it's nice to see you but why lie?"

"Icy as always, Princess." Nico slipped his hand out of his black pant pocket and extended it to Poppy. "I don't believe we've met. I'm Nico."

Despite the glare Ramsey flashed her way, Poppy shook his hand and giggled. "I'm Poppy McGuinness. Ramsey's best friend and co-worker."

"It's nice to meet you, Poppy McGuinness." He smiled and Ramsey rolled her eyes when Poppy shivered.

"Ramsey and I were just talking about you."

Ramsey coughed, choking on the one piece of breadstick she managed to eat. She glared at Poppy, a warning look, but her friend either didn't notice or was too tipsy to care.

Nico flashed a wicked grin at Ramsey, "All horrible things, I'm sure."

"Actually," Poppy rattled on before Ramsey could kick her under the table, "she was telling me about how you two first met. Do you remember the first time you met Ramsey?"

Nico seemed surprised by the question but recovered quickly. "I recall her being lost on campus." A waiter approached Nico and handed him his to-go order. "Thanks, Mike." Nico grabbed the bag and turned his attention back to the women. "Well, it's been a pleasure meeting you, Poppy. Chilling as always, Elsa."

Slithering his way out of the dining room, Nico left, probably well aware he pissed Ramsey off.

"That's it? Just lost?" Ramsey fumed, crushing the partially eaten breadstick in her hand. Poppy opened her mouth to say something, but Ramsey held her hand up silencing her. "I'll deal with your betrayal tomorrow at work."

She slammed a twenty-dollar bill on the table, downed the last bit of her wine, feeling dizzy. She stood up and nearly fell over but snatched the back of her chair to steady herself.

Poppy's mouth was wide open. "What are you doing? Where are you going?"

"I'm going to confront him." Ramsey snatched her purse and straightened her shoulders.

"Rams-"

"I'll see you tomorrow, Pop." Before her friend could protest, Ramsey slipped out of the restaurant, ready to smack that smug look off of Nico's handsome face.

Six

Nico

When Nico walked into his favorite Italian restaurant, the last person he ever imagined seeing in the hole-in-the-wall eatery was Ramsey Price. Ruffling her feathers with the vodka tonic was a guaranteed way to get her attention but the rage in her eyes when Poppy asked about when they first met was hard to miss.

Of course he remembered first meeting Ramsey. He thought about it more often than he cared to admit. When he first laid eyes on the lost freshman, all he could think about was how breathtakingly beautiful she was. Those grey blue eyes of hers would consume his dreams and he was more than happy for the haunting.

When he made it back to his dorm room that afternoon, he bragged to Sean all about this stunning girl he was going to ask out. *She's perfect*, he had told his roommate. And she was, except for the fact she was his best friend's little sister.

Seeing Ramsey walk into the restaurant where he was supposed to meet Sean's sister stopped his heart. What were the odds he'd run into her twice in the same day? But when she headed straight for their table and Sean stood up to hug her, Nico's stomach sank. He couldn't date his friend's sister. Sean had made it explicitly clear to him and their other male friends that they weren't allowed to put the moves on her.

Her smile nearly brought him to his knees. But instead of showing her how excited he was to see her again, he pretended he didn't know her. Seeing the light fade from her brightened eyes gutted him. Had he been a man, he would have admitted right then to Sean that his sister was the same girl he'd been gushing his heart over all afternoon, but his friendship with Sean was too important to risk.

Nico was at odds with his dad about his decision to go to college and pursue a business degree to open a bar. He wasn't interested in taking over the family moving company. He'd been at school for two years and neither his father nor mother had attempted to speak with him. His sister, Guiliana, was more than happy to keep him updated on the family, extended cousins included, but it still didn't make their disappointment and rejection hurt less.

Sean was the only family he had and even though his heart ached at the thought of Ramsey not being his girl, he wouldn't risk what he already had.

Days later when Sean brought up the girl he'd met the first day of the semester, Nico panicked and lied, saying the girl gave him the wrong number. They never spoke of it again. And now, it was too late to right his wrong.

"Hey! Hey, Nico!"

Stirred from his memories, Nico turned around when he heard his name. An odd sound coming from Ramsey's lips. Those lips he'd obsessed about kissing for eight years. She beelined straight for him, angry as usual.

He looped a finger through his belt loop, firmly putting his mask in place when he grinned, "Stalking me now, Price?"

"Where do you come off?"

"What?"

She stomped up to him and pointed a finger to his chest. "Sending that stupid vodka tonic. Introducing yourself to my friend like you aren't the absolute worst."

He pursed his lips and cocked his head to the side. "I love it when you talk dirty to me."

Ramsey opened her mouth to retort but swallowed her insults when she swayed dizzily to the side of the sidewalk. She reached her hand out to place against the brick building. He extended a hand to catch her wrist, but she slapped him away with a hiss.

"Don't," she frowned in warning. "Don't try to be all nice now that I've called you out for being a dick."

"A dick?" He chuckled, running his fingers through his dark hair. "I bought you and your friend drinks and said hello. How does that make me the worst?"

"I thought you were a nice person when we first met. But you..."

"You're drunk. Let me get you home."

"You'd like that, wouldn't you?" she spat like a spoiled child.

"It would be a very trying experience for the both of us." Nico rubbed his eyes, the takeout bag of delicious food growing heavy in his left hand. "Look, my place is a couple of blocks from here. If you want to walk with me, I'll have Sean come pick you up."

"I don't get it," she whispered, not looking up at him.

"It's not a difficult concept. You put one foot in front of the other and -"

"Not walking, you dick. *You.*" She met his gaze and he saw pain in her hardened eyes. "I don't understand you."

Nico paused before asking, "Do you want to?"

"Yes. No. No. I ... No." She leaned her back against the building and rubbed her temples in obvious frustration. "You're just messing with me because I've had a couple too many drinks tonight."

"I've been nothing but a gentleman. You scoffed when I offered to get you home two different ways, yet you're still following me home."

Ramsey clutched her stomach when she burped. "I should have eaten something."

Nico's mouth fell wide open. "Wait, you're telling me you were in the best Italian place in town and didn't order any food?"

"We were about to when you showed up and ruined my night," she spat venomously.

"Look," Nico huffed, "I've got enough in here for two people. If you'd like some and can make it to my apartment without falling flat on your face, you're welcome to join me."

Ramsey eyed him suspiciously but didn't say a word. He would have preferred her to just insult him and walk away before staring at him in complete silence.

He broke the standoff first. "As fun as it is to just stand out on the sidewalk with you while my food gets cold, I'd rather not waste my entire night doing this weird, passive aggressive tango with you."

After a few seconds staring at him, Ramsey finally pushed up from the wall. "Fine.

"Fine, you're coming with me, or fine, I can go?"

"Fine, I'll go with you." She marched up beside him and motioned for him to lead the way.

"Well, come on then, Price."

Nico wasn't quite sure if having her alone in his apartment was the best idea. They'd never been alone before. Sean or Cali had always been with them, and he'd been able to maintain his distance. With her in his home, sharing a meal with him, looking stunning in that little black dress and heels...

He had to quit thinking about her dress before the thoughts of what she looked like out of it started to creep in. Even though the walk was only a few minutes, it seemed longer. Nico's heart raced as he stopped in front of the main entrance and entered his code to get inside the building.

She hadn't said a word to him the entire walk. But he was impressed she managed to walk the entire way in those high heels without stumbling, tipsy or not.

"This is me." He motioned with his head for her to follow up the two flights of stairs to his apartment door. Still she didn't say anything but he could sense she was observing, possibly even judging, her surroundings.

He unlocked his door and held it open with a splayed hand for her to walk in first. She flashed him a dirty look and he huffed and walked in first, letting her stew in the hall. She didn't wait long before entering.

His place was a direct representation of himself. Brick walls, black and white photography he had taken displayed around the sparsely furnished apartment, with a leather sofa and white geometric area rug laid out over the oak floors. Though it lacked color, it still felt cozy. At least, that's how he hoped it felt to anyone who walked in. Although the only people who had ever visited his place were his mother and sister, and Sean.

He sat at the four seat dining table and emptied the take-out bag of its Italian goodies. The apartment was instantly filled with the scent of garlic, herbs, and tomato sauce. He inhaled with a satisfied smile before walking into his galley kitchen for two plates and utensils.

"Would you like something to drink?" He paused at his refrigerator, waiting for her response.

She looked over at him and nodded, "Water."

He quickly filled two glasses with ice water and brought everything to the table where Ramsey was already sitting.

She was in his seat, but he wasn't going to have her move, so he sat in the chair across from her.

After splitting the food and offering her a plate with chicken parmesan, salad, and a breadstick, they silently began to eat. He watched her cut a piece of chicken and soak it in more tomato sauce before slipping the morsel into her mouth. She closed her eyes and let out a small, glorious moan.

When she opened her eyes, she met his awaiting gaze and offered him a tight-lipped smile. "Thank you."

"Did you just say thank you?"

"I'm not incapable of having good manners, Narcissa."

There was the Ramsey Price he knew all too well.

"Well, for what it's worth, you're welcome. I'm not the worst after all." He smiled and she shook her head in response.

"How do you figure?" She bit into her breadstick as if she hadn't eaten all day.

"If I was the worst like you claim, I would've left your drunk ass outside and had all this food to myself."

"So," she took a sip of water and glanced around his apartment, "this is your place?"

"Go ahead," he stabbed his fork into his salad.

"What?"

"No snarky remark about the manly furniture or how you hate the fact that the windows are too big and probably let skin-scalding light inside during the day? I know how your kind hate direct sunlight."

She tilted her head and rolled her eyes. "Haha. Very funny. A vampire joke."

"Vampire joke?" Nico shook his head. "No. It's because you're pale. And pale people like you and Sean burn."

"I almost threw this breadstick at you," her nostrils flared and accentuated the silver hoop ring piercing.

He leaned forward and said in a low, warm voice, "I've seen you throw a baseball, Price. I'm not afraid of a direct hit."

Ramsey pinched her fingers over the bridge of her straight nose. "Why do we do this?" she huffed.

"Do what?" He took another bite of his salad. Since childhood, he always ate his greens before his protein.

"Bicker and pick at each other like a couple of old people?"

Nico smiled and shrugged, "I thought we were just having a good old-fashioned conversation."

She stared at him, her eyes watering the longer they remained silent, until she finally asked, "Do you only remember meeting me because I was lost?"

He put his fork down and leaned back in his seat. "Is that what this is about?"

Ramsey maintained eye contact but said nothing.

"You had your hair in a braid. And you were wearing black denim jeans with a *Rosie the Riveter* t-shirt and red converse." Her eyes brightened as he spoke. "You looked so lost, so worried that you were going to be in trouble for being late to your first class. And I was just happy to help you."

"You remember all that?" she whispered.

Nico nodded, not sure what else to say without pouring his heart out to her. Which could not happen under any circumstance.

"Why did you act like you didn't know who I was when I met you and Sean for dinner that first night?"

"I don't know." *Liar.*

She stiffened and he instantly wished he could take it back. "I know I came on strong back then. I thought you might have been attracted to me, but I realize I misread your kindness for something more." She pushed her seat back, scrapping loudly against the floor. "This was a bad idea." She stood up too quickly and swayed sideways. Nico jumped up and grabbed ahold of her, clasping at her waist to steady her.

"How much did you drink?" He whispered against her ear. Her back was plastered against his chest, and he was afraid she would be able to feel his heart thrashing in his chest.

"I don't remember," she didn't attempt to flee from his gentle hold. "I had a few glasses of wine and that vodka tonic."

Nico could have stayed welded to her all night long and not uttered one complaint. But he snapped to his senses and when he was sure she wouldn't fall over, he released her. "I'll call Sean."

"Don't," she whipped around to face him, resting her hand on the back of her chair. "He hates when I do this."

Nico scratched his head, grimacing. "Alright. Then I'll get my keys and drive you home."

"If Sean sees me this drunk, he'll go all big brother on me. I don't need the lecture."

If he didn't know any better, he would have thought she was looking for a reason to spend the night. And he was willing to oblige. "You can take my bed. I'll sleep here on the couch."

She folded her arms over her chest. "I'll take the couch," she announced in true stubborn fashion.

"Don't be ridiculous," Nico snorted. "You're my guest. Take the bedroom. It's got its own bathroom, so you will have plenty of privacy."

She looked down the hall to where the bedroom door was half open. Her gaze returned to him and a bought of playfulness flickered in her eyes. "Is this how you treat all the women you bring home?"

Nico wasn't one to bring women back to his place. He wasn't really one to date. Casually, but nothing serious. But she didn't need to know that. He ate the distance between them. "Is that how you want me to treat you?"

To her credit, she didn't step back when he approached and stared down at her. "You feed them, charm them with that devilish smile, and then offer them your bed for the night?"

"Seems like you think you have me all figured out."

Ramsey shrugged. "Good thing I'm not like any of them. I know exactly what you are."

"Take the couch. Take the bed. I don't care. I'll sleep wherever you don't." He leaned forward until his lips skimmed her ear. "You can't say I wasn't a gentleman."

He heard her breathing quicken. She glanced up at him, their lips inches apart. "Good night, Nesta."

He smiled and whispered, "Good night, Banshee."

Ramsey turned on her heel and walked to his bedroom. He couldn't help watching her strut away, her heels clicking with each step, her hips swaying side to side. He was almost in a trance when she reached the door and closed it.

He rubbed a hand through his hair and busied himself with cleaning up their finished dinner. Once the table and kitchen were spotless, he went to the linen closet and retrieved a pillow and blanket reserved for any guests, though no one had actually stayed to use them. He sank into the leather couch and turned the television on before realizing he was still in his button-down shirt and black pants. He tried to lay down but shook his head immediately. He wouldn't be able to sleep unless he had some sleep pants on. He thought about sleeping in just his boxers but didn't need her making any snide comments if she found him that way. Shoving the blanket off, he marched for his bedroom door and knocked.

He could hear her feet hit the floor and the bed squeak as she stood up and made her way to open the door.

"What?" She whipped it open to reveal her wearing one of his Phillies t-shirts. His eyes scanned from her face all the way down to her mid-thighs, where the coverage ended.

Nico cleared his throat which put a smug smile on her face. "I forgot to grab something to sleep in. Is that my shirt?"

"You didn't expect me to sleep in my dress, did you?" She tilted her head, clearly toying with him.

He planted his hands on the doorframe and leaned closer to her. "I'm just surprised it didn't rip against your scales, you goblin."

Ramsey opened the door fully before leaning against the doorframe, not intimidated by his six-foot-two frame in the slightest. "By all means, get yourself something to sleep in," she purred. "Lord knows I don't want to walk out in the morning and see you naked."

"And realize no other man will measure up?"

She crossed her arms over her chest, his t-shirt pulling up slightly. She scoffed, "Please."

His eyes bounced from her smooth thighs up to her predatorial, hungry eyes. "Begging already, Price?"

"You wish," she flicked her long, platinum hair behind her back. He could smell the lavender and vanilla scent waft up and he fought the urge to close his eyes and soak her in. He knew the shirt she was wearing was going to smell like her well after she was gone. His gaze drifted from her eyes to her mischievous grin. "Ah, ah, ah, Natalie. No touching."

He wasn't about to give her the satisfaction of knowing the affect she had on him. Before he lost the nerve, he ripped his shirt over his head and smirked when her gaze drifted up and down his muscular torso. He winked. "Same applies to you, harpy."

He pushed past her, his chest rubbing against her arm as he made his way across the bedroom to his dresser. He grabbed a plain black t-shirt and some plaid sleep pants. He faced her, noting the haziness in her grey-blue eyes, and started to unzip his pants.

"Watch if you want to, Price, I'm not shy."

As if snapped out of her stupor, Ramsey turned her back to him right before he pulled his pants down. He was oddly satisfied by winning this round of the *uncomfortable game* but a part of him wished she had stood her ground and watched. Maybe he would have lost that battle of the wills.

Once he changed, he made his way toward the door and stood with his chest a few inches from her back. He leaned forward and whispered, "Guess you'll be having sweet dreams tonight, Princess."

"You beast." She didn't move or look at him, but he could feel the electric pulse between them and knew if he didn't leave right then and there, he'd be staying the night with her cuddled in his arms.

"I'll be in the next room if you need anything." He slipped around her and closed the door and breathed for the first time since he saw her wearing his shirt.

That woman. That woman made him feel things without even laying one finger on him. If she ever found it in her heart to reciprocate those feelings, he would come undone in a heartbeat.

Seven

RAMSEY

Ramsey woke up in a foreign bed that smelled like cedar and whiskey. A scent that reminded her an awful lot of Nico Giovanni.

Her eyes flew open as she shot up in the soft black and white sheets. The bed smelled like Nico Giovanni because she was in Nico Giovanni's apartment, sleeping in his room. She glanced down and saw she wasn't in her little black dress but was wearing what she could only assume was one of his Phillies t-shirts. She slapped a hand over her face. She hadn't been that drunk in a long time and of course she had to get sloppy in his presence.

Although, when she thought about it, she realized last night had been the first time they'd ever been together by themselves. She remembered enough of their time together to know she didn't make an absolute fool of herself, but her skin still flushed when thinking about Nico's sculpted chest and how he changed a few feet away from her. She had wanted so badly to watch, to stand her ground, but for some reason she couldn't explain, or maybe wasn't willing to admit to herself, she turned away with a heat rising in her lower belly.

The bedroom door was still closed and when she looked at the alarm clock on his nightstand, she saw it said six-thirty in the morning. She had just enough time to sneak out of his apartment, get home to shower and change, before heading into work where Poppy would get the tongue lashing of a lifetime.

As quietly as possible, she slipped Nico's shirt off and laid it on his remade bed. Putting her dress on but forgoing the heels until she slipped out, she opened the bedroom door and made her way toward the living room. She expected to see Nico drooling on the leather sofa but instead Nico was already awake and making breakfast. He poked his head up when she entered the main area, and he saluted her with a whisk.

"Good morning, Mother Gothel. Did you want some eggs or were you planning to snack on a few children on your way to work?" His sly grin made her heart feel like melting chocolate, and she flashed him a scowl to mask the fact she was picturing him shirtless.

"Are you always this trying so early? Or is this just for me?" she cooed to hide her blush. Why did he look so enticing at six-thirty in the morning? Curse him.

"Like any other woman can make my balls shrivel up upon first shriek." He winked and she thought her uterus just about exploded.

"If it keeps you from spawning more monstrous Giovanni's, then I should be given a medal." She sat on one of two stools that sat against the bar area of his galley kitchen. She put her shoes on, no use in pretending she could sneak out now.

Nico chuckled and handed her a cup of coffee. "Here."

"Poisoned?"

He rested his elbows on the counter like he did at his bar whenever he was sparring with her. "Beneath me."

"You'd like that," she purred, but then pictured what it would feel like to have him hovering above her, kissing her slowly down her neck...

"Do you need me to drive you home?" His voice sliced through her naughty thoughts, and she cleared her throat hoping he hadn't noticed her change in demeanor. "What time do you need to be at work?"

"I start at nine." Ramsey sniffed the coffee before taking a sip.

"Did you really just sniff the coffee?" he sounded amused.

She winked. "One can never be too careful."

Nico rolled his eyes, trying and failing to hide his smirk. "Do you need a ride or not?"

Ramsey shook her head. "I'm a big girl. I can get home on my own."

"Alright." Why did he sound disappointed?

"I better get going." She put her half-full cup of coffee on the counter and grabbed her purse and phone, noticing she had a few text messages from Sean. She couldn't wait to explain where she'd been all night.

Nico bobbed his head, sipping from his own mug. For a second, she thought about what he would do if she rounded the counter and kissed him. She wondered what his facial hair would feel like against her smooth skin. She wanted to rub her hands up and down the ridges of his abs and draw her fingernails down his muscular back. She didn't get a close enough look at the script tattoo etched vertically over his ribcage, but she'd like to get close enough to read it for herself. He cleared his throat, once again drawing her from those thoughts.

Ramsey stood up, her heels clicking on the wide plank wooden floors. The way he was looking at her as if she was the answer to the million questions running through his tormented mind made her want to shoot him one last insult so all he would think about the rest of the day was her, but instead she said, "Thank you."

He smirked, seeming to be snapped free of thoughts of his own. "For not smothering you in your sleep?"

"I'm serious." She stared deeply into his chocolate brown eyes, hoping he understood she was grateful. "Thank you for letting me stay here last night. You didn't have to do that."

"You're welcome." He leaned against the wall of cabinets and smiled. It wasn't a grin that was wicked or mischievous, but one that seemed relieved that she was being genuine.

She turned on her heel and left, hoping he didn't notice the desire in her eyes. Maybe it wasn't the wine last night that had her chasing after him. Maybe it was her stupid college crush rearing its ugly head. Maybe it was because her relationship with David had crashed and burned. Maybe she was just lonely. Or maybe, she still had feelings for Nico Giovanni and that just wouldn't do.

Once Ramsey had hailed a cab and was on her way back to the rowhouse she shared with Sean, she tapped her phone to read her brother's text messages.

8:48pm: Are you still at dinner with Poppy?

10: 03pm: It's really late. Are you ok?

11: 49pm: Please don't tell me you're with David.

1: 17am: If I don't hear from you by noon, I'm going to call Nico and start a search party to find you.

Ramsey rolled her eyes and smiled. Sean might only be a couple of years older than her, but he took his big brother duties seriously. But when she skimmed over Nico's name again, her heart fluttered. She couldn't tell Sean she had spent the night at his best friend's house. He'd always acted weird whenever his high school buddies had crushes on her and she didn't want him uncomfortable with her sleeping in Nico's bed.

She scrolled through her favorite contacts and pressed Sean's picture. It was nearly seven in the morning. He'd be up by now getting ready for work. Or sharpening his pitchfork to ready himself to lead the search party in his quest to track his little sister down.

Sean answered on the second ring, and she could tell he was trying to hide the panic and rising anger in his voice. Had he slept at all? "Ramsey? Where are you? Are you alright?"

"Good morning to you too, Sean." She tried to lighten the mood but that wasn't the right course of action.

"Look, I understand you're an adult and can do as you please, but I was worried about you all night. It's not like you to ignore my messages."

"Sorry, Sean." She rubbed her face, wishing she could tell him the truth. "I got a little tipsy at dinner and..." I ended up staying with your best friend who I think I might have feelings for.

"Rams?" Sean's voice echoed in her ear. "Rams, are you there?"

She shook her head. "Sorry. I'm here. I got tipsy at dinner and crashed at Poppy's place. I'm on my way home now to get ready for work."

Sean was so quiet she thought they'd lost connection but then he said, "You were at Poppy's?"

She felt like she was fifteen again lying to her parents about being at her high school best friend's sleep over when she actually went to a senior's party.

"If you're asking if I was actually at David's place, no. I wasn't." At least that wasn't a lie. "He and I are done."

Her brother sighed. "I believe you. Sorry, I just don't want to see you get back with him when he clearly doesn't make you happy."

"Yeah." Ramsey rested her head against the headrest and closed her eyes. She hadn't been happy with David. Why had she stayed? "Well, I'm almost home. I'll see you soon."

Eight

RAMSEY

"Ramsey! I'm so sorry about last night. Are you still upset with me?" Poppy nearly tackled her to the floor the second she walked into the archives office.

Ramsey smiled at her short friend and shook her head. "No. I was a little tipsy. I just needed a good night's rest." The thought of sleeping in Nico's bed, in his shirt, with the image of him shirtless was going to toss and turn in her mind throughout the day.

Poppy sighed in relief. "Good. I was a little tipsy myself. Otherwise, I would have kept my big mouth shut when it came to that gorgeous Italian Stallion."

Ramsey walked to her workspace and put her belongings on top of her desk as she checked her work phone for messages. "It's too early in the morning for one of your moods."

"What do you mean one of my moods?" Poppy popped her round hip to the side and attempted to look upset but failed miserably.

Ramsey leaned back in her seat and placed her hands behind her head. "When you get all hot and bothered by a man you find handsome, you get all flustered and say the weirdest sexual phrases."

"Ah-ha!" The redhead pointed her index finger at Ramsey. "So, you *do* think Nico is handsome!"

"I said *you* thought he was handsome." Ramsey started fiddling with paperwork on her desk so Poppy couldn't see her blush.

"Well, it's a shame I might never see him again" Poppy sat at her desk which faced Ramsey's and pouted. She opened her top drawer which she used for snacks and popped a pretzel in her mouth. "Perhaps, I'll dream of him."

"Never see who again?"

Ramsey and Poppy whipped their heads toward the door and saw Nico leaning lazily against the doorframe, hands buried deep in his pockets. Dressed in his signature all black, he smiled, and looked just like a mobster in a Martin Scorsese movie. Poppy just about choked on her pretzel and started coughing furiously. Ramsey quickly got up and patted her back until she settled down.

"You alright?" Ramsey asked and Poppy nodded, eyes watering.

"Who would it be a shame never to see again?" Nico pressed, knowing full well they had been talking about him from the smug look on his face.

"Uh..." Poppy's eyes bugged, and Ramsey sighed.

"No one," she stated matter of fact. "What are you doing here?" She folded her arms over her chest, squaring her shoulders to his.

Nico ran a finger up and down the doorframe and a shiver ran down her spine thinking of what that finger could do to her.

"So, this is where you work?" He looked around the cozy office for two.

"Yes," she nodded. "Again, what are you doing here?"

Nico ate the distance between them with a smirk. She refused to shrink back and stood her ground. He pulled his hand out of his pocket and flashed a pair of earrings in front of her.

"You left these at my place. Thought you'd want them back."

Poppy's mouth dropped open but before she could say anything Ramsey shoved the earrings away from her.

"And if I said these weren't mine?"

"I would call you a liar," he said in a low, seductive voice.

She wouldn't give him the satisfaction of seeing the affect he had on her. She was in control of herself, and she would rather be caught naked than admit she found him attractive. "Well, they're not mine." *Lies.* They were her earrings and not only that, they were her favorite pair.

Nico bit his bottom lip and leaned closer until his lips were an inch from her ear. "Considering I haven't had a woman other than you, my mother, and my sister over in a very long time, I call bullshit."

She didn't know why learning he hadn't entertained an-other woman in a long time made her heart leap, but the traitorous organ rejoiced. Pulling away to look him in the eye, she flashed a devilish smile. "Dry spell, Nora?"

"Offering to quench my thirst, Succubus?"

Poppy squeaked a laugh and Ramsey turned her focus back to her redhead friend.

"Isn't there something you should be doing?" Ramsey shot her a warning look.

Poppy hopped up from her desk, grabbing a few manila folders Ramsey knew were empty. "Right. Yeah, I'll leave you to it."

Once she was out of earshot, Ramsey whipped back toward Nico who was now sitting in her chair, kicking his feet up on her desk. He tucked his hands behind his head and smiled when she huffed.

"Why are you really here?"

"I told you." He nodded toward the silver earrings on her desk, "To return your earrings."

She reluctantly snatched them and looped them in her ears. She hadn't realized how naked she felt without them until they were firmly back in her ears. "This could have waited until tomorrow when you picked me up for our road trip."

"Maybe." He shrugged and smirked. "Perhaps I was curious to see where you worked."

"Nosy Nancy." She smacked his black sneakers off her desk and perched herself on the edge. When she crossed her legs, she noticed him staring at her outfit.

"Like what you see, Natasha?"

"Do you always dress like a librarian?" Nico waved a hand up and down her body. "Buttoned blouses, tight skirts, heels.

Just throw your hair up in a messy bun and put on some black rimmed glasses and you are a lot of men's fantasy."

"And are you one of them?"

"Maybe I am."

A crash sounded on the other side of the wall followed by a cough. Poppy. Ramsey rolled her eyes and shouted without looking behind her, "Poppy, you alright?"

"I'm fine," Poppy sheepishly answered as they listened to her pick up a pile of books she'd knocked off the shelf while attempting to eavesdrop.

"So," Nico cleared his throat, drawing Ramsey's attention. He stood up and started walking up and down the rows of bookcases. He put his finger on a shelf and swiped as if looking for dust. He wouldn't find any. Even though they were in the archives section of the museum, Ramsey was a stickler when it came to cleanliness and dusted religiously.

"So, what?" Ramsey followed him; arms still folded over her chest.

"What exactly do you do?" He fingered a tattered book spine and Ramsey hip checked him out of the way and neatly put it back in its spot with a frown.

"I am an archivist," she said. "I maintain, control, organize, and collect records for the museum."

Nico leaned against the metal shelf. "So, in other words, you're a big nerd."

"In simple terms. Yes." She squared her shoulders to his, popping her hip to the side. "I suppose I should have just said that so your puny brain could comprehend."

Nico walked toward her, so she was forced to back up against the bookshelf. He planted his hands on either side of her, eating the distance that remained between them. He flashed a deliciously wicked smile down at her and whispered, "How about a private tour of the museum?"

His chocolate brown eyes had specks of green scattered throughout that she hadn't noticed before. Not that she was normally this close to him, but with the lamplight hitting his face just right, the little details were hard to miss. She steadied her breathing. Being pinned against the bookshelves by a handsome man was most book loving women's fantasy, but she was not going to give him the satisfaction of watching her yearn with desire. This was Nico after all. He wasn't interested in her; he just liked to ruffle her feathers. She wasn't going to allow the feelings she had for him eight years ago continue to beg for resurrection.

"I'm sure you can schedule something at the front desk," she deadpanned.

"I meant with you."

"Don't you have work to do?"

"That's the funny thing about owning the bar," he whispered as if he was telling her a secret he didn't want anyone else to know. "I hire a staff to work when I'm not there. Crazy. So, any other excuses or do you want to just give in and show me around?"

"If you don't take him, I will!" Poppy's voice startled Ramsey causing her to jump. She scowled, fully aware of how close she and Nico were.

Nico stepped away from Ramsey until his back was against the opposite bookshelf. He smiled, "Thanks, Poppy."

"Yes, thanks, Poppy." Ramsey spotted her friend at the end of the row and tried to compose herself, knowing she was probably blushing. "You aren't going to leave unless I give you this tour, are you?"

Nico's smirk was answer enough.

"Fine," she swatted imaginary dust from her skirt. "Let's get this over with.

"The French and Indian War, otherwise known as the Seven Year's War, was an expensive endeavor for the British Monarchy and that resulted in new taxes on the colonies without representation. The Stamp Act of 1765 and the Townshend Act of 1767 were met with colonist protests which resulted in British troops shooting at a mob, killing five, which became known as the Boston Massacre of 1770. The Tea Act of 1773 followed. During a cold winter night in 1773, a group of men disguised themselves, boarded merchant ships in the Boston Harbor and proceeded to dump three hundred and forty-three cases of tea into the water. It later became known as the Boston Tea Party -"

Nico whistled; his hands buried deep in his pockets. Ramsey turned to look at him. "Problem, Niecy?"

"For someone who likes American history so much, you're boring the piss out of me, Price."

Ramsey's nostrils flared and she slammed her hands on her hips. "I don't *like* American history. I *love* it. And if you would let me finish without rudely interrupting you might love it too." She waited for him to respond but when he stood there staring at her with a blank expression, she sighed and rubbed the heels of her palms against her eyes. "Alright, look. How about we try a different approach?"

"I'm listening."

"I won't throw anymore dates and numbers at you." Ramsey glanced around the exhibit, which was oddly lacking summer patrons, probably due to it still being early. "I'll just take you to my favorite exhibits instead. How does that sound?"

Nico smiled and motioned for her to continue. "After you."

Ramsey led him to a room that had a replica of an elm tree standing in the center. She watched Nico circle it before he looked at her. She could see the questions in his eyes, and she answered before he had a chance to ask.

"This is a Liberty Tree. The first one was an elm in Boston, and it was where the Sons and Daughters of Liberty would meet from 1765-1775."

"You promised no more dates." Nico teased but his smile was warm, as if he really didn't want her to omit those details.

Ramsey found herself smiling back. "Well, the idea of Liberty Trees caught on and other colonial towns adopted the concept. Soon, it became a symbol of resisting tyranny."

Nico closed the gap between them and nodded his head in approval. "And why do you love this part of American history so much?"

It had been a while since someone had asked her that question. She took a second to mull it over before saying,

"Because a group of men and women fought for their right to live, worship, and forge a path so they and their children could be free. During a speech, Patrick Henry once declared, 'Give me liberty, or give me death,' and that not only resonated with his neighbors and peers, but it called out to me, too."

"Why is that phrase so important to you?"

Because all her life, Ramsey had felt the burden of her parents' and society's expectations weighing her down and at times, she felt as if she were drowning. Graduate high school. Graduate college. Get a job. Own your own place. Own your car. Be debt free. Date a successful man. Marry that successful man. Have that successful man's babies. Retire. Die. All in that order. Not at any point had she been instructed to live.

But she couldn't tell Nico any of those things. He might not understand or worse, he might laugh at her. Or even worse than that, he might agree with those expectations, and she'd have to take one of the swords on display and stab his cold, black heart.

"Ramsey?" Nico's voice dragged her back from her crippling thoughts.

"I just like the phrase." She cleared her throat and brushed past him to go to the next exhibit.

They continued through the *Revolutionary War Museum* as she showed him all the powder horns men would carry into battle. Most of them had been etched and engraved with the owner's names and decorative scenes such as houses, ships, and animals. She told Nico all about the weapons that the colonists used and how inferior their militia, compromised of soldiers and civilian riflemen, was compared to the British Regulars.

When they finally came to the room where a copy of the Declaration of Independence was displayed proudly even Nico seemed to pause to take the room in, as if his breath had been stolen. He was quiet for a long time before Ramsey realized he was taking the time to read through the document that fifty-six men had boldly and rebelliously signed. Those men decided to take a stand against tyranny and fight for the liberty and freedom their ancestors had come to the New World in search of hundreds of years prior.

"We hold these truths to be self-evident, that all men are created equal, that they are endowed by their Creator with certain unalienable Rights, that among these are Life, Liberty, and the pursuit of Happiness." Nico looked back at her and smiled. "No one writes like that anymore. It's beautiful, powerful, and revolutionary at the same time."

Ramsey was for the first time in a long time, lost for words. She felt as if he'd seen to the deepest parts of her soul and understood her passion like others didn't. Not even her ex-boyfriend, David, had shown a sliver of interest in her work. All she could do was stare at Nico until the sound of approaching patrons echoed from the adjoining room. She cleared her throat and motioned with her head for him to follow her out.

They silently walked side by side until they reached the exit.

"This is where I leave you," she said turning to face him. "I hope I didn't bore you."

Nico smiled and shook his head; the slight movement caused a few strands of dark hair to fall across his forehead. "You didn't bore me." He scratched his stubble and started walking toward the door. "You might have converted me."

"Converted you how?"

He glanced at her over his shoulder, not breaking his stride through the lobby, "I think I could find myself falling in love with American History."

She wasn't sure how to respond to that and stood there dumbstruck. It wasn't until he flashed his signature devilish grin that she snapped out of her stupor.

"I'll see you tomorrow, Price."

Ramsey stood there for a few more seconds watching him until he disappeared before venturing back down to the archives. Nico hadn't been terrible to be around that morning. And he hadn't been terrible the night before. Were she and Nico becoming... friends? After eight years of believing he couldn't stand her or that he only saw her as Sean's irritating little sister, were they finally connecting?

She opened the door to her shared office and Poppy pretended not to notice her walk in as she clicked away on her keyboard.

Ramsey sat at her desk and scooted her chair closer so she could finally start working on a few projects before leaving for the long weekend in Maine. Poppy hadn't said a word for several minutes and Ramsey was afraid she might combust if she didn't allow her to ask her questions.

"You may ask three questions," Ramsey said, eyeing her across the room.

"Soooooo," her friend flashed a toothy grin, planting her elbows on her desk and cupping her chin in her hands, "you spent the night with him?"

"You devil," Ramsey smirked. "I crashed at his place to sleep off my drunkenness."

Poppy hopped up and rounded her desk to hover over Ramsey's workspace. "Does he have a six or eight pack?"

"I wouldn't know." Ramsey lied and she knew that Poppy knew she was lying. The truth was, every time she closed her eyes, she could see the defined ridges of all six of his abs and the ribcage tattoo etched in his tan skin. "Now, can we get back to work, please?"

"I still have one more question." Poppy straightened to her full five-foot-three-inch height and crossed her arms over her busty chest. She looked like an angry fairy. All she was missing were her wings and some pixie dust.

"Alright, ask your question, Pop." Ramsey set her pen down and leaned back in her chair. "You're clearly bursting."

"Do you still hate him?"

Ramey was surprised by her question. She expected Poppy to ask something outrageous like *does he have a brother?* When she thought about Nico, she wasn't sure if what she felt toward him was hatred or just the pain and embarrassment of rejection. Maybe both. What was frightening, was that she was beginning to question what type of feelings she had for Nico and that wasn't something she really wanted to know the answer to. At least, not yet.

"Well?" Poppy's eyes were wide in hopeful anticipation. "Do you still hate him?"

"You're too meddlesome for your own good, Pop."

"So, that's a no." The redhead grinned and if Ramsey could see inside that brain of hers, all she'd probably see were unicorns, rainbows, and glitter. And perhaps the Chippendales.

"I think I'll reserve my answer for when I come back from Maine. A lot can happen in five days."

Nine

RAMSEY

The second Ramsey got home from work, she kicked her heels off, went to the kitchen, grabbed a handful of snacks, and walked up to her room, grateful her bedroom was on the second floor and not the third, and began packing her bag for the long weekend in Maine.

Five days.

Five days dealing with her six brothers and their families. Five days dealing with her overly involved and overbearing mother. Five days of having to answer the never-ending questions about David, her dating life, when she was going to get married, and why wasn't said boyfriend attending the wedding.

Suddenly, packing for five days seemed overwhelming and she pushed all the clothes she'd pulled from her closet to one side of her queen bed and scrunched up in her blankets. She swiped the remote off her nightstand and flipped through the channels until she landed a documentary about George Washington. One of her favorites. She'd watched it so many times, she could probably quote it word for word.

A soft knock on her door drew her attention and she reluctantly muted the television.

"Come in."

The wooden door squeaked open, and Sean poked his head inside. When he saw her wrapped in her favorite fluffy blanket his smile faded. "Rough day at work?"

Ramsey shook her head. It wasn't work. Work was the one place where there was order, structure, and routine. It was her safe space. It was everything else in her life that was a mess. Her two-year relationship over in a blink of an eye. A five-day vacation normally made people jump with joy, but she was dreading every second. Whatever was going on with Nico that filled her with irritation and embarrassing desire was also on her list of things beyond her control.

She hadn't realized Sean had sat on the edge of her bed until she felt the dip of her mattress under his weight. She met his concerned gaze and slipped the bag of chips out from underneath her blanket and offered him some. He took a handful and popped one in his mouth. She knew he wouldn't press her for answers because eventually she always told him what was bothering her.

"Are you sure you can't drive to Maine tomorrow?" she asked.

"Sorry, Rams, but I can't." He scratched his fingers through his short, reddish-blonde hair. "Is this about driving with Nico? Cause if you'd rather not, you can just wait to drive with me and Cali in a couple of days."

"No, it's not Nico. He's fine." Ramsey mentally swatted the picture of him half-naked out of her head. "Honestly, I'd rather fend off a pack of wolves in my underwear than deal with mom's passive aggressive wrath if I don't help her prep."

"Then what's bothering you?" He popped another chip in his mouth and crunched loudly.

Ramsey shrugged. "Five days is a long time."

"It'll be over faster than you realize, and you'll be back in that dungeon you call an office in no time," he smiled. And the thought of being back at work warmed her.

"Five days with our family having to explain again why I'm not married will be an eternity, Sean. You know that."

"Screw them, Ramsey."

"Sean!"

He grabbed her hand and squeezed. "You think I cared when mom pressed me to hurry up and find a girl to marry? No."

"You're also her sixth son," Ramsey pointed out, patting the top of his freckled hand. "I'm her only daughter. There are different expectations of me. If only she'd had seven daughters instead. Maybe I could have flown under the radar."

Sean barked a laugh. "Mom with seven daughters would have been torture for Dad."

Ramsey smiled thinking of their dad. Apart from Sean, most of her time growing up had been spent with him. He didn't treat her any differently than her brothers. She'd learned to hunt, fish, work on cars, and even studied economics, politics, and law from her dad. He never once pressured her to get married and even shed a few tears when she moved out of their family home. She had to admit, despite the nonsense the rest of her family brought to the table, she was excited to see her dad again. Maybe they could sneak away for an early morning hike together or down a bottle of scotch in his impressive library.

"Well, I'm at least excited to see Dad." Ramsey took a sip of her water bottle. "He won't badger me with a thousand personal questions."

"You think Melissa will be there?" Sean asked, scrunching his nose as if he'd smelled something rotten.

Ramsey shuddered. "I hope not. She basically ruined Christmas last year."

Melissa was their brother, Phineas', on-again-off-again girlfriend and simply put, she was a mess. They'd met years ago on one of the planes their pilot brother flew. She was a high-maintenance flight attendant who was loud, flirtatious, and every word that flowed from her mouth was insincere. It would have been easier, and more worthwhile, to have a conversation with a toad than Melissa Cooper.

"If she is there, hopefully she remembers which brother she came with this time." Ramsey's snide remark garnered a hearty laugh from Sean.

"Phineas does have a way with picking women, doesn't he?"

"If you're suggesting Captain Phineas Price picks women with anything other than his coc-"

"Ramsey," Sean shook his head in brotherly warning. He didn't like her using crass or rude humor, so she changed her wording.

"Fine," she snorted. "If you're suggesting Captain Phineas Price picks women with his lower extremities, then you'd be correct. He's never brought home a woman who could string two coherent sentences together let alone be a genuinely decent human."

Sean snickered, "You're in a rather judgmental mood this evening."

"Is it judgmental or blunt?" Ramsey quirked an eyebrow and Sean finished the last of his chips.

"Well, either way," Sean wiped his hands on his pants which drew a scowl from clean-freak Ramsey, "if she's there, play nice."

"Always," she smiled, but she and Sean both knew she didn't mean it.

"Last time you saw her, you two exchanged some...words."

"And I'll exchange more than words with her if she tries to shamelessly flirt with you in front of Cali again."

Ramsey couldn't help but think of the last family gathering that past Christmas. Melissa had arrived with Phineas, late as always, and toward the end of the evening was trying her damnedest to convince Sean to sleep with her. Even though it was clear that Cali and Sean were engaged. Sean politely declined as to not embarrass Melissa, but Ramsey wasn't that sort of person. She called the flight attendant out, making sure every member of the Price family caught an earful. Melissa demanded Phineas take her home, insisting Ramsey was belligerent, and he obliged. She hadn't spoken to Phineas since and it didn't bother her one bit.

"Promise you'll play nice." Sean's voice sliced her from her thoughts. "For Cali. We don't need any drama during our wedding weekend. You know how she hates a lot of attention as it is."

"Fine. I'll do my best. For Cali's sake," Ramsey crossed her fingers over her heart but kept two fingers twisted behind her back.

"I know what you're doing," Sean sighed, fighting to hold back a smile.

"What do you mean?" Ramsey cocked her head to the side, feigning confusion.

"Let me see the hand behind your back."

"What?" Ramsey lifted her hidden hand for him to see, uncrossing her fingers. "You mean this hand?"

"You're a child," Sean laughed as he stood up.

"Well, I am the baby of the family."

Sean walked to Ramsey's closet and pulled out one of her Phillies t-shirts and tossed it at her. She caught it before it smacked her in the face. "Put that on and get dressed. We're going to a Phillies game tonight."

"You have tickets?"

Sean grinned and pulled four tickets out of his pocket. "Consider this my apology for not being able to drive you to Mom and Dad's tomorrow."

"Four tickets?" Ramsey narrowed her eyes.

Sean counted them out as he said, "One for you. One for me. One for Cali. And one for Nico."

"Nico's coming?" she asked, trying to mask her odd excitement when hearing his name.

"Yeah," Sean nodded. "It was actually his idea."

"His idea?"

"I told him I felt bad about sending you to Mom and Dad's on your own and wanted to get you something to apologize. He suggested going to the Phillies game tonight. Said you'd enjoy the experience rather than a physical gift." Sean paused and rubbed his chin while her traitorous heart leapt. "Unless he was messing with me, and you would have preferred something else."

Ramsey shook her head quickly. "A baseball game is perfect. Thank you, Sean." She kissed his cheek and pushed him out of her room. "Now get out so I can get dressed."

Ten

Nico

When Nico suggested Sean take Ramsey to a Phillies game, he hadn't expected his best friend to purchase him a ticket and insist on him joining them. He couldn't say no to Sean, but he wasn't sure how Ramsey would react to him being there. He'd be lying if he said he wasn't interested, even excited, to see her twice in one day, but he couldn't show her that. He might scare her off or worse, she might use it as ammunition to make fun of him and he wasn't sure he could handle that type of humiliation.

Nico's thoughts kept floating back to seeing Ramsey at the museum earlier. He couldn't rid himself of the image of how beautiful she looked – how enticing she was. He didn't think himself to be into the librarian look, but after spending an hour with her touring the museum, he basically had to sprint out of there before his knees gave out and he fell before her like a knight paying homage to his queen.

He'd wanted to kiss her in the archives room when he'd pinned her against one of the bookshelves. And the way she'd looked up at him, he knew if he leaned forward an inch, she would have met his advances with one of her own. But then Poppy popped up and rattled him. He'd waited eight long years to kiss her, to hold her, to call her his. He could wait a little longer.

Nico was brought back to the present when he heard Sean call out his name. He glanced at his watch and smiled. He didn't have to wait long in front of one of the entrances into Citizens Bank Park before Ramsey, Sean, and Cali showed up. The members of the Price family were sticklers when it came to punctuality, and he made sure he was early, not wanting to give Ramsey any reason to be irritated with him before their long road trip the next morning.

"Fancy seeing you here." Always the first to greet someone, Cali hugged him tightly before Sean dapped him up.

"Thanks for inviting me." Nico's gaze shifted from Sean to Ramsey and his heart lodged in his throat. If he thought she looked gorgeous this morning, then he was sure to bow down to her tonight. Her red Phillies baseball hat sat atop her loose platinum blonde hair and her lips were painted the same shade of red. Ripped-at-the-knees denim jeans, a Phillies t-shirt that hugged every curve, and high-top sneakers; everything about her was casual and put together at once, right down to her expensive watch and black nails. She looked like a hot witch who just happened to like baseball.

He knew he was staring. He knew Ramsey knew he was staring. And yet, he couldn't tear his eyes away from her. Then she smiled and he nearly came undone.

"Damn, I must be looking good if it rendered you speechless, Nannette." Her voice jarred him from his stupor.

Nico thought maybe they could move past their banter after their time together in the museum, but clearly, she wasn't ready to give that up yet. He was willing to play; he'd gotten pretty good at it after two years. He flashed her his signature grin and smoothed his hair down, slipping his baseball cap on backwards. "I was just wondering if you're here, who is scaring the crows away from eating our crops."

Ramsey narrowed her eyes at him with a smirk. How he wished he could read her mind, just once, to know what she was thinking. How she really felt about him.

"A scarecrow joke," Ramsey brushed past him, her fingers trailing through his, sending a shiver down his spine. "How original," she whispered and the urge to pin her arms over her head and claim her lips caused his heart to beat faster.

Nico shrugged, "I aim to please."

Sean had bought the best tickets he could short notice, and they were incredible seats. They were a few rows away from the field along the first base line. Sean claimed the aisle seat and Cali sat next to him. Ramsey scooted past the couple, making sure she didn't spill her beer, and took the third seat, leaving Nico the fourth seat to Ramsey's right.

Ramsey leaned close to Nico and whispered, "Sean told me coming to the game was your idea."

He turned his head slightly to meet her gaze. His first instinct was to deny it, but she wouldn't believe Sean lied about it. So, he bobbed his head and took a sip of his beer. "It might have been."

"Well," she batted her eyes beneath the rim of her hat, and he imagined pulling her onto his lap and kissing her slowly from her lips down to her... "It was a good idea." It seemed like it took great effort for her to admit, and it made him smile which garnered her rolling her eyes. "See, this is why I don't compliment you."

"What else would you compliment me about?" His eyebrows bounced playfully.

She snickered and shook her head. "And give you an even bigger head? You'll float right out of the stadium."

"Try me. A compliment for a compliment."

She stared at him for a second before tucking a few strands of hair behind her ear. "Is this another one of our little games?"

"It's either the compliment game or we can go for another round of the uncomfortable game," he rubbed the back of his neck, making sure to flex his bicep, and smiled when she noticed and quickly looked out toward the field.

"Fine." She glanced back at him and those grey-blue eyes of hers gave him goosebumps. "A compliment for a compliment. I already gave you one. So, now, you have to say something nice about me." Her Cheshire cat grin made him laugh. "How hard will this be for you, Noelle?"

Nico set his arm next to hers on their shared armrest. Her skin was warm and soft, and she smelled like vanilla. If only she knew complimenting her wasn't a difficult task. His dilemma was which one to start with.

He rubbed the stubble along his jawline.

"Is it really that troubling for you?" she chuckled.

Nico met her gaze; the brim of her baseball cap nearly touched his forehead. "I think you're funny."

Ramsey rolled her eyes and huffed.

"What?" Nico tilted his head up. "What's wrong with what I said?"

"Are you setting yourself up for a joke?"

"No," he rubbed the heels of his palms against his eyes. "What are you talking about? What joke?"

"You say you think I'm funny," Ramsey leaned back in her seat, stretching her legs in front of her, "and when I think you mean it, you say, 'I mean, funny looking.'" She faked a deep laugh and Nico covered his mouth to keep from laughing.

Once he composed himself, he shook his head. "I know that sounds like something I'd do, but I mean it. I think you're funny. And smart. And beautiful. And you look great in Phillies colors."

She sat in silence for what felt like an eternity before she asked, "You mean all those things?" He nodded, eyes fixed on hers, hoping she would see he was telling her the truth. Expressing, even if just a miniscule amount, how he felt about her.

She leaned toward him, her lips hovering over his ear. "That might work on other girls, but I'm not so easily swayed by the charms of men."

A warmth flooded his body and the urge to prove her wrong consumed him. "You don't believe me?" Nico turned his head, his forehead brushed against the brim of her hat.

"Not a word."

"I guess I'll have to prove you wrong."

They held one another's gaze and if this is what electricity felt like shooting through his body, he didn't want the feeling to stop. There was something behind those grey-blue eyes that had him wishing he could read minds. What was she thinking right that moment? Whatever flashed across her face was gone a second later and she shrugged with a typical Ramsey smirk.

"Don't hurt yourself trying, Nova." Her attention was now fully fixed on her plastic cup filled with beer and on the baseball players running out onto the field. "I won't lose any sleep waiting on you."

The Phillies pulled out a 3-2 win and surprisingly, Ramsey hadn't given him too hard of a time during the game. They'd sparred with their words several times and argued over which baseball position took the most skill to play, but other than that, hanging out with her had been enjoyable.

It had taken hours of prodding, but Ramsey finally relented and gave him her new cellphone number and he promised he'd use it for good and not for pranking.

After parting ways with Sean, Cali, and Ramsey, Nico made his way to his bar to check on his staff before they insisted he go home and enjoy his vacation in Maine.

Was he excited about travelling with Ramsey? He'd be lying if he said he wasn't, but he was nervous too. Since college, he'd kept his distance, and made sure to keep his actions purely platonic for Sean's sake. The last thing he needed was this near decade old crush to put a wedge between him and his best friend.

When Sean asked him if he'd be willing to drive Ramsey to Maine, he wanted to say no. But the treacherous part of himself screamed yes and willingly agreed to Sean's plan. There had been a chance Ramsey would have picked flying over letting him drive her, but he knew she got nauseous on planes. The last trip she'd taken was to Hawaii with David and when she got back, she swore up and down she'd never get on another plane unless it was absolutely necessary. There had been turbulence, screaming babies, gassy passengers, and the sway and bumps throughout the flight prevented her from getting a wink of sleep. When she stepped off the plane in Hawaii, it took her nearly the entire vacation to get her bearings back and before she knew it, she was flying back to the mainland.

From how Ramsey told the story, David hadn't been much help or fun during their tropical getaway. He remembered her sitting in his bar, wearing a body curving black dress with strappy black high heels and was dripping in diamonds, apology gifts from David. She looked like she should have been on a red carpet somewhere, not slouched on a stained barstool in his tavern. But there she was, sitting with Sean and Cali, wondering if she was even good enough to be with someone like David.

It had taken all of Nico's willpower to prevent him from wrapping her in his arms and kissing her from head to toe, showing her how a real man treated the woman of his dreams. But he'd kept quiet except for when she quipped at him and he'd returned the jabs, knowing it helped her in some way. He'd do whatever he could to put a smile on her face, even if it meant she saw him as her brother's irritating and obnoxious friend from college instead of mounting him and claiming him for herself.

As Nico packed a bag for their road trip, he racked his brain for any excuse he could think of as to why he and Ramsey shouldn't be alone in a car together, but all he could think about was making sure she got to her parents' house safely and on time to avoid her mother's wrath. He had it bad for her and she wasn't even his. He could only imagine what he'd be willing to do to make her happy if she were his girl.

Ramsey Elizabeth Price was going to be his undoing and he was more than willing to accept his fate.

Eleven

RAMSEY

Ramsey could have taken the day off since she was leaving for Maine that morning, but she couldn't help herself. She would worry all weekend long if she hadn't come in to finish a project and organize her desk for her absence.

She and Poppy shared their usual morning cup of coffee together before they said their goodbyes. Once Ramsey was done cleaning up and finalizing some paperwork, she'd be meeting Nico outside for their road trip. Poppy had a meeting to go to and then she was going to get ready for a date, promising Ramsey she'd text her later about it.

In the quiet of their shared office space, Ramsey nearly jumped out of her skin when her phone rang. She quickly searched her purse, cringing as it echoed throughout the archives. All she needed was for Old Man Jenkins to shuffle into her space from across the hallway fussing about the noise. He was so old she and Poppy would joke that he fought alongside Washington. He was in charge of all the museum staff from the tour guides to the gift shop workers to the volunteers for occasional events. In all honesty, she was going to miss the old man once he retired the following year. He was crotchety but he did his job well.

Thankfully, she got to her phone before it could spur Old Man Jenkins into action and when she saw Cali's picture pop up, she immediately answered instead of sending it to voicemail.

"Hey Cali," Ramsey tucked her cell phone between her ear and shoulder, continuing to organize papers on her desk. "Is everything ok?"

"Ramsey, please tell me you haven't left for Maine yet?" Cali sounded borderline panicked and out of breath, like she'd been running a marathon.

"Not yet." Ramsey glanced at her office door that was propped open, thinking she heard shuffling shoes, but her elderly colleague didn't appear. "Why?"

"I need you to do me a huge favor!"

"Anything." Ramsey straightened, her full attention on Cali.

"I was supposed to pick up my wedding dress today but I'm going to be at work late and the shop will be closed by the time I get off. I would ask Sean to pick it up, but I know he'll peek. He can't help himself." Cali rattled on, and Ramsey could picture her future sister-in-law pacing up and down the hospital hallways in her scrubs, rubbing her fingers across her forehead.

As a nurse, Cali was the best of the best. She was great under pressure and saved countless lives in the ER and

Ramsey loved when she would share the outrageous stories about some of her patients. But when it came to having all the attention on her, Cali panicked. Ramsey was there the day she picked her wedding gown and being the sole focus in the boutique shop nearly brought Cali to tears.

And she wasn't wrong about Sean. He would definitely peek. When they were kids, every Christmas Eve, Sean would go searching the house for his presents and when he found them, he'd open them just to rewrap them before their parents could bust him. He hated surprises and he'd go out of his way to figure out if someone was throwing him a birthday party or gage what someone was preparing to give him for the holidays just so he could match the effort.

"Do you need me to pick your dress up for you?" Ramsey shook the memories free and focused on the task at hand.

"And take it with you to your parents' house." Cali exhaled a breath. "I'm sorry. I wouldn't ask if I could do it myself."

Ramsey waved a hair in the air, even though her future sister-in-law couldn't see it. "It's not a problem. I'll let you know when I pick it up."

"You are a lifesaver!" Cali squealed. "Thank you!"

"No problem." Ramsey finished straightening her desk and beamed in pride. "You're right by the way. Sean would definitely peek."

Cali's laugh echoed through the phone. "Absolutely." A beat of silence passed before she said, "I hope you enjoy the road trip with Nico. Hopefully you two can get along for seven hours."

"We'll figure it out." Ramsey managed to respond, but with Nico fresh in her thoughts, she became nervous of being stuck in the car with him. What would they talk about for seven hours? Would they just sit in silence the entire time? What kind of music did he like? What if he was a terrible driver and she was stressed the entire way?

Ramsey realized they'd both been silent for far too long and she knew Cali had something else she wanted to say but was holding back. "Out with it, Cali."

"What do you mean?"

"Every time you get really quiet on the phone it's because you are debating on whether you should say what you're thinking. Go ahead and tell me."

"I don't want to upset you," Cali said softly.

Ramsey perched her thigh on the edge of her desk and swung her leg. "Nothing you could say will offend me. I have six brothers and an invasive mother."

Cali nervously chuckled. "Ok." She sighed, as if she were summoning the courage to spit the words out. "I think if you gave Nico a chance, you two would be perfect for each other."

Ramsey's chest tightened. She hadn't expected Cali to say that.

"Ramsey?" Cali's voice was higher in pitch, concern lacing her tone. "Are you there?"

"I'm here."

"See, you're upset."

Ramsey shook her head. "No, Cali. I'm fine," she croaked cheerfully to ease her friend's mind. "I just didn't expect you to say that is all."

"Nico is a good guy," Cali pressed on. "I think if you let him, he could make you happy." Someone in the background mumbled something to Cali and she huffed a response. "Sorry, Rams, I have to go. Duty calls. I'll talk to you tonight."

As soon as Cali hung up, her words hovered over Ramsey like a thick, heavy rain cloud.

If you let him, he could make you happy.

She was used to people disappointing her, letting her down, putting her last – she was used to being unhappy. She wasn't sure she would even recognize a happy or healthy relationship if it bit her in the butt. But then again, when she watched her brother with Cali, she could feel their love for one another. It was like staring at the moon – the glow and wonder of its presence, the comfort it brought.

Her phone buzzed in her palm, and it made her jump. She looked down at the screen and saw Nico's name. She glanced at her watch and saw it was already ten in the morning. She pushed her desk chair in and answered his call as she walked out the door.

"Hey, before we head out of town, I need to make a quick stop."

"I've told everyone I know who I'm with and where I'm going," Nico's sultry voice washed over her like a much-needed hug. "If you murder me, they'll know who did it."

Though she was alone in the hall, she tried her best to hide the smile that spread across her face.

"I'm not going to hurt you," she cooed. "But I can't promise you won't hate me."

Twelve

Nico

Never in a million years did Nico think he'd be sitting in a bridal shop. There were so many shades of white it was alarming. He stood in the center of the boutique with his hands buried deep in his pockets afraid if he ran a finger across the bodice of one of the delicate gowns it would disintegrate.

The three bridal consultants working that morning watched him as Ramsey signed the paperwork to pick up Cali's wedding dress. Ramsey had whispered right before they entered that the shop didn't see a lot of men come in, so it explained why one saleswoman eyed him suspiciously. The second woman looked him over with a hungry gleam in her eyes. He wasn't unaccustomed to that look from women, but he stuck close to Ramsey just in case she tried to approach him. And the third was an older woman helping Ramsey and she didn't even give him a second glance.

"We'll have her dress wrapped up and ready to go in a few minutes," the older woman smiled. "Please," she motioned to the chairs in front of a podium surrounded by mirrors, "make yourselves comfortable."

"Thank you," Ramsey bobbed her head and motioned for Nico to join her.

Nico sat down and watched Ramsey look around in the reflection of the mirror. She didn't seem overwhelmed by the countless options, she seemed almost sad. And then he remembered how she thought David was going to propose and instead she left him. He was still unsure of where the two of them stood but he was grateful that he was even spending time alone with Ramsey. He could only hope she felt the same way.

One dress caught Ramsey's eye and she slowly walked over to it and ran a gentle, tentative finger down the skirt. It was simple looking compared to the other grand dresses on display but for some reason it screamed of Ramsey. There were no frills or beads or lace – it was a plain, white dress with off the shoulder sleeves and a silky skirt.

"Why don't you try it on?" Nico suggested before he realized he'd even said it. She glanced at him and there was a sadness in her eyes that he wished he could erase.

"When Cali was here trying on dresses, I saw this one and fell in love with it." Ramsey returned her attention to the ivory gown. "I thought I'd be able to try it on soon but..."

Nico shifted in his chair. He'd upset her. But instead of her lashing out she said nothing, and that was worse.

"I'm sorry, I shouldn't have said anything."

Ramsey shook her head and mustered a small smile. "It's ok. Not your fault."

One of the consultants – the hungry-eyed one – came to check on them and noticed Ramsey's hand lingering on the dress of her dreams. "Would you like to try it on? It would look perfect on you!"

"Oh," Ramsey protested, "I'm not here for myself."

"When are you two getting married?" she asked, her gaze raking up and down Nico's body. "Or are you not together?"

Ramsey opened her mouth but before she could get a word out, Nico interrupted. "Go ahead, honey, try the dress on." He flashed a smile at the consultant, "We're not a traditional couple. She doesn't mind me seeing the dress before the big day."

The look on Ramsey's face should have stopped his heart but he wasn't interested in dealing with the unwanted attention or advances of the shop attendant. Ramsey once again tried to protest but the saleswoman put her professional mask on and swept her into a dressing room, taking the coveted dress with her.

Nico knew he'd pay for this on the trip, but he was oddly excited to see what Ramsey looked like in a wedding dress. With black being her favorite color to wear, it had him curious to see what white would look like against her skin.

He only had to wait a couple of minutes before the consultant stepped out of the room with a grin that took up most of her face. "Your fiancée is stunning." She motioned for Ramsey to exit the dressing area and to step on the podium in front of Nico. "Come on, dear. Don't be shy. You look gorgeous."

When Ramsey rounded the corner and walked toward the podium, his heart nearly exploded in his chest. She looked heavenly, other-worldly. Her hair cascaded over her bare shoulders as she took a step up onto the small, circular pedestal. The attendant helped her fluff out the train and Ramsey stared at herself in the mirror. The entire room was so quiet, you could hear the church bells several blocks away chiming the time.

"What do you think?" Nico only realized the saleswoman was speaking to him when Ramsey cleared her throat and stared at him in the mirror.

He held Ramsey's gaze. She was pleading with him to be kind; he could see it in her blue-grey eyes. If only she knew he would remember her in this dress for the rest of his life. That no other woman would surpass her beauty, wit, and drive. That she was his entire world. But she couldn't know. She would push him further away and he'd waited eight years to get close to her.

"You look beautiful," he managed to say in a barely audible whisper.

Ramsey looked taken aback. "You think so?"

He nodded and stood up. He circled around to stand in front of her and looked up into her hazy eyes. "I think you're the most beautiful woman I've ever laid my eyes on."

Ramsey tilted her head slightly, quickly glancing at his lips before returning to meet his gaze. The attendant clapped her hands loudly, breaking whatever spell they'd been un-der. "You are a lucky man!" she cried.

Nico smiled, his eyes never leaving Ramsey's. "I am."

"Ramsey?" A shrill, southern voice rang out when the small bell over the front door dinged. "Ramsey Price, is that you!?"

Ramsey's eyes widened and whatever joy that had been on her face was wiped clean. She slowly turned toward the brunette; horror written across her face. "Jessica, it's been a long time."

"I knew it was you!" Jessica waved her hand up and down Ramsey's frame. "This looks gorgeous on you! I didn't know you and David had gotten engaged. I figured he'd take an ad in the newspaper to declare his love! Let me see the ring!"

Nico could sense Ramsey panicking and his need to protect her rushed through his body. He hadn't realized his fists were clenched when he took a step forward but before he could say anything, Ramsey cleared her throat halting him.

"Actually, David and I broke up."

Jessica's mouth dropped open. "Oh, you poor thing. Did he dump you? He dumped you, didn't he?"

"I -"

"It's ok," Jessica didn't let Ramsey get a word in and Nico wished he could snap his fingers and make the woman disappear. "It's hard being with successful men sometimes. It is our duty to make their lives easier, but they don't always appreciate us." She rolled her eyes and snatched Ramsey's hand, patting it like a child's. "You're strong. You'll get through this. Maybe he'll see he made a huge mistake in letting you go."

"He didn't let me go," Ramsey growled, anger flooding her features as she ripped her hand from Jessica's grasp. "*I* dumped *him*. Now, if you'll excuse me, Jessica, Nico and I have plans." She grabbed Nico's hand and pulled him toward the dressing room, away from Jessica's prying eyes and irritating voice.

Nico allowed Ramsey to drag him into the small changing area. Once she slammed the door behind them, she squatted on the floor, the skirt pooling around her, and started breathing heavily. She was having a panic attack. His sister, Guilianna, had them all the time as a teenager. He dropped down to the carpeted floor, gently took her hands in his, and forced her to make eye contact with him by tilting her chin up.

"Breathe with me," he said softly. "Inhale, exhale. Inhale, exhale." Together they breathed rhythmically until Ramsey was calm. "Are you alright, Ramsey?"

"You used my name?" She looked surprised, almost relieved, he'd used her actual name and not one of his many tit-for-tat pet names.

"Would you prefer I didn't?"

They were so close to each other. One brave push and his lips would claim hers. They'd ruin that wedding dress before she even had a chance to walk down an aisle.

Ramsey's bottom lip quivered, and he placed his hand against the wall behind her head, steadying himself. The air seemed to get sucked out of the dressing room, leaving them breathless and wanting. Ramsey perused his face gingerly. What she was searching for, he didn't know, but he didn't mind the attention, in fact, he relished it. He yearned for it.

When her knee bumped into his, it sent his heart skyrocketing to the moon. Her breath hitched when he started to lean closer, but she didn't stop him.

What was he doing?

Was she tilting her head to meet him halfway?

He'd thought about kissing Ramsey for years – thought about what her lips would feel like on his, what her body pressed against his would do to him.

Inches. They were inches apart as her eyes closed and his heart thrashed in his chest.

A knock on the door startled them. "Miss? Are you alright? Do you need some help out of the dress?" The saleswoman's voice was dripping in concern which seemed to irk Ramsey's nerves.

"She's fine," Nico answered, mentally uttering every curse word in the English language. "We'll be out in a minute." He turned his attention back to Ramsey who had rested her head against the wall where his hand was still rooted. Fighting the urge to stroke his fingers through her hair, he said, "I'm going to step outside. If you need me, let me know."

As if his comment sobered her from her stupor, she nodded, and allowed him to help her to her feet. He slipped out of the room and paced outside the dressing room, making sure no one came near the door. His need to protect her was an odd sensation. It seemed primal, like it had been programmed into his DNA to watch over her and keep someone from shattering her heart.

Nico noticed Jessica chatting with the bridal consultants, but he couldn't overhear what they were whispering about. He could take a good guess and probably not be far off. Their eyes flicked over toward him, and their tongues started wagging again. He wanted to know who Jessica was to

Ramsey, but he wouldn't bring it up. His curiosity wasn't more important than her mental health.

The dressing room door flew open, and Ramsey's tough exterior and no-nonsense mask was firmly back in place. She went into the changing area looking like a heavenly creature and she emerged a dark and powerful queen ready to slay her enemies. She glanced at him and tilted her head toward the front door, signaling she was ready when he was. He pressed his hand against the lower part of her back and ushered her out. Ramsey grabbed Cali's wrapped dress from the older attendant and muttered a goodbye to Jessica before stomping down the city sidewalk toward the parking garage where Nico's truck was.

"Let me," he extended his hand to grab the heavy garment bag and surprisingly, she allowed him to take it from her.

They walked a block silently before Ramsey spoke. "Jessica is engaged to one of David's colleagues. I never liked her. Now I hate her."

"That makes two of us," Nico scoffed which put a small smile on Ramsey's forlorn face. "I'm sorry that happened. I never would have suggested you put the dress on -"

"About that," she interrupted, throwing a hand on her hip. "What the hell was that? You acted like we were together."

"That blonde saleswoman was eyeing me the second I step foot in that shop," he explained. "I wasn't really in the mood to deal with that angsty feminine energy."

"You think too highly of yourself," Ramsey teased, rolling her eyes.

"Well, for what it's worth," he bumped his shoulder into hers, garnering her attention, "you did look beautiful in the dress."

Was she blushing?

"Thanks," she tucked hair behind her ear. "I guess it was kind of fun to finally see what I looked like in it." She made eye contact with him again, but something flashed across her face, causing her to frown.

"What is it?"

She shrugged, flicking her finger across her nose ring as they walked through the parking garage to his truck. "Nothing."

Nico hung the dress up in the back seat of the four-door truck before opening Ramsey's passenger door.

She crossed her arms over her chest, popping a hip to the side. "What are you doing?"

"Being polite?" he squinted.

"You're holding your punches."

He glanced around the parking lot to make sure no one overheard her or misunderstood. "What are you talking about?"

"This," she waved a hand at the door he propped open. "Opening my door, carrying Cali's dress, calling me Ramsey. You're holding your punches and that makes me feel like shit."

"I'm trying to be nice."

"Well, stop being nice!" Her tone surprised him, and he recoiled. "Treat me like you would anyone else!"

"I don't treat anyone else the way I treat you, Price!" he snapped, and she stood there open-mouthed. "Just," he exhaled, running a hand through his hair. "Just get in the truck. We have a long drive ahead of us."

Nico left her door open and walked to his side of the vehicle. He'd never raised his voice to her before and he felt awful. His heart was bubbling with angst and his feelings for her were starting to overwhelm him. Nothing would make him happier than for Ramsey to straddle him and claim him as her own. To share her innermost thoughts and feelings with him. To let him in. To give him a shot at making her happy. He was sick of seeing her sad, lonely, and put on the back burner. She was so focused on David, the man who forgot her birthday every year they were together, that she was blind to him standing there, waiting, willing, begging to treat her the way she deserved. She was his queen, but she would only ever treat him as a court jester. Someone to poke fun at, someone to verbally spar with, but not someone to give her heart to.

He made a mistake when they were in college, and he'd regretted it every day since. He should have told her how he felt about her years ago. But eight years later, still harboring the same feelings for her and sitting on them, made him hate himself. He hated that he would put himself through this torture. And now that she was single, and they were alone together, he couldn't bring himself to confess. All he kept seeing was David's face and he knew that even though Ramsey had dumped him, he wasn't sure she wouldn't go back to him if he put a ring on her finger.

Nico slammed his door shut, stabbed the keys into the ignition, and the truck roared to life. Before he threw the vehicle in reverse, Ramsey grabbed his forearm and squeezed.

"I'm sorry I snapped at you," she whispered, her eyes glued to the dashboard. "I don't want you treating me like I'm weak."

"Price, you're one of the strongest people I know." He leaned his head back until it connected with the headrest. He closed his eyes and sighed. "I won't pull my punches if it means that much to you."

"I just want things to go back to the way they used to be." Her words stung but he nodded in agreement.

"If that's what you want," he turned his head and met her gaze, "then that's what it'll be."

She nodded and with that, he silently drove the car out of the parking lot and didn't say another word until they hit the interstate.

Thirteen

RAMSEY

Ramsey had dreaded the road trip with Nico for days but not for the reason she now found herself squirming in the passenger seat of his black truck. In the parking garage when she snapped at him and he raised his voice in response, it rattled her. She'd been yelled at before by her six brothers, his tone didn't bother her. It had been the pained look in his eyes that stole her breath. When he'd said her name, it felt like a whispered prayer. She wanted to beg him to say it again. She wanted to hear her name slip from his lips. For a brief second, she felt her walls tumbling down in front of him and she couldn't allow that to happen. They were getting dangerously close to being open with one another and that would mean she would have to address her unwanted resurfacing feelings for him.

Sitting two feet away from Nico might as well have been miles. They hadn't uttered a word to each other since they'd pulled out of the parking lot, and it was slowly driving her insane.

She wished he'd look at her so she could initiate a conversation, but he didn't. As if he was purposely remaining silent until she broke the standoff first. Reaching out to him was the last thing and the only thing she wanted to do. But if she did, she might lose some game he was playing, and she didn't like losing.

They hit a bump in the road and the bounce slammed the side of her head into the window.

"Ouch!" Ramsey rubbed her head.

"Are you alright?" Nico asked, glancing over at her, meeting her gaze for the first time in hours.

"I'm fine," she nodded before he refocused on the road. She exhaled a sigh of relief. It wasn't a full-blown conversation, but it was a start. She cleared her throat. "How much longer?" Internally, she cringed at the question. She sounded like a petulant child asking, *Are we there yet?*

She spied a half smile on his face and loved that it crinkled the corners of his eyes. She shooed the urge to run a finger across his stubbled jawline and tore her eyes from his face. *What was going on?* She'd not looked at Nico like that since college. Was there a full moon? Was she ovulating? What was going on?

"We should be there in a few more hours," his voice sliced through her thoughts. "Why don't you like long car rides?"

"Semi-trucks make me nervous." The words slipped out before she thought better of it. She'd unwittingly armed him with ammunition to tease her about. As if just speaking of the trucks summoned them, a moving truck zoomed by

Nico's vehicle. Ramsey gripped the center consul and the door handle, closed her eyes, and took a deep, calming breath. When she felt Nico grab her left hand, her eyes flew open. Staring at his tan hand clasping hers while he continued watching the road as he drove made her heart beat faster. Once the semi-truck was ahead of them, he quickly turned to catch her awaiting gaze.

"I don't like them either," he said softly.

He was being kind again and she should scold him, she should fuss at him for holding his punches, but for some reason she couldn't bring herself to do it. What was even more unlike her was she liked his hand holding hers. She wished she could curl her fingers in his, but this was just him feeling sorry for her. Not just sorry about her fear of large trucks barreling down the interstate, but what happened in the bridal shop.

Internally, she screamed when Jessica Farrow, blabber-mouth of the south, walked into the store. Jessica was engaged to David's colleague, Ellis Tucker, and he spent less time with his fiancée than David did with her when they were together. Truthfully, Jessica didn't care if Ellis so much as looked at her, so long as she got the expensive wedding of her Alabama heart's dream. She acted as if the diamond perched on her left hand weighed the entire left side of her body down, but Cali sported a larger engagement ring and saved lives day and night at the ER without so much as blinking. Ramsey never liked Jessica and when her shrill, southern voice echoed in the boutique while she was standing on a pedestal in a wedding dress she had no business trying on, she just about fell over and died of embarrassment. And with

Nico standing in front of her, looking like he wanted to take his time undressing her, she was positive – in fact, she'd bet every damn dollar in her banking account – that by this time tomorrow, Jessica would have told everyone in Philadelphia what she saw and heard.

"Ramsey?" Nico pulled her back to the present. "Are you hungry?"

He said her name again, sending goosebumps rippling over her skin.

"Ramsey?" He asked once more time, patient but looking for an answer.

She cleared her throat, hoping she wasn't blushing. "I could eat."

Nico bobbed his head, as if that was exactly what he wanted to hear. "I have the perfect place to stop."

Ramsey was surprised when Nico pulled off the interstate, drove down the road a couple of miles to a small town she'd never heard of, and pulled up to a food truck in the middle of their downtown strip. Without giving him too much of a hassle, he convinced her to get out of his truck to try some of the best food he'd ever had.

"Barbeque?" she asked once they made it to the late lunchtime line.

He looked down at her with a smile. "Don't tell me you don't like barbeque, Price."

She grimaced but before she had a chance to explain she'd never tried barbeque before, he'd already figured it out.

"Never?" Nico's eyes widened in wonder. "You've never had barbeque before? Ever?"

Ramsey shook her head and shrugged. "Barbeque was never high on my list of cuisines to try." They took a couple steps forward, moving with the line. "How did you even know about this place?"

"After holiday or summer breaks I would drive myself up to Boston for college and would always make it a point to stop here. I found it by pure luck." He took another step toward the food truck; they were next in line. "I needed gas and hopped off the exit and followed the signs. After I filled up, I saw this food truck and decided to try it. Now, anytime I have to drive this way, I stop."

"Nico!" The food truck owner bellowed from his tiny window; arms outstretched in welcome. "Long time, no see!"

Nico smiled and stepped up to the counter. "It's good to see you, Gus."

Gus peered over at Ramsey and shot her a friendly smile. "I see you're not alone this time. Who is this?"

"This is Ramsey," Nico started the introductions. She was curious to see how he would explain who she was to him and by the look in Nico's impish gaze, she knew it wasn't going to be good. "She's a hitchhiker I picked up earlier today."

Ramsey rolled her eyes and Gus roared in laughter. "If you're telling me good looking women like her are stranded on the side of the highway, sign me up."

She extended her hand for the foodie to shake. "It's nice to meet you, Gus. I'm actually his best friend's sister."

Gus winked at her. "I figured as much. We don't get a lot of models coming through our little town."

"You flatterer." Nico shook his head at Gus.

"If this one doesn't treat you right," Gus tossed a thumb Nico's direction, "you give me a call and I'll punch him right in the nose."

"Oh, don't you worry about me, Gus," Ramsey shot a mischievous look at Nico. "I have six older brothers. Nico doesn't stand a chance."

Nico smiled at her, and a warmth pooled in her lower belly. She shooed the feelings away, blaming it on her obvious hunger, and pointed at a picture hanging above Gus. "I'll try number four."

"So, two number fours then?" Gus asked and Ramsey whipped her head to look at her traveling companion.

Nico nodded. "Two number fours, one check."

"Coming right up." Gus scurried to prep their to-go meals.

"Did you want a number four?" she asked.

"It's what I normally order whenever I come here."

What were the odds of that happening?

"At least I know it's good then."

He tilted his head, "Is that a compliment?"

"What?"

"You trust my taste in food?" Nico leaned against the side of the barbeque food truck, crossing his arms over his chest, a smirk snaking across his face.

Ramsey rolled her eyes but before she could utter a retort, Nico pointed at her and teased, "You keep rolling your eyes like that and they might get stuck that way."

"Thanks, Grandma." Ramsey snorted, "You're the reason I'm even rolling my eyes."

"Oh, Princess, if I was giving you a reason for your eyes to roll back in your head, you wouldn't complain."

There it was again. The hunger of desire in his eyes. A tingling sensation rippled through her body, leaving goose-bumps in their wake. She couldn't be imaging the sexual angst between them. What had changed between them over the last week? For years, they couldn't stand one another, and now she wasn't sure what exactly she was feeling. It could just be carnal attraction – she had just ended her relationship days ago and probably needed a release. But why Nico? She hadn't thought about her crush on him in years, even when she sat across from him at his bar. Now, all she could think about was straddling him in the back seat of his truck, running her fingers through his hair, biting his bottom lip, and forgetting about Maine completely.

"Two number fours." Gus' voice ripped her from her sinful thoughts.

She cleared her throat and flashed a smile at the food truck owner. "Thank you, Gus."

"You're welcome," he returned the smile as Nico paid their tab. "You two be sure to come see us again real soon."

Nico grabbed their white to-go boxes and led her back to his parked truck, lowered the tailgate, and patted for her to sit. Her gaze bounced from the bed of the truck to Nico, and he stared at her curiously.

"Do you need me to help you up?" he asked, probably realizing she was in tight pants and couldn't jump the distance.

Part of her didn't want to admit she needed his help, but the other part of her, the traitorous part, wanted to feel his hands on her waist.

"Price?" he asked, lowering his head to meet her gaze. "Do you need help or not?"

Ramsey bobbed her head, brushing her hair out of her face. "Yes."

"Yes, what?" he smirked.

Damn him. That devil would want her to beg him.

She started to roll her eyes and caught herself, not needing him to make another comment. Slamming her hands on her hips, she glared up at him. "Would you lift me up there," she gritted her teeth, seething at his cocky grin. "Please."

Nico slid his hands along her waist and effortlessly hoisted her up. He plopped her on the edge of the tailgate. Her hands were resting on his shoulders, and he was standing between her legs. They were so close; her thighs tightened slightly around his hips, and he accepted the invitation, eating the little bit of distance that remained between them.

Ramsey slowly dragged her hands from his muscular shoulders down the length of his arms until she flattened her palms on the bed of his truck and pulled herself away from him. This couldn't happen between them. She was just lonely, maybe even bored. If she put the moves on her brother's best friend, Sean would act all weird around her and that was the last thing she wanted.

If Nico was disappointed by her scooting away from him, he didn't show it. He hopped up next to her and passed her food. Barbeque brisket with a side of homemade mac and cheese and a buttered roll. It smelled incredible and with a tentative first bite, the smoked meat melted on her tongue. She closed her eyes and released a small moan. Why hadn't she tried barbeque before? The mac and cheese exploded in her mouth, and she gobbled it up faster than was polite. It was then she remembered she wasn't eating alone and dared a glance at Nico. But he wasn't watching her stuff her face, he was too busy enjoying his own lunch.

"That good huh?" he smirked without looking up from his plate.

She felt her cheeks burning bright red. Her mother had always warned her not to devour her food like a starved animal. *Men don't want a woman with an appetite, dear.* Her mother's voice echoed in her head, and she silently chastised herself for letting the love of food get the better of her. But then again, why was she so concerned about impressing Nico? He'd seen her chugging beers and challenging Sean or any other bar patron to a drink off and didn't think twice about his opinion.

"Sorry," she lowered her plate from her lap to the tailgate.

"Sorry for what?" Nico met her embarrassed gaze.

"Scarfing my food like I haven't eaten in weeks."

He straightened and squared his shoulders to hers. The serious look on his face made her stop fidgeting. "Don't ever apologize for having an appetite."

"But you said, "that good huh?""

"Yeah," he motioned toward her plate, "cause you moaned when you started eating."

"I didn't moan," she glanced across the parking lot, looking anywhere but his face. She couldn't let him see the humiliation blooming in her soul.

"You moaned, Price," his voice was soft, seductive in his teasing. "I liked it."

She turned her head toward him, "What?"

Nico shrugged lazily, ripping a portion of his bread roll apart and slipping the morsel into his mouth. "Tells me what you like and don't like." His eyes darted to meet hers. "Now I know."

Fourteen

Nico

Nico wished he could reverse time, just for a few seconds, to feel her thighs tighten around his hips again. To see the look in her glossy eyes as she dragged her fingers down his arms, shooting bolts of electricity through his body. What he would give to hear her moan one more time, even if it was just over liking their barbeque lunch.

What was she doing to him?

He'd trained himself to keep his feelings hidden, to keep his face neutral when she walked into his bar, to keep up with the tit-for-tat sparring sessions when all he wanted was to wake up with her lying next to him. All the years of thinking of her as he fell asleep and not getting involved in a serious relationship because the dream of her one day being his was too tempting, even if it was next to impossible. She had ruined him and didn't even know it. No other woman would measure up to her and it wouldn't be fair to date someone while looking at Ramsey like she was the sun, the moon, and the stars.

"Want one?" Ramsey held out a silver wrapped piece of peppermint gum and he grabbed it, his fingers grazing hers.

"My breath smells that bad?" he snickered as he chewed.

She shrugged as she slipped a piece in her mouth. "I was fully prepared to let you breathe your dragon breath all over my parents but figured I'd save you the embarrassment since you paid for my lunch."

"I suppose I should thank you," he side-eyed her with a smirk, "but I'm not that nice."

"Says the guy driving me all the way to Maine because I don't like flying." Though she was teasing, he heard something in her voice that made his soul ache.

"So, you don't like semi-trucks and you don't like flying." He hoped she would take the bait and open up to him about her fears, but he wasn't going to be so lucky this time.

"I don't like either. The end." And by the tone in Ramsey's voice, he knew it was best to drop the issue. For now.

The car in front of them swerved to avoid a divot in the road and Nico followed suit but was a smidge too late in his maneuvering and smacked the pothole. His truck bounced and by the unevenness of the vehicle, he knew he busted one of his tires. Thankfully, they were no longer on the interstate and were on backroads not far from Ramsey's childhood home. The two-lane road was lined with trees and provided greatly appreciated shade as Nico veered off to the shoulder to check the damage.

Throwing the truck in park, he slipped out and made his way to Ramsey's side. The front right tire was flat as he suspected. She rolled her window down and leaned out to see what he was looking at.

"Flat?" she asked, and he bobbed his head.

Nico walked back to his side to turn the truck off and threw the parking brake into place, then made his way to the silver storage box in the bed of his truck. Reaching inside, he dragged a tire changing kit out followed by the spare tire. Ramsey hopped out and pulled her hair back into a neat ponytail as he put the tools he needed next to the ruined tire.

"It'll take me a few minutes and then we'll be back on the road," he reassured her as he slipped the jack underneath the vehicle.

"Do you have something to stick in front of the other tires to make sure the truck stays in place?" Her question threw him off guard.

"I have a few bricks in the storage box," he nodded.

Without a second's hesitation, Ramsey found the bricks he'd mentioned and wedged them in front of the three good tires to make sure the truck didn't move.

Nico went to work on removing the hubcaps. "You know how to change a tire."

"My dad taught me," she said, wiping her hands together. "He never treated me any differently than my brothers. Whatever he taught them, he taught me."

"Smart man." He put the hubcap to the side and started cranking the jack. Ramsey squatted next to him. Her pants were so tight they outlined the curve of her hips and hypnotized him.

She pointed at the truck. "I think it's high enough."

He shook his head and refocused on the task at hand. Ramsey handed him the wrench so he could remove the nuts.

"Thanks," he smiled, doing his best to hide how impressed he was with her but failing. Once the nuts were off, he took the damaged tire off and then replaced it with the spare. "So," he grunted as he put the new tire on. "You know how to change a tire and drink men twice your size under the table. What else did your dad teach you?"

Ramsey's laugh sent a warmth surging through his chest, and he met her amused gaze. "Well, he taught me how to hunt, fish, grill, and how to drive. He also taught me politics, economics, history, and mathematics. Although, I really wasn't a fan of the last one."

Just when he thought she couldn't surprise or impress him more she went and proved him wrong.

Nico tightened the nuts and replaced the hubcap. "And what did your mom teach you?"

The smile on her face faded and he wished he could take the question back. He knew Anne Price could be a lot to handle and her expectation of all her children was exceptionally high. But with Ramsey, it was much higher seeing she was the youngest and only daughter. He felt stupid and his shoulders tensed.

"I'm sorry," he said softly, "you don't have to answer-"

"She taught me how to carry myself in a professional manner. She taught me that cleanliness is next to godliness. And she taught me that first impressions matter." Her eyes bored into the very depths of his soul and the last comment stung.

He'd made a terrible first impression years ago and he'd spent the last eight years trying to make up for it and obviously, he was failing miserably.

She stood from her crouched position, snatched the toolbox, and put it back in its place in the storage box. By the time Nico threw the busted tire and jack in the bed of the truck, Ramsey was already buckled in the passenger seat ready to go.

He had more ground to make up with her than he originally thought, but he was willing to put in the extra effort if it meant winning her heart in the end.

Fifteen

RAMSEY

As they pulled up the gravel driveway, through the pine trees lining either side of the path, Ramsey's heart beat at a quickened pace. *Five days.* She could do this. Her childhood home came into focus once they rounded the bend, and it flooded her with a familiar comfort. The grey shingles, white trim, wrap around porch, large windows, and ocean for a backdrop made the Price Mansion picture perfect.

But someone standing in the open front door caught Ramsey's eye, and it rattled her already fraying nerves.

Anne, Ramsey's mother, waved from the front porch as they parked in the circular driveway. Even though they were supposed to arrive a couple of hours earlier, her mother seemed happy to see them. Nico motioned Ramsey to go greet her mother while he grabbed their bags, so she walked up the five wooden steps to the patio landing and hugged her mother, hoping she wouldn't question her about David.

"Hello, Ramsey, dear." Anne embraced Ramsey tightly, kissing both her cheeks, before glancing over her daughter's shoulder. She pouted but didn't look surprised. "Where's David? I was looking forward to meeting this mysterious boyfriend of yours."

And there it was. That had to be a record. Literal seconds before diving headfirst into her personal life. "He had to work."

"Again?" By her mother's tone, Ramsey knew she didn't believe her.

"We're actually no longer together because of his schedule."

"Oh, Ramsey." Anne hugged her again, patting her back as if she were burping a fussy baby. "You don't have to lie to me. I know you've felt pressured to get married, but some of us are late bloomers."

"Mom, I'm twenty-six -"

"Don't remind me, dear." She released Ramsey from her grip and smiled. "How about you finally let me set you up? My friend, Diane, has a son who is a doctor."

Ramsey crinkled her nose. "That won't be necessary." She knew Diane's son from high school, and she had no interest in being within spitting distance of that train wreck of a human.

"I insist," Anne looped her arm in Ramsey's. "After all, it's hard to be so dedicated to your career and try to date. I didn't mean to make you feel as if you had to make up a relationship to please me."

"Make up? I didn't," Ramsey sucked in a breath to keep from snapping five minutes into her five-day vacation. "You know what? You don't need to fix me up with anyone because I *am* dating someone."

"Oh, Ramsey. This is getting embarrassing."

Ramsey crossed her arms over her chest, feeling like a child throwing a fit. "I'm serious."

Anne flashed a smile, rubbing Ramsey's shoulder. "Ok, dear," she said softly. "Who is this *new* mystery man?"

If Ramsey could have punched herself in the face she would have. How stupid could she be? Of course her mother would ask about who this new man was, but the problem was there was no man. She heard Nico slam one of the truck doors and his shoes crunch up the gravel driveway. Could Nico be any louder? And then it hit her. He wouldn't like it. But she couldn't go through the long weekend with her mother parading her around the wedding meeting every eligible bachelor from her hometown.

"It's Nico," she croaked hoarsely before she could talk herself out of it.

Anne, for the first time in years, was rendered speechless. "Nico?" She glanced at him climbing up the steps completely unaware of the situation he was about to walk into.

Ramsey nodded, forcing herself to smile. "We didn't say anything because it's still new and we didn't want to overshadow Sean's day." Believable. At least she hoped it was believable.

"Really?" Her mother arched an eyebrow. "You two are dating?"

"Why is that so hard to believe?" Ramsey threw her hands in the air. "You want me to prove it to you? Fine."

"Hello, Mrs. Price," Nico smiled at Anne, "It's good to see you ag -"

Before losing her nerve, and with her mother eyeing them suspiciously, she grabbed his face and kissed him. He dropped the luggage and to her surprise and relief he kissed her back. His lips were soft, and his kiss was hungry. His hands trailed up her arms and cupped her face. She felt as if her insides were nothing more than goo and if her mother wasn't standing there, she would gladly melt into him.

Her mother!

She reluctantly forced herself to push away from Nico's face and clear her throat. "I'm sorry, *babe*," she whispered, trying to catch her breath. "Mom didn't believe me when I told her we have been secretly dating so we didn't overshadow Sean's wedding weekend."

Nico shot her a look that promised retribution and demanded an explanation, but he thankfully played along. "That must have come as quite the shock."

"How long have you been seeing each other?" Anne asked, breaking her short-lived stupor.

"About a week," Ramsey quickly answered before Nico could.

Nico wrapped his arm around her waist, pulling her close to make her uncomfortable. "It's been that long already?" He smiled into her hair. "I feel like we just kissed for the first time."

Ramsey shot him a warning look and forced herself to laugh. "What a sense of humor you have, *darling*," she patted his face a little too hard and he released her. She turned back toward her mother and rolled her eyes. "What?"

Anne scratched a finger through her salt and pepper hair that was fashioned in an elegant updo. "This is very interesting."

"You still don't believe me, do you?"

"Oh, I believe you, dear." Anne flashed a small smile. "I'm just surprised it took you so long."

Ramsey was taken aback and was unsure of what to say in response. "What are you talking about?"

Absent-mindedly, Anne muttered, "I owe your father $50."

Ramsey held a hand up. "Wait a minute. Are you betting on my dating life?"

She chuckled and shook her head. "No, dear, of course not. I merely bet your father years ago you'd never date your brother's best friend. I thought for sure I'd eventually wear you down so I could set you up. But somehow, your father knew you two would end up together." She looked back and forth between them. "I suppose you will be wanting to share a room then?"

Ramsey coughed out a nervous laugh. "Mom-"

Nico pulled her closer and kissed her temple. "That would be great. She can't seem to keep her hands off me."

Anne grimaced but quickly donned the perfect hostess' smile. "Well, you can have your old room, Ramsey. I'll let you two get settled before your father and brothers come back from fishing."

Sixteen

RAMSEY

Silently, Nico and Ramsey walked through the grand foyer of the Price family's Portland mansion and made their way to the grand wooden staircase. The polished railings and cushioned window nook overlooking the ocean hadn't changed since Ramsey moved out eight years ago. Spending her summer break catching up on her reading, she would read anything she could get her hands on: Fiction, Non-Fiction, Historical, Romance, Political. If it was in English, she'd read it.

But as she and Nico made it to the top of the stairs, with her mother watching from the open foyer below, skepticism still rooted in her icy-blue eyes, Ramsey intertwined her fingers in his and pulled him down the paneled hallway. All the doors were closed, but she had lived in this house her entire life and knew that her room was the second door on the left. She opened the door and scurried inside.

She dropped her bag on her queen mattress, still fitted with one of her great-grandmother's handmade quilts, and whipped around to face Nico who had just closed the bedroom door. Snatching one of the pillows, she chucked it at him. He easily side-stepped it with wide, curious eyes.

"What the hell do you think you're doing?" she whispered furiously.

"Me?" He slapped a hand to his chest in disbelief.

"We can't share a room."

He took a small step toward her, keeping his voice low. "But you can kiss me and say we're a couple?"

She folded her arms over her chest, popping a hip to the side. "You didn't seem to have a problem with pretending at the bridal shop."

"That was different." Nico stroked a hand through his dark hair and sighed. "What exactly do you think is going to happen when Sean gets here and outs you as a liar?"

"What if he believes we're dating?"

He flashed her a look. "You're too smart to say something that stupid."

"Is that a compliment?" she teased but he shook his head, worry seeping into his Italian features.

Nico absent-mindedly chewed his bottom lip and the desire to be the one biting his lip surged through her body. "Sean will kick my ass if he thinks I've been secretly banging his little sister."

His comment brought her back to the present situation. "Am I so repulsive?"

He tilted his head. "Do you really want me to answer that?"

"I hate you," she hissed and marched for her window seat and plopped down, keeping her bed between them.

"Can we stop for one second," Nico held up his hands in surrender. "Stop all of this," he motioned back and forth between them and took another step forward, "and tell me what's going on. Why did you tell your mother we are dating?"

"I'd rather go skinny dipping than explain myself to you."

Nico leaned against the wall, burying his hands in his pockets. "That works for me, too."

"You're disgusting." But the thought of them skinny dipping put a small smile on her face.

She could feel Nico's eyes on her, so she met his awaiting gaze. There was something different in the way he looked at her. There wasn't any judgment or sarcasm behind those brown eyes, but she couldn't put her finger on what it was. Whatever he was thinking or feeling remained a mystery to her.

"What's going on?" he asked.

Ramsey dragged her fingers through her platinum locks and sighed. "I panicked," she confessed, and it felt oddly freeing to admit to him.

"About?"

But then again, he didn't need to know everything she was feeling. "None of your business."

"I think it is my business. You've wrangled me into your web of lies. I at least deserve to know what's going on in that head of yours."

That was fair. She'd roped him into her schemes, and he deserved to understand why, even if it did pain her to open up and be honest.

"My mother was expecting to meet David this weekend." She shrugged, "He's cancelled every time he was supposed to visit, and she thinks I made him up to get her off my back about dating. I shouldn't have dragged you into this. I was being stupid. How am I an adult and still afraid of disappointing my mother?" Ramsey glanced up from her sneakers and saw he hadn't moved. She stood up and marched toward him, aiming for the door. "I'll go tell her the truth and get you another room -"

"Sit down."

Ramsey stopped. "I don't take orders -"

"Shut up for one second," he waved his hand, straightening from his reclined position. "I'm thinking."

Ramsey crossed her arms across her chest and smirked. "Don't think too hard or you'll hurt yourself."

Nico paced in front of the bedroom door a few seconds before turning to her, a determined gleam in his eyes. "You're not going to tell her anything."

"But-"

He suddenly grabbed her hands and pulled her to sit next to him on her bed. "I need you to listen to me for once in your life, Medusa."

"What a lovely pet name," she rolled her eyes.

"I'll go along with us pretending to be a couple."

Even though her heart thundered in her chest at the possibility of them acting like they were together, she narrowed her eyes at him. What did he want in return? "Why?"

"Several reasons."

And there it was. Now, she needed to know what this charade was going to cost her. "And your reasons?"

"One, it'll be fun to make you squirm," he said with a mischievous smile. "Two, you'll owe me big time. And three, I know what it's like to disappoint a parent. If I can help you avoid that judgment another weekend, I don't see the harm."

That was oddly vulnerable of him to admit.

"Wow, that's ... nice of you," she squared her shoulders to his. "Why are you being so nice?" She had to be sure his kindness was not being offered because he thought her to be weak or incapable or worse, a failure.

He squeezed her hand which she had forgotten was in his grasp, and said, "I would like to think, maybe, you'd do it for me."

"Honestly," she pulled her hand free, "I probably wouldn't."

"Then, take this moment to realize, I'm a better person than you."

Ramsey laughed which put a smile on his face.

"So," he cleared his throat, "if we're doing this, we're going to have to act the part of a real couple."

"Nicolette-"

"Let me rephrase," he interrupted with a huff. "We need to act the part of a *loving* couple. Calling me girl names won't convince them you're in love with me."

"We've been *dating*," she used air quotes, "for a week. No one expects us to be in love already."

"We might have started *dating*," he mimicked her hand motion, "a week ago, but we've known each other for eight years. They will suspect we've harbored secret feelings for a while now."

The memories over the last eight years of them meeting, finishing school, moving, seeing one another on the rare occasion when Sean brought him around, to them living in the same city flashed in her mind. She'd had a crush on him years ago and when she realized he didn't feel the same way about her she buried her feelings. Why, all of a sudden, was she wishing they were doing more than just sitting on a bed together?

"Right," she nodded, forcing herself to focus.

He cocked his head to the side, his eyes roving over her entire face. "What is it?"

"Nothing." She shook her head and inhaled a deep breath. "Ok. I suppose we will need to know simple things about each other."

He leaned back on the mattress, resting his back against the mountain of throw pillows. He tucked his hands behind his head, his biceps bulging, making it difficult to concentrate. "Such as?"

Ramsey had to look anywhere but his muscular arms. "I don't know. Favorite food, favorite color, pet peeves, favorite pastime, favorite snack, greatest fear, do you have tattoos?"

Nico shrugged, "All of those are easy."

She clicked her tongue. "What are you talking about? There's no way you know all the answers to those questions."

Nico sat up and leaned closer to her. Their knees were inches apart and he stared deep into her eyes. "You like to say your favorite food is sushi, but we all know you're a sucker for a burger and side of fries. Your favorite color is obviously black, although I don't think it actually qualifies as a color so much as the absence of it. You hate when people chew too loud. Your favorite pastime is going to baseball games with your brother or reading another Revolutionary War history book. Your favorite snack is Hot Cheetos, you are terrified semi-trucks, and you have one tattoo you think no one knows about on the side of your hip."

For the first time in years, Ramsey was stunned into silence. She had no rebuttal. All she could do, inches from a man she claimed to hate, was sit in awe that he answered every question right and fight the urge to slam her lips against his. She felt seen.

Nico's gaze bounced between her eyes and her lips as he whispered, "Got anything harder?"

Ramsey struggled to find her voice. "How do you know all of that about me?"

"It's called the power of observation, Princess."

The cockiness in his answer slapped her out of her stupor. "I couldn't answer all those questions about you."

"Would you like me to help you out?"

Ramsey nodded. "I guess I would need to know if my family is going to believe us."

He flashed a devilish smile. "Let's make this interesting."

She arched an eyebrow. "Ok."

"I'll let you take one guess for each question. For each one you get right, I'll do anything you want during this weekend trip. Each one you get wrong; you'll do something I want."

"So if I told you to jump into the ocean naked?" she asked playfully, though a hunger flashed in his eyes.

"I'd do it. And if I told you to eat your weight in potatoes, you'd have to do it. Do we have a deal?" He extended his hand for her to shake.

Ramsey shook it. "Is anything off the table?"

Nico smirked, still holding her hand. "I'm not shy, Price."

"Neither am I," she purred.

"Alright," he released her hand and once again got comfortable. "My favorite food."

She knew this one. "Chicken Parmesan."

"Don't be too proud of yourself. That was easy." He was right. It was easy. Nico wouldn't shut up about his love for Chicken Parmesan.

"Next one. Next one."

"Favorite color."

Ramsey squinted, trying to get a read from him but he offered nothing. "Blue," she guessed.

He flashed a perfectly straight smile. "Red."

"Dang it. Ok, next question."

"What is one of my pet peeves?"

Ramsey closed her eyes so she could think and not be distracted by the curve of his jaw or how tempted she was by his lounged position. Her eyes shot open when she was ready to guess. "You hate when people crumple napkins into balls and leave them on the floor."

He rolled his eyes, smoothing his hair back. "I'll give you that one."

"You didn't give me anything. I got it right."

"You're also one of those people," he squinted, and she shrugged in response.

"Only because I know it annoys you," she smirked.

"You wicked creature," he cooed, and it sent a shiver down her spine.

"You flatter me." She cleared her throat and motioned for him to continue. "Next."

"Favorite pastime."

Ramsey didn't hesitate. "Going to Phillies games."

"Wrong."

"You're a big, fat, liar."

"I like going to games once in a while, but I really enjoy photography."

Ramsey rolled her eyes and leaned back on her elbows, throwing her head back with a huff. "This again? It's easy, you point and click."

Nico rolled onto his stomach, lying next to her. "One of these days, I'll show you some of my photographs and you might be impressed."

"Doubtful."

"Favorite snack." Their faces were so close she could smell the mint on his breath.

"Nuts," she whispered, and he laughed.

"That's too vague. That's like if I said your favorite snack was chips. You have to be more specific."

Ramsey let her back hit the bed and the mattress bounced. His face hovered above hers. "Fine." She closed her eyes to think although she could sense he was scanning every inch of her face. "Dang it. You eat them at the bar all the time. I can see you eating them. What kind are they?"

"Picturing me eat," he purred. "Sexy."

"Shut up. I'm trying to think." Feeling defeated, she flippantly guessed, "Cashew?"

"Pistachios," he whispered, staring at her with a gleam in his eyes.

She groaned and rubbed the heels of her palms against her face.

"I'm up, 3-2," he playfully taunted her. He rested his chin in his palm and smiled. "I can't wait to make you sing opera style in front of everyone."

Ramsey stuck her tongue out at him. "Next?"

"What is my greatest fear?"

She maintained deep eye contact with him, as if she could draw the answer out of him. "Would you tell me if I guessed right?"

"Why wouldn't I? I've been honest so far." *He wasn't wrong about that.*

"Men don't normally admit their fears."

Nico shrugged, "Maybe not. But if you guess it, I won't lie about it."

She wiggled her eyebrows. "Why don't you just tell me?"

He chuckled softly and rolled over on his back. "And give you ammunition for the future? Pass."

"Fine." Ramsey rested on her side, supporting herself with an elbow, and studied his face. She thought she saw something flash in his eyes, but whatever he was thinking, his face was blank a second later. "Rats?"

"They make me weak in the knees."

"Did I get it right?" She hovered over him, excited.

Nico shot her a look. "No. I'm a 6'2" city boy. Rats are basically pets."

Ramsey's hair curtained around his face. "Then what is it?"

Nico twirled a piece of her hair between his index finger and thumb. "Nice try," he replied softly. "Last one. I'm up 4-2."

Ramsey wanted to press him to tell her his greatest fear, partially to make sure he wasn't lying about being afraid of rats and two, because she was genuinely interested in what he feared. She wasn't in dangerous territory anymore. She was deep behind enemy lines.

"Let's hope I get this right," her voice came out raspier than she intended.

Nico smiled, "Do I have any tattoos?" They both knew she knew the answer to this question.

Ramsey's mind flashed back to seeing Nico in his apartment and the tattoo scrawled up his ribcage. She'd thought about it every night since. "You have at least one."

"So, we end this 4-3," he grinned up at her and she narrowed her eyes.

"Are you smiling at me like that because you beat me?"

"I'm actually impressed you got three right. But no. I'm just thinking of all the embarrassing things I could dare you to do."

"Keep in mind," she cooed, "I can do something far worse if you want to play the game that way."

He arched an eyebrow as if compelling her to tell him all her secrets. "What's the worst thing you could have me do?"

Ramsey flashed a mischievous grin of her own. "Propose to me, in front of my entire family."

Nico slowly sat up, forcing her to move with him. "That's one way to get me down on my knees. Is that what you want?

Me on my knees?" He slid off the edge of the bed and knelt before her.

Her breath hitched. "What are you doing?"

He leaned close, whispering in her ear. "You think you can outdo me in the uncomfortable game? You have no idea what you're getting yourself into, Ramsey."

Nico said her name like it was a dark, dirty secret. She hated him. Hated that he made her shiver. Hated that she wanted to feel the taste of his lips again. Hated that she felt a pang in the pit of her stomach. But he had rejected her years ago. Making it perfectly clear he wasn't interested in hanging out with her. If he wasn't

Sean's best friend, she wouldn't have seen him again and been reminded of the humiliation.

Pulling away from her, he met her gaze. "Wow, I don't think you've ever gone this long without saying something."

That stupid, smug, handsome face of his. He thought he had gotten under her skin, but she knew how to trump this. She was not accustomed to losing. And she would be damned if she lost to him of all people.

"Kiss me," she dared.

"So, this is how you're going to play?" The huskiness in his voice sent a welcome shiver through her body.

She smirked, "Unless I've made you uncomfortable. You can always -"

Nico slammed his mouth against hers, swallowing her insults. He was hungry; unrelenting. He pushed up from his kneeling position and climbed on top of her. She relished the weight of him over her and raked her hands across his chest. He slipped his tongue inside her mouth, and she moaned, hating that she enjoyed his kiss but loving it at the same time, craving more. She ran her fingers through his hair and felt him grab ahold of her thighs.

Stars. She was seeing stars with each passing second of their locked embrace. More. She needed more of him. And she needed it now. Her hands found the buckle of his belt and she started to unhook it, but Nico pulled away before she was ready for him to and hopped off the bed. She pushed herself up on her elbows and stared at him, hazy eyed and confused. He smiled as he smoothed his hair back from where she ruffled it.

"Two dares left, Medusa. Use them wisely." He winked and slipped out of the room.

Seventeen

Nico

Nico had to get out of that room before he completely lost control. He'd wanted to kiss her for eight years and they'd kissed twice in a span of thirty minutes. If that's how their dares started, he was afraid of where it could end.

Could she tell he'd dreamt of being on top of her, holding her, kissing her until she begged him ...

He raked a shaky hand through his hair. When she moved to Philadelphia two years ago, he was surprised that the feelings he'd had for her in college, hadn't gone away like he suspected, but they'd been hibernating. When she walked into his bar, wearing a pencil skirt and heels, looking like a sexy librarian, he almost came undone in front of everyone.

Now that he had his own successful business and had known Sean for ten years, maybe his best friend would be okay with him asking his little sister out on a proper date. But the first thing Ramsey said to him was, "You've aged." And he knew then she hadn't forgotten how he'd avoided being alone with her in college. Their snarky, tit-for-tat banter was all he was going to get from her and if that was what she was willing to give, he would soak all of it up. So, he responded, "Like a fine wine."

Two years later, and they were still singing the same song. Except he'd missed his chance to ask her out when David got to her first. Nico respected she was out of his reach, but that didn't prevent him from thinking about her daily.

He'd imagined what kissing her would feel like and he'd fallen terribly short of reality. She was amazing. Her lips were soft, and she kissed him like her very survival depended on it. If he hadn't left when he did, he was positive they'd be tangled beneath the sheets, and that's not how he wanted such an intimate moment to go down. On one of her dares.

And then there was Sean to contend with. Either way, his best friend was not going to be happy about this. If he suspected they'd actually been secretly dating, he'd be mad they kept it from him. But if and when he realized it was all a lie, Sean would be pissed they were using his wedding weekend to deceive the entire family.

"Sean's going to kill me." Nico muttered to himself, standing on the back patio overlooking the ocean.

"He doesn't know you're banging our sister?"

Nico whipped around and saw three of Ramsey's brothers and their father sitting in the outdoor lounge area in their fishing gear. He hadn't noticed them when he barreled out of the house and was grateful he didn't say anything incriminating.

"Patrick, that's your sister. Have a little class." William Price chastised and extended his hand to Nico with a warm smile. "The Mrs. just told us you and my daughter are finally dating. Took you long enough, Nico."

"Umm, yeah, thanks. She's terrific." Nico smiled, and nodded his head at Patrick, and the twins, Connor and Collin. "Any luck out there?"

"Anne is cooking our haul for tonight's dinner as we speak." William waved a freckled hand for Nico to follow him inside. "We can't wait for you and Ramsey to tell us all about how you finally started dating."

Nico smiled to keep from panicking. "I'm sure Rams is excited to tell you." *Rams?* He had never once in his entire time of knowing Ramsey called her Rams. She might even punch him if she heard him use it.

"Great. Well, go on up and tell my daughter that dinner will be ready in an hour. But I expect to see her well before that."

"I'll go tell her right now."

Not wanting to answer any more pressing questions from Ramsey's brothers, he marched back up the front staircase, passed the window seat overlooking the water, and walked up to the second door on the left side of the hall. He sucked in a breath before he knocked softly on the wooden door.

He heard the mattress squeak and made a mental note of how loud it was before Ramsey shuffled to the door and swung it open. They stared at one another and the hunger he had for her before, the hunger he thought he got under control during his brief walk on the patio, flooded him like a broken dam. Her hair was slightly disheveled from their make out session but by the gleeful look in her eyes, he knew she was putting her mask back in place. How he wished she would just surrender and realize that they would be perfect together.

"Hey," Nico rasped.

"Hey," she whispered, a small smile creeping across her face. "Back for more?"

Foolishly, he thought she would let her guard down after what happened between them, but she resurrected the banter. He could play along for a little while longer. Hopefully his feelings wouldn't fog his brain.

"Thought I'd give you time to take a nice cold shower after blowing your mind with just a kiss."

"If you say so."

Her cheeks were flushed, and her pupils were still thundering with longing. She wanted him. But unless she said so, he wasn't going to kiss her again. Although, every inch of him wanted to pin her against a wall and make her scream his name.

"I ran into your dad and three of your brothers."

She seemed to sober at that. "What happened?"

"Your dad is really excited we're dating. I would like to think it's because he likes me so much, but it might be pure joy of finally getting rid of his spinster daughter."

She flinched at that. He hit a nerve not meaning to and instantly felt bad.

"I'm sorry," he quickly apologized, "I didn't mean to hurt your feelings. I was just joking."

"It's going to take a lot more to hurt my feelings than that." She was clearly lying which made him feel worse.

"Ramsey -"

"Nicolas."

"You used my actual name." It was weird.

"And you used mine."

They stared at each other. It was so quiet; he could hear Mrs. Price prepping dinner downstairs in the kitchen and Ramsey's brothers taking a crack at billiards in Mr. Price's library. He couldn't tear his eyes away from Ramsey's even if he wanted to. Blue, but almost grey, they bore into his very soul and wouldn't release him from her spell. She took a step to him, closing the distance between them.

Was she going to kiss him?

He hoped she would. But he wasn't sure he'd be able to just kiss her and not want anything more to happen between them.

She slipped her hands underneath his shirt, and he let her fingers roam over his chest, along his abs, and held his breath when the tips of her fingers clutched at his waistband. He should stop this. He should take a step back. Did she want him? Or was this part of the uncomfortable game they liked to play? Should he use one of his dares to see how far she'd go to win?

Her chest rose and fell sharply, and he knew this wasn't a game. This was carnal need and desire for them to be tangled up. Her lips parted, and he leaned toward her without being able to stop himself. He wanted to taste her again. He wanted to grab her wrists and pin them above her head and take complete control. Wanted to hear her say his name again and equate his name with pleasure and not irritation.

"Nico."

Hearing his name come from her mouth nearly brought him to his knees. He still hadn't laid a finger on her smooth skin, and she had this power over him. To bring a grown man to his knees. A queen and her conquered prey.

"Say my name again," he rested his forehead against hers.

"Nico," she breathed against his neck and goosebumps rippled across his skin.

"You're playing a dangerous game, Ramsey."

"Maybe I like dangerous."

"Nico!" The voice jolted him, and he took a step away from Ramsey. "It's been a long time! How are you?" Liam, one of Ramsey's middle brothers and a successful doctor in Boston, clamped a hand on his shoulder.

"No hello for your sister, Liam?" Ramsey stepped into the threshold; arms crossed.

"Oh, did I interrupt something?" Liam flashed a coy smile. "Jen and I just got here, and they told us you two were dating."

"So, you thought you'd just run upstairs and knock on our door and catch us having sex?" Ramsey huffed, crinkling her nose.

Liam and Ramsey stared at each other, clearly feeling the other out. Then Liam laughed and Ramsey wasn't too far behind. They hugged and her brother kissed her forehead.

Nico let out the breath he'd been holding since Liam crept up and scared him.

"How have you been? I feel like I haven't seen you in years." Liam pulled away and scanned his sister like one of his patients, looking for anything out of the ordinary.

"Other than fulfilled and happy?"

"All due to Nico, I'm sure." Liam winked and Nico was surprised he wanted her answer to be yes.

Ramsey glanced up at Nico and smiled. An actual, full-blown smile. Not her typical tight-lipped grin. He didn't think she could look any more beautiful and then she went and smiled at him.

"I suppose he has something to do with that." And just like that, his heart burst, and she turned her attention back to Liam. "How's Jackson?"

"The terrible twos are exactly that. Terrible." Liam motioned a hand for them to follow him down the stairs. "Come and see for yourself. I can already hear mom bubble wrapping the house as we speak."

Without looking back at him, Ramsey snatched Nico's hand in hers, and led him down the steps. She slowed, distancing them from Liam. She leaned up and whispered in his ear, "You sure about this?"

He knew she was asking if he was still up for pretending to be her boyfriend. But what she didn't know, was he was wanting them to be together for real and it pained him to know that after the weekend was over, they'd go back to their wicked-tongued banter. He mustered a smile and puts his lips against her ear.

"I'm sure."

Eighteen

RAMSEY

Holding Nico's hand steadied her. They were about to walk into the lion's den, and she was going to have to answer a million questions about her and Nico dating. *Finally dating*, as they all kept putting it. Why did they all expect this to happen? And why was she the last to hear of it?

They were going to be really disappointed when they found out she and Nico were lying. *If. If* they found out they'd been lying. She honestly wasn't sure what would be worse at this point. For the family to find out she and Nico weren't actually dating or when they broke up shortly after Sean's wedding.

But the most frightening thing about the entire situation, was she didn't want to break up with Nico. She found her feelings for him to be stronger than they had been when they were in college, and she wasn't sure what she was going to do when the jig was up. It had taken her years to get over her crush and she still hadn't quite recovered from the humiliation of his silent rejection. Now, having felt his lips against hers, having rubbed her hands across his muscular torso, and picturing him doing unspeakable things to her, it was going to be a million times harder to get over Nico Giovanni.

As she rounded the staircase and made her way through the two-story foyer to the family room with floor to ceiling windows boasting an incredible view of the ocean in their backyard, she found members of her family scattered throughout the room.

Collin, the oldest of the Price kids and a successful lawyer, sat in one of the armchairs that framed the stone fireplace nursing a beer. He had met his wife, Grace, in high school and they'd been inseparable since. Grace was a wonder in the kitchen, and Ramsey figured that's where the perky blonde was now, helping Anne with dinner. Their two kids, Troy and Travis, were a wild duo that thrived on chaos, and she could hear them screaming in the backyard along with Connor's three kids.

Connor, Ramsey's second brother and Collin's identical twin, was watching the kids sprint around the grassy yard like a concerned mother hen. His wife, Kristen, was his partner in life and business. They'd been the ones to take over their father's boat building business when William had retired several years ago. They had three girls, Hannah, Sarah, and Rebekah: all Bible names to Ramsey's mother's delight.

Patrick took up the armchair flanking Collin's. His wife, Quinn, who he met at their engineering firm in Portland, sat on his lap with a wide smile, laughing at whatever joke her husband had cracked. Patrick was always the funniest of the Price Seven and it's what Quinn claimed was her favorite thing about Ramsey's third brother. They had been married for six months and the newlywed smell was still fresh.

Ramsey and Nico followed Liam, her fourth brother and incredibly sought-after plastic surgeon in Boston, into the room to the horde of smiling faces. His wife, Jen, bounced Jackson, their two-year-old son, against her hip. Jen's smile lit up the entire room and she beelined for Ramsey with an arm outstretched for a side hug.

During Ramsey's stint living in Boston, Jen had been her saving grace. She would grab coffee with her sister-in-law whenever she had a spare minute and enjoyed catching up on all the family gossip. She released Nico's hand and wrapped her arms around Jen, squeezing as tightly as she dared with Jackson in her sister-in-law's grasp.

"I've missed you," Jen greeted her cheerfully and it flooded Ramsey with much needed warmth.

"I've missed you, too," Ramsey pulled away from her and opened her palms to see if her nephew would come to her. After a moment's hesitation on Jackson's part, he reached for her and she snuggled him, kissing his cheek. "I've missed you most of all, Jack Jack."

"Missed him more than your ole dad?" William clutched his hand to his chest, feigning pain. "Say it isn't so!"

Ramsey rolled her eyes and perched herself on the arm of the couch next to her dad and planted a kiss on top of his head. "You came in a very close second, Dad."

"Well, at least this time you didn't come empty handed," Patrick teased, ignoring Quinn's slap against his arm. "We were all taking bets to see if you'd bring a date this time."

She hated when her brothers did this. Joking about her love life – or lack thereof – never sat well with her. But if she showed any sign of weakness or vulnerability in a house filled with brothers, they'd be like sharks in the water and sniff out the bloody wounds and feast.

"Well, I hope you lost all your money," she forced herself to joke.

"I'm sorry, Ramsey," Quinn looked embarrassed by Patrick's inconsiderate comment. "I told him he shouldn't joke about it."

Ramsey waved a dismissive hand in the air. "Don't worry about it, Quinn. Patrick's been an ass since we were kids. I'm used to it."

Patrick frowned but the rest of the Price men roared in laughter. Collin and Connor started rattling on about how Patrick would cry whenever he didn't get his way or when he got scared, he'd piss his pants and let the pee drip down his leg. Satisfied with paying her insensitive brother back for calling her out, she turned toward the doorway remembering Nico was still standing there, lazily leaning against the doorframe. She waved him forward and he pushed himself up and walked toward her.

"So," William patted the cushion next to him for Nico to sit, "You have to tell us all about how you two finally started dating."

Again, with the *finally* business. She would have to steal a private moment with her dad and question him about it later.

Nico sank into the couch next to her dad and rested his hands on top of his knees. Those hands of his. How she wanted to feel his touch again. A tingling sensation spread up her spine as she flashed back to them in her bedroom moments earlier. She craved the roughness of his fingers dragging across her skin and exploring her body.

Someone cleared their throat, and she abandoned her thoughts. Glancing around the room, she saw all eyes were on her. She turned to look at Nico and he flashed her a small, encouraging smile.

"I'm sorry, I didn't hear the question."

Everyone erupted in laughter, and she wasn't sure why. What had she missed the few seconds she'd zoned out?

"What's so funny?" she looked to her dad for answers.

William patted her knee, stilling it from bouncing. "We asked you to tell us how you two started dating."

"Oh, right, how we started dating," Ramsey's eyes darted to an amused looking Nico. He offered her no assistance and she wanted to smack the smug look off his face. She was on her own for this one. "Well..." An idea sparked and she grinned at Nico like the Cheshire Cat, which wiped the smile off his face. "Well, it's a boring story but unfortunately for my boyfriend, an embarrassing one."

Nico's eyebrow quirked and she pressed on before he could interject. "Sorry, honey, they want to know the story, so I have to tell them." She stood up from the arm of the couch and resituated Jackson on her hip, swaying back and forth as he rested his head against her shoulder. "So, for months, Nico had been begging me to go out with him. I mean begging like his life depended on it." She risked a quick glance Nico's way, and he was leaning back, relaxed, not looking remotely bothered by her lies. He met her gaze and winked. Why was she now the one nervous?

"Then what happened?" Jen asked, intrigued by the story.

Ramsey found her voice again, hoping whatever retribution she was going to face was worth the price. "He came to Sean's place late one night, practically on bended knee, crying, begging me to give him a chance. I couldn't take seeing him that way anymore, so I said yes, and here we are."

"Desperate," Patrick snickered, spurring the brothers to laugh.

"Well, that is quite the story," William cleared his throat, side-eyeing Nico to his right. "I would imagine you'd like a chance to share your side of events?"

Nico smirked and shook his head to Ramsey's surprise. "No, I think she summed it up pretty well."

William looked taken aback. "There's nothing you want to add?"

Nico tapped his chin, pretending to be deep in thought, and Ramsey knew deep down in her soul, that he was about to use one of his dares on her.

"You know what, Rams," she cringed when she heard her nickname ooze from his lips, "you did forget something. You forgot about the song you sang to me after our first date."

She tilted her head to the side, and he flashed a devilish smile. "What?"

"Oh, don't be shy, babe," Nico pressed. "She loves this song. She sings it every night before we go to sleep. Go ahead, sweetheart. Sing it for everyone."

"Oh, I couldn't possibly -"

"I insist," Nico stood up and wrapped an arm around her waist pulling her against him and whispered in her ear so no one else would hear, "I *dare* you."

Her heart sank. Everyone knew Ramsey was the furthest thing from a singer. Nico moved away from her slowly, and her breathing hitched as she felt his chest pull away from her back. She loathed him. Flicking her eyes up to meet his, she promised he'd pay for this later.

"Go ahead, Ramsey," Liam encouraged her with a brotherly smile. The doctor had always been the kindest of her six brothers.

"Yes," Nico echoed. "Sing for them, Rams."

She clutched a now sleeping Jackson tighter in her grasp, realizing for the first time just how heavy her nephew was. Or maybe it was the crushing weight of the looming humiliation she was about to endure.

Songs. Songs. Songs. Ramsey racked her head for any song she could think of and the only one to pop in her mind sent her into a full-blown panic. She cringed and prayed she'd think of another song, but with her family watching her, and Patrick egging her on, she gave her best out-of-tune rendition of the *Star-Spangled Banner.* With each stanza of the National Anthem, she died a little bit more on the inside, until the entire brutal moment was over. It felt like she'd been screeching for hours, but after about ninety seconds, she received an awkward applause.

Patrick howled in delight as Quinn swatted at him furiously. "Ramsey," he wheezed, wiping tears from his eyes, "Ramsey, please tell me this is some weird joke. Please, please tell me you do not sing the National Anthem nightly before you two bang one out."

"Patrick!" Quinn's cheeks were beat red.

"Do you make him dress up like George Washington just for good measure?" Patrick's laugh spurred others to join in the levity. "I knew you loved American History but damn."

Ramsey shot Nico a vicious look, but his smile and the crinkle at the corners of his eyes made her heart skip beat. She didn't know if she wanted to punch him or kiss him. Damn him.

When Ramsey's mother came around the corner and announced dinner was ready, she was both relieved and irritated. Once their dinner was over, Nico was in for a good tongue lashing. She'd make sure he didn't pull a move like that again.

Nineteen

Nico

Apart from the National Anthem incident, dinner went off without a hitch. Everyone in the Price family already knew him from his college years and once they'd gotten the fact he and Ramsey were dating out of their system, conversation veered away from their personal lives for other topics like business, vacations, kids, if Phineas was going to bring his on-again-off-again girlfriend, Melissa, for the weekend, and Sean's upcoming wedding.

Once dinner had been eaten and the kitchen and dining room cleaned, everyone headed to their designated rooms for the evening. William claimed they all needed to get a good night's rest because he had a bunch of fun water activities planned for tomorrow.

Nico and Ramsey trekked up the stairs silently until he tugged their shared bedroom door open and let her walk inside first. As he closed the door, he started humming the

Star-Spangled Banner and earned a vicious glare from his fake girlfriend.

"You think you're so funny," she snorted, throwing a pillow at him which he caught with a chuckle.

"Come on," Nico tossed the pillow back at her. "You did start it, you know."

She opened her mouth to say something but then snapped her lips shut. Shaking her head and mumbling obscenities under her breath, she pulled a blanket off her mattress and put it on the narrow window seat. Slamming a pillow down at one end of the nook, she pointed at it and said, "That's where you can sleep."

"You're joking." The window seat was no more than four feet long and was about a foot deep. "I am not sleeping there."

Ramsey folded her arms over her chest, pursing her lips in that stubborn way of hers. "Well, you certainly are not sleeping with me."

"Is this because you had to sing the National Anthem," he couldn't help the laugh that slipped from his lips. "Price, I'm sorry. I didn't realize the first song you'd think of was the *Star-Spangled Banner*."

If he was being honest, that was hands-down the funniest moment of his entire life. Now her family thought they were *that* into American History. His cheeks started to hurt he'd been smiling so much.

"You realize I'm going to hit you with something so much worse tomorrow, right?" Ramsey busied herself with building a pillow barrier down the center of the bed. At least she'd abandoned the notion of forcing him to sleep on her window seat.

"I welcome the challenge," Nico dug through his bag until he found a dark grey t-shirt and plaid sleep pants. He tore his shirt over his head when she gasped behind him, forcing him to face her half naked.

"What are you doing?" Ramsey spat indignantly, though her eyes were raking over his entire torso.

"I'm getting ready for bed."

"You're not changing in front of me."

"That would look extremely suspicious if one of your family members caught me changing in the bathroom instead of our room." By the look on Ramsey's face, she knew he made a good point. "You face that way," he pointed at the wall behind her, "and I'll face this way. We'll both change and no one has to see what they don't want to see."

She mulled it over before huffing in agreement. "But no peeking."

"You're the one staring at my bare chest, Price."

Ramsey whipped around, but not before gazing at his abs one more time. He smiled as he faced his side of the room and quickly slipped on his pajamas.

"Are you decent?" he asked before turning around.

"Hold on." He heard one foot hit the floor followed by the other. "Done."

When he turned around, she was standing on the opposite side of the bed wearing a loose tank top and cotton shorts. "You wear knee high socks to sleep?" He spied the Phillies logo and smiled.

"What of it?" Ramsey sneered as she slipped under the covers on her side of the pillow mountain.

Nico shrugged as he got comfortable on his side. "Didn't picture you as a sock person is all."

"What does that even mean?" Ramsey poked her head over the stack of pillows between them. "Do you not wear socks?"

"I do." He met her gaze. "With shoes."

She rolled her eyes and sank back down. "Keep to your side of the bed. And I swear if you start to snore, I'll kick you out."

"What if you snore?" Nico asked, knowing the question would rile her up.

"I don't snore."

"Oh really? And how would you know?"

Ramsey didn't respond and was so quiet he wondered if it was even possible she had fallen asleep that quickly.

"David told me I'm not a snorer," she said softly. "He was a light sleeper; any little noise would wake him up."

A lump formed in Nico's throat, and he closed his eyes. Why did he always seem to ask questions that made her uncomfortable? He wanted her to open up to him and he feared he was pushing her further behind the wall she'd built up around herself to keep safe.

"Good night, Price," he managed to spit out before he turned on his side, facing the wall.

He felt the pillow against his back lift, so he flipped to his other side and found Ramsey staring at him.

"You alright?" he asked when she didn't say anything.

"Truth or dare," she said, and his heart thrashed in his chest.

Nico flashed back to earlier when she dared him to kiss her and as desperate as he was to see what else she would dare him to do, he found he was more interested in seeing what she wanted to know about him.

He planted his elbow on top of his plush pillow and rested the side of his stubbled face in his palm. "Truth."

"What does your tattoo say?" Ramsey didn't hesitate, armed with that question, as if she'd been trying to figure out what the script running up and down his left ribcage said for a while.

"*Ad astra per aspera.*"

"I was never very good with Latin. What does it mean?" She mirrored his body language, tucking her chin in her hand.

"It means, '*Through adversity to the stars*'," he was oddly impressed she knew it was Latin.

She searched his face, for what he wasn't sure, but either she found what she was looking for or let it go. "So, do you speak Italian?"

"Not fluently to my parents' dismay," he shrugged. "I know enough to get by and understand more than I let on." He winked drawing a tight-lipped smile from her. "Do I get to ask you a question now?"

"Sure." She seemed hesitant, but also like she didn't want to back down from a potential challenge. This woman's competitiveness fueled him.

"What does your tattoo say?" Nico glanced down her blanket to where the curve of her hip was. "The one on the side of your hip."

"Give me liberty."

"Or give me death." He recognized the quote from when she was giving him a tour at the museum. "Patrick Henry."

She looked at him and seemed impressed. "You remembered."

Nico bobbed his head, truly coming to realize how much she desired to be free from societal expectations or maybe just her mother's expectations. It was a strong enough desire that she had the Revolutionary's words permanently etched into her skin.

"Tell me about your family." It wasn't a question, but his body warmed with the thought that she was trying to get to know him better. He didn't like talking about his family with anyone, but he wasn't going to forgo her request.

"My parents moved here from Italy when they were teenagers. They'd just gotten married and decided they wanted to start a new life and have a family here in the States." Nico shifted his weight and tugged his blankets to get comfortable since he would be in that position for a few minutes. "I'm the oldest and my sister, Giulianna is three years younger than me. My father started his own moving truck business-"

"Wait," she slapped a hand down on the bed. "Are you talking about Giovanni's Movers? *If they give you the boot, we'll give you a hand?*"

Nico smiled; he couldn't help it. She nailed their slogan, and it was so random that she even knew it. "The one and the same."

She laughed, "So, you grew up in the moving business, I take it?"

"Yeah. I worked throughout the summers and during the weekends." He raked a hand through his hair. "My Pops wanted me to take over the family business after I graduated college, but I told him while I was at school I had no interest in taking his place. It wasn't in me. But opening up my own bar, that's where my passion lied."

"Was he upset?"

He was furious. Borderline ready to disown Nico. "He wasn't happy about it."

"But he's happy for you now, right?" Her eyes searched his and her hopeful smile faded.

Nico shook his head. "I actually haven't spoken to him much over the last few years. I see him for holidays and special occasions and that's about it. Even then, we don't speak unless it's about the family business."

"That's..." Ramsey slid her hand across the mattress and grazed the tips of his fingers with her own. "I'm sorry, Nico."

"It's alright," he dragged his thumbs across her knuckles. "My sister talks to me almost daily. And my mom has come around knowing that I'm happy and successful. Giulianna is trying to convince my Pops to let her run the family business. She likes ordering men around."

That drew a giggle from Ramsey and before he realized it, they were both laughing. He loved the sound of her laugh and how her eyes closed when she smiled widely.

"I think she and I could be good friends," she wiped a tear from her eye and Nico nodded.

"I think she would adore you, Price." *Like he did.*

With the moon being their only lighting source, Nico and Ramsey quietly soaked one another's facial features in, like they had never examined one another before. Her platinum hair nearly glowed in the moonlight, and he knew she would never look more angelic than she did that very second. She was a vision and letting his eyes freely roam her face stole his breath.

Nico wanted to whisper his true feelings for her in her ear. Wanted to run the tip of his hand along the curvature of her jaw and wherever his fingers touched, he wanted to leave a trail of kisses.

Was Ramsey's face inching closer to his? Or was that all in his imagination?

Just when he thought she was going to kiss him, something sparked in her eyes, and she retreated back to her side of the bed. She laid flat on her back and stared at the ceiling.

"Goodnight, Nico."

"Goodnight, Ramsey."

Tonight had been the closest he'd come to infiltrating the fortress that was Ramsey's heart. Maybe tomorrow, she'd finally let him in.

Twenty

RAMSEY

Last night had been a little too intimate and Ramsey had to make sure that didn't happen again. Getting to know Nico was one thing but finding herself having butterflies in the pit of her stomach when she opened her eyes and saw him sleeping next to her was another issue entirely.

Doing her best, not to stare at his peaceful, albeit handsome face, she slipped out of their bed to change. Double checking to make sure his eyes were still closed, she slipped her pajamas off, and pulled some athletic shorts and a loose tank from her suitcase knowing her dad had water activities planned that morning. Just before she was able to pull the new shirt over her head, Nico's voice rang out behind her causing her to jump. She hid herself behind the outfit she'd picked out.

"And where are you off to so early?" He smirked, mischief in those brown eyes of his.

"Turn around!" she hissed. "Don't peek!"

"Do I make you nervous, Price?" he purred, his elbow propping his head up, making his bicep look incredibly enticing.

"It'll take a lot more than your unwanted gaze to make me nervous, Nora."

The taunting in her voice spurred him to slip out of the bed and approach her, his eyes glued to hers. To her credit, she didn't shrink back, and stood as tall as her frame would allow, even though he still had several inches on her. Once he was within a foot of her, he looked down at her, planting his hands on either side of the wall behind her.

"If I wanted to make you nervous, Princess, I could."

"Do I detect a challenge, Norelle?" she cocked her head to the side, doing her best to ignore the excitement pooling in her lower belly.

Nico leaned closer, brushing his stubbled jaw against her cheek, drawing a raspy gasp from her lips. "You couldn't handle me, sweetheart."

"If you think you're going to make me uncomfortable by invading my personal space," Ramsey dug deep for the un-wavering confidence in her voice, "then I'm afraid you'll be sorely disappointed."

He pushed away from her with a grin plastered across his face. "I like that about you, Price, never backing down from a challenge."

"Good thing I don't care what you think about me," she quickly slipped her tank on, followed closely by her running shorts. "I suggest you dress comfortably. If my dad has his way, we'll be out on the water thirty minutes after breakfast."

Ramsey brushed past Nico as she made her way to the bedroom door. She only realized once she'd shut the door that she left her shoes in the room. "Damn it," she muttered. She turned around and burst through the door to find Nico standing in nothing but his boxers.

Ramsey couldn't help herself. Her eyes wandered up and down his muscular body, appreciating every single ab, and now that she knew what his tattoo meant, it looked even better etched in his olive skin.

Nico stood up straight, not bothering to cover up. "Now who is the one peeking?"

The subtle tease in his tone ripped her from her thoughts and she quickly scurried for her shoes on her side of the bed, purposely averting his gaze. "Forgot these," she made it a point to show him her sneakers, before bolting for the door again.

Once she closed it, she rested her back against the door to catch her breath. She'd seen men's bodies before – why was *his* body the one to make her knees weak? She felt like one of those damsel-in-distress females she read about in books when she was growing up. Always fanning over the male love interest as if he was the oxygen she desperately needed to breath.

Snap out of it, Price, she chastised herself. Catching her breath, and getting ahold of her raging hormones, she commanded her body to stand up and walk down the steps for breakfast, but before she had a chance to react, Nico opened the door behind her, and she fell backwards into his arms. With his hands firmly rooted to her waist, she looked up as he glanced down at her and he smiled.

"Damn, Price, if that's how you react to seeing me shirt-less, I can't imagine what you'd do if you saw the rest of me." He winked and her face flushed in anger. No, embarrass-ment. No, lust? She wasn't sure anymore.

"Let go of me," she fussed as he lifted her back to a standing position.

"Have I made you *uncomfortable*?" Nico asked, stuffing his hands in his short pockets.

He even looked good in basketball shorts and a t-shirt. It really was unfair how attractive Nico was – especially since she wasn't supposed to be having real feelings for him.

"Let's just eat breakfast, pretend to be a happy and loving couple, and get this day over with." Ramsey stomped down the steps and Nico rushed to catch up, slipping his hand in hers. She flicked his hand away, frowning. "What do you think you're doing?"

"You just said we needed to be a happy and loving couple. Forgive me, but the last time I checked, I do believe couples hold hands."

She rolled her eyes, knowing she wouldn't win this battle of wits and her stomach was about to growl like a starved lion. "Fine." She slapped her hand back in his and pulled him down the steps.

"Would you slow down?"

"Why?"

"You're racing like all the food will be gone by the time we get down the steps."

Ramsey shot him a look, not slowing her pace. "Are you forgetting that I have six brothers? If you didn't get to breakfast first, you got the scraps. And if we're going to be doing this *love-tango*, then I'll need as much energy as I can get."

"Loving me is that difficult, huh?" He teased but let her pull him down the hallway until they made it to the dining room. Most of the Price family was already eating, but thankfully there was plenty of food left.

"Good morning!" William chimed, setting his newspaper to the side.

Ramsey kissed her father's cheek and sat down on his left. Nico claimed the seat next to her.

"Where's mom?" she asked.

"She is getting her hair done," her dad answered with a smile. "She'll be back this afternoon."

Once Ramsey and Nico piled food on their plates, she could sense she was being watched. She glanced up from her plate and stared at Patrick across the table and she could tell he was itching to say something.

"Yes, Patrick?" she stuffed her mouth with a spoonful of eggs. "You have something you wish to say?"

Everyone's attention flew to Patrick who was now cackling, wiping his red face with his linen napkin. "We were wondering when you two lovebirds were going to come down for breakfast. We thought you might forgo this morning's water activities for activities of another kind." He bounced his eyebrows up and down, clearly insinuating they were going to skip the family activity for intercourse.

William shook his head. "Patrick, you're too old to be making remarks like that -"

"Dad, it's just a joke," Patrick protested. "Ramsey knows I'm just kidding around."

Ramsey shrugged lazily as she spread raspberry jam over her toast. "I'm sure if you need any tips, Patrick, Nico would be more than happy to explain what it takes to please a woman."

Nico spit out his orange juice and coughed, while Liam, Connor, and Collin cackled at their end of the table. Their wives weren't too pleased with the turn of conversation that morning, but Ramsey really didn't care. If Patrick wanted to play, she was more than happy to oblige.

"You're not going to say anything to your daughter about her remarks?" Patrick stared at their father, but William waved his son off and laughed.

"If you don't want someone shitting in your backyard, don't unlock the fence." Ramsey's dad clapped his hands together, "Are we excited to go kayaking?"

Ramsey turned her attention to Nico who had been quiet at the table. "Have you been kayaking before?"

He met her gaze, "I went kayaking a couple years ago."

"Great," she bobbed her head, finishing her plate and downing the last of her orange juice. "I don't feel like having to save you from drowning. Way too much effort."

"Glad to know you care," Nico teased, standing when she did.

She shrugged, "Just being the best girlfriend I can be."

Twenty-One

Nico

Once everyone cleared their plates from the dining room, they met in the backyard where William had all the kayaks waiting for them.

"Make sure you put these life vests on and stick with your partner. Just in case the water gets a little bumpy, I don't want anyone alone," William instructed, marching up and down the line looking each one of them in the eye. "Does everyone understand? Any questions?"

Everyone was familiar with kayaking, so they nodded in agreement before slipping life vests on. Nico noticed Ramsey was having trouble getting one of her buckles to work so without thinking, he took the straps from her, pulled her closer, and snapped her in. When their eyes met, he felt a warmth spread through his body and he fought the urge to kiss her.

"Thanks," she cleared her throat, taking a step back from him.

"You're welcome."

The plan was to kayak toward Cushing Island. The small isle was visible from the Price's backyard, so it wasn't going to be too tough of an activity. Pushing off from the embankment, the group consisting of William, Collin, Kristen, Liam, Connor, Patrick, Quinn, Ramsey, and Nico set off.

The weather was perfect. Bright blue skies, cool water, the sun beaming down on them. It was between two and three miles to paddle to Cushing Island and the views of the mainland were worth the soreness in his muscles.

William took great pride in guiding the group around and even had them stop at the coffee shop to get refreshments before their journey back to shore. Apart from joking with Ramsey's brothers and his upper body enjoying the break from kayaking, the trek around the island was uneventful. It was beautiful to be sure, but his favorite part was watching Ramsey interact with her family.

He learned the second Sean moved into their freshman dorm that the Price family was large but that they were also close. Sean would receive care packages, letters, cards, and even the occasional gag gift throughout the school year. Sean was great about including him in whatever snacks or goodies he received from home, but a piece of Nico died each time he went to his mail slot and saw it empty.

Ramsey's laugh rescued him from the sad memories of his college days, and he smiled, relishing in the sound of her happiness. He watched her shove Liam. Whatever he said had everyone cackling as they headed back to where they'd left their kayaks a couple hours earlier.

"You've been really quiet, Norma," Ramsey slowed her pace to fall in line with him. "You alright?"

"Concerned about me?" Nico wiggled his eyebrows up and down with an impish smirk. "Be careful, Price, I might think you care."

"I'm not a monster, Giovanni." Ramsey elbowed him playfully in his ribs. "At least, not often."

He laughed softly, cracking his back once his kayak was within sight.

"You didn't answer my question," Ramsey pressed, grabbing his forearm and turning him to face her. "You alright?"

The look in her eyes nearly stole the breath from his lungs. Normally a blue-grey, her eyes were a bright, vibrant blue and he was rendered speechless. She looked like a water nymph with that platinum blonde hair and dark eyebrows. In the sunlight, he could see she had freckles over the bridge of her nose, and he wanted to kiss each and every single one.

"Giovanni?" she narrowed her eyes at him.

"I'm fine, Price," he shifted his weight foot to foot, readjusting his backwards baseball cap. "Bet I can beat you back to shore."

"Is that a dare?" She brightened when he nodded his head, and she cracked her fingers. "Don't cry when I destroy you."

Still a short distance from shore, and paddling neck and neck with Ramsey, Nico heard his phone ring. He'd buried it in a pocket on his life vest and slipped it out to see who was trying to get in touch with him.

"Your girlfriend?" Ramsey teased when he smiled at the name that popped up.

"Jealous, Price?" By the look in her eye, he realized she was jealous and part of him rejoiced knowing she must have some type of feelings for him but the other part of him wanted to snatch her in his arms and reassure her she was the only woman on his mind. Instead, his attention was drawn back to the video chat alert, and he swiped the green button, accepting the call.

"Ahh, there he is," a female voice crowed, and Nico noticed Ramsey's shoulders stiffen. "How are you doing? Where are you?"

"I told you I'd be in Maine for a long weekend."

"That's right! I forgot that was this weekend." The brunette smiled at him, and he returned with a grin of his own. "I miss you. When do I get to see you again? When are you coming back to Philadelphia?"

Nico should have explained the second he accepted the phone call that Ramsey had nothing to worry about, but maybe a little jealousy was good for her. At least then she'd realize she was attracted to him and wanted him to herself.

"I'll be back Monday," Nico returned his focus to the screen. "Giulianna, have you met Ramsey?" He turned the camera toward Ramsey, paddling through the water. She didn't seem to appreciate being included and shot him daggers with her eyes. "Ramsey, this is my sister, Giulianna."

The tension in Ramsey's upper torso vanished and she waved, flashing his sister a smile. "It's nice to meet you, Giulianna."

"*That's* Ramsey!" Giulianna squeaked, tossing her shoulder-length dark brown hair out of her face to get a better look. "You're just as beautiful as Nico said you were!"

"You told your sister about me?" Ramsey glanced at Nico, and he cleared his throat.

"I might have mentioned you," he shrugged casually, but if his sister kept revealing his secrets, he'd have to toss his phone in the water and just buy a new one later.

"Mentioned you?" Giulianna scoffed. "I think he talks about you more than -"

"Gules," Nico turned the phone toward him and frowned. "I think you've said more than enough. What'd you call about?"

"Sean just called me," she propped the phone against something and started doing her make up.

"What'd he call you about? Is he ok?"

"He wanted to see what I knew about you and Ramsey dating."

Nico's stomach dropped and he risked a glance at Ramsey who also looked as if she was going to throw up.

"What did you tell him?" He was hoping, praying, that his sister kept her big oversharing mouth shut. He'd talked to her about Ramsey for years and she had always told him to man up and ask her out. Giulianna knew too much and if she told Sean just a fraction of what he'd spilled to his sister about, he was screwed.

Giulianna applied mascara, unfazed by the nervous edge in his tone. "I told him I had no idea you two were dating. Why didn't you tell me?"

"It just sort of happened recently," Nico rubbed the back of his neck. "I promise I'll tell you all about it when I'm back in town." He knew Giulianna would fight him for more information, so he decided to change the subject instead. "How are Mom and Pop doing?"

Giulianna rolled her eyes and groaned. "Mom is good. Pop is driving me crazy."

"What's wrong?"

"You know Pop is retiring in the next year or two and I keep telling him I want to take over, but he keeps saying, 'we'll talk about it soon'." She huffed, snapping her make-up kit closed and picking the phone back up. "If he hands the company over to someone else just because they're a man, I'll scream."

"You deserve the company, Gules," Nico reassured her, even though he knew their Pop had no intention of handing over the company unless a man was involved. He was old school and would preach until his dying breath that women should be the caretakers and men should be the breadwin-ners. If only their Pop knew Giulianna would rather burn half the city to the ground before letting the family business fall into someone else's hands.

"Of course I deserve it. Let's hope the old man sees that too." There was a beep on Giulianna's phone. "I'm going to have to let you go. We'll talk soon, okay?"

"As soon as I'm back in town, we'll grab dinner," Nico promised.

"As long as you're buying," she teased, and he rolled his eyes. "It was nice to finally meet you, Ramsey," she called out and Nico turned the phone back to her. "Don't take any of my brother's shit, either. He talks a big game, but he's nothing but mush on the inside."

Ramsey chuckled and he faced the screen again. "Thanks for that."

"No problem," she winked and then ended the call.

Nico slipped his phone back into his life vest pocket and smiled thinking of his sister. She was just as no nonsense as he was, and her brain was built for running a business. She commanded attention whenever she walked into a room, but she had the sweetest and most generous heart. She deserved the world and he wished he could do more to help their Pop see she was the right person to take over once he retired.

"She seems nice," Ramsey's voice sliced through his thoughts and he smiled at her.

"Unfortunately, you two would probably be best friends if you two ever met face-to-face."

"Why would that be unfortunate?" she flashed him a quizzical look.

"I can barely manage you two separately. I can't imagine the havoc you two would wreak together. Especially when it comes to me." His laugh spurred her to cackle, wiping tears from her eyes. "I'm glad you think that's so funny, Price."

"So," she got ahold of herself as they kept paddling back toward the Price house. "You talk about me?"

"Someone has to warn the population about you," he winked at her which drew another laugh out of her.

"I hate you," she snickered.

"No, you don't."

The joy in her face slowly dissipated and he wondered if he'd said the wrong thing.

"What's wrong, Price?"

"She said Sean called her about us," she rubbed a hand over her face. "Either someone called him to tell him, or..."

"He's here." Nico knew where she was headed, and he'd be lying if he said he wasn't a little bit worried about Sean. He'd been concerned since Sean asked him to drive Ramsey to Maine that he'd not be able to resist acting on his feelings, but when Ramsey wrangled her into this fake dating scheme, he couldn't help but agree. Even if it was just pretend, he wanted, needed, to have a chance to put a smile on her face.

"Alright, everyone," William's voice boomed from the front of the pack. "Almost there!"

Reluctantly, Nico joined the rest of the group as they paddled the rest of the way back to the Price mansion. Nico squinted his eyes as they neared the dock, seeing someone standing there waiting on them. His stomach dropped the moment he recognized the man on the embankment was Sean.

Twenty-Two

RAMSEY

Sean stood on the dock in the backyard with his arms folded across his chest. Ramsey knew by the look on her favorite brother's face that Giulianna was right. He'd definitely heard about her and Nico dating, but she was hoping and praying he'd gone along with it and not outed them for being liars.

As desperately as she wanted to head back out to the ocean for another few hours and avoid this confrontation, she and Nico rowed up to the shore and Sean helped Ramsey out, his blue eyes fixed on her and her alone.

"I didn't expect you and Cali to make it here until tomorrow," Ramsey smiled brightly when she hugged him, but when he didn't squeeze her until she couldn't breathe like he normally did, she knew this wasn't going to end well. "Is everything alright?"

"Mom told me and Cali your news," Sean's gaze darted to Nico who stood on the dock next to her quietly. "I think we should talk."

Nico nodded his head, rubbing a hand along the back of his neck, but this wasn't his lecture to endure. It was hers. She stepped between the best friends, placing her hand on Sean's chest, and whispering so her other brothers and their wives wouldn't overhear. "Sean, not here, please."

Sean looked at her and nodded before turning and walking back up toward the house.

"Looks like someone is in for a big brother lecture," Patrick joked as he helped Quinn out of their rowboat.

Ramsey closed her eyes, counted to ten, and resisted the urge to two-hand shove Patrick in the water, and marched after Sean, ready to take her lickings like a Price. But before she stepped foot off the dock into the grass, Nico grabbed her arm and turned her around to face him.

"I'll go," Nico glanced over her shoulder, looking at a retreating Sean, before meeting her gaze again. "It's me he's mad at, not you."

"He wouldn't be mad at you at all if I hadn't gotten you involved," she shook her head, patting his hand still wrapped around her bicep. "I'll calm him down. Trust me. It's better this way."

"Rams -"

"Quit being stubborn, Nelly, and just let me take the heat for this."

"We'll go together," he offered. Something in his eyes was hauntingly protective.

Noticing her family members still on the dock watching them, she squeezed his hand and leaned in close to his ear. To her brothers and their wives, it would look like she was giving him a peck on the cheek, but instead she whispered, "I'm going to tell Sean the truth. I would never come between your friendship with my brother."

She turned on her heel and stomped up the gradual hill to the house, dreading every second. Ramsey and Sean were fondly known as Bonnie and Clyde growing up because they were inseparable and always seemed to find themselves in some kind of trouble. Remembering the two of them having to meet their parents in their dad's study to endure an hour-long lecture followed by whatever punishment they saw fit for their crimes oddly brought back warm memories of her and her brother.

But this time, she wasn't marching with Sean to face the wrath of their parents. She was about to face off with him and hoped he'd give her a chance to explain what was going on before he ripped into her.

Sean had disappeared inside the house a minute before she did, but she already knew where he'd be waiting. She weaved through the halls of the first floor until she came to a door in the kitchen that led to a small garden their mother liked to plant her herbs for cooking. It wasn't a large space, but it was fully enclosed with a stone fence and manicured hedges, so they'd have the privacy she'd asked for.

He was pacing up and down the gravel path. On either side of the ten-foot-long pathway were wooden boxes filled with rosemary, cilantro, oregano, basil, and parsley. It smelled heavenly. From childhood, Sean had loved coming to sit on the two-seater wooden bench at the end of the trail, against the stone wall, to think or escape the others for a few minutes of peace and quiet.

Ramsey stopped in the entrance with arms folded over her chest. She took a deep breath but before she could say anything, Sean said, "When were you going to tell me?"

"Sean -"

"I would have preferred to hear it from you or from my best friend of all people instead of listening to our mother crow on about how she lost fifty bucks to our dad on some stupid bet." Sean quit pacing and stared at her.

Was he smiling?

"Are you alright?" She arched an eyebrow, concerned he'd snapped, and his face was now broken. "You're smiling."

Sean motioned for her to speak, "Just waiting for an explanation. I thought we were closer than this and that you felt you could come to me about anything. I guess I was wrong."

She stepped to him. "It's not what you think."

"Then please, explain to me how my sister and my best friend have been dating secretly behind my back and didn't feel the need to tell me. Wait," he held his hands up, "were you seeing each other while you were dating David?"

"No!" Ramsey shook her head. "I'm not a cheater, Sean."

"Then how- ?"

"We're not really dating," she hissed, cutting him off. "We're not dating, Sean, it's all a lie."

"Wait, what?"

"When we got here Wednesday, mom did her typical thing where she asked about David and when I told her I broke up with him, she thought I'd made him up completely. She wanted to set me up with her friend's son, and I just couldn't go through another wedding being paraded around like a prized cow." She rubbed the heels of her palms against her eyes and groaned. "I told her I was already dating someone else and when she asked who, I panicked and blurted Nico's name, kissed him, and then convinced him to pretend to be my boyfriend for the weekend so I could avoid the drama." Ramsey glanced at Sean who had remained quiet. "So, it's not real. We didn't keep anything from you, and we didn't mean to hurt your feelings, Sean. If you're going to be angry with anyone over this, be angry with me and not Nico. He only did what I asked him to do."

Sean scratched the back of his head. "So, you and Nico aren't dating?"

"No." It hurt her heart to admit aloud and stung that her brother's mood seemed to brighten at the confession.

"Am I the only one who knows?"

"You can tell Cali if you want to, but please, keep this between the four of us," Ramsey pleaded and plopped down on the bench, burying her face in her hands. "We're in too deep as it is, and I don't want mom finding out and the entire situation ruins your wedding."

She felt Sean sit next to her and drape his arm across her shoulders. Pulling her close to him, she rested her head on his shoulder.

"Are we friends again?" she asked softly.

Sean squeezed her. "We're always friends." He pulled away from her and leaned forward to meet her gaze. "Why'd you step between me and Nico?"

"He would have let you take whatever anger or aggression you had pent up inside of you out on him even though he didn't deserve it."

"You spared him?" His brow quirked. "Ramsey, did you do something nice for Nico?"

She shoved him and laughed. "Hard to believe, but I am capable of doing the right thing, even for someone I can't stand."

By the look on Sean's face, both of them knew her feelings for Nico were the furthest thing from disdain. Something had changed between them, but she'd have to bury those feelings. Not just to protect herself, but so Sean wouldn't be upset and feel awkward about the whole situation.

"So, what do you say?" Sean smiled. "Should we get back to everyone else before their tongues get tired of gossiping about us?"

Ramsey hopped up and readjusted her Phillies hat. "How would you like me to play this? Should I pretend like I've been crying from facing my big brother's wrath? Or should I just keep quiet the rest of the night, as if I'm deep in thought?"

"How about, we enjoy ourselves, and quit pretending?" He bumped her with his hip. "Everyone is happy you two are dating. Let's keep it that way."

She was surprised but grateful Sean would play along for her sake. "I suppose Nico will be able to sigh in relief that you aren't going to deck him."

Sean offered her his arm and she looped hers through as they walked back inside. "He thought I was going to punch him?"

"I don't know," she shrugged. "Isn't that what guys do? That's what you six idiots do when you're mad at each other."

"We don't fist fight anymore, Ramsey," Sean shook his head, smirking down at her. "I would like to think we've matured and are beyond that phase."

They walked out to the backyard where the women were sitting around a roaring firepit roasting marshmallows for smores with the kids. But off to the side, Ramsey and Sean's brothers, father, and Nico were gathered in a small circle arguing about which action hero was more lethal in a fight. Collin and Connor argued in favor of Arnold Schwarzenegger. Patrick insisted Chuck Norris was the ultimate fighter. Liam and their dad put their faith in James Bond, and Nico looked ready to fight them all to his dying breath that Jason Bourne was the best choice.

"I stand corrected," Sean sighed and Ramsey laughed. "I guess we're not as mature as I thought we were."

"You're all wrong," Ramsey shouted, interrupting their debate and garnering their full attention. Nico flashed her a warm smile that made her insides feel like goo.

"Oh, you think so?" Patrick put his hands on his hips, amusement written across his face. "And who would you pick as the ultimate fighter?"

"John McClane, hands down." She pointed a thumb at Sean and scoffed, "Sean said Ethan Hunt."

"What the hell, Sean?" The men erupted, shouting back and forth about their great hatred for the *Mission Impossible* character.

"Thanks for that, Rams," Sean rolled his eyes. "They'll be texting me Ethan Hunt memes from now until Christmas."

Nico slowly approached them, hands in his pockets. "Everything alright?"

Sean looked at his friend and extended his hand, "We're cool, man."

"Quinn!" Patrick shouted at his wife, "Sean said Ethan Hunt was the ultimate action hero! Can you believe that?"

"I didn't say that," Sean rubbed a hand down his face. "Ramsey was messing with you." He walked toward the circle to defend himself and Ramsey couldn't help the smirk that slithered across her face.

"How mad was he?" Nico whispered, standing so close to her that his arm brushed against hers.

"A hell of a lot less than I thought he'd be." She bumped him with her hip, drawing his gaze, and realized how much she craved his attention. "Everything's fine. I promise."

"I trust you," he bobbed his head with a small smile.

Twenty-Three

Nico

And Nico found that he meant it. He did trust Ramsey, more than anyone else. That should have made him nervous, but it brought him an odd sense of peace. More shocking than his unwavering trust in her, he couldn't believe she thrust herself between him and Sean, willing to take the brunt of her brother's anger over them dating. Well, fake dating, but still. She protected him, shielded him like a lioness protecting her mate, and it filled him with a longing to do something to repay her kindness.

He slipped his fingers in hers, hoping she wouldn't pull away, and was relieved when she twisted her hand into his. "Hey," he whispered, and she glanced up into his eyes. "I dare you to go swimming with me."

Ramsey's eyebrow quirked. "Right now?"

"Right now." He held his breath. Would she back down from the challenge since her entire family was enjoying the warm night?

"Oh, Giovanni," Ramsey purred, and he just about crumbled to his knees before her. "I'll do you one better," she smiled, throwing her hair up in a messy ponytail. "I'll race you down there."

"You're on, Price." He kicked his shoes off and she did the same.

They took their stances.

"On the count of three," she said, and he nodded in agreement. "One, two, three."

Ramsey took off like a bullet that had just been fired from a gun. He knew she liked to go for morning runs several times a week, but he greatly underestimated how fast and light on her feet she was. He bolted after her, hot on her heels. She started laughing as he crept up on her but was clearly determined to beat him to the water. Nico stumbled when he saw her strip her tank off, but not to be outdone, he also ditched his top in the grass.

They splashed into the ocean at the same time, each claiming victory over the other.

"I won and you know it, Giovanni," she waded, spritzing water in his face. "Admit defeat."

"No way," he shook his head, splashing water back at her with a smile.

Ramsey's laugh was a symphony to his ears, and he could listen to the music of her soul for the rest of his days and die happy.

She dunked her head beneath the waves and when she emerged, she slicked loose strands of hair back. Meeting his gaze, she cocked her head to the side and her smile faded. "Why?"

"Why what?" Nico floated closer to her.

"Why dare me to swim? Don't you think you wasted one of your precious dares on something silly?"

He shook his head, swiping a rebellious strand of hair stuck to her cheek. "I have you right where I want you, Price."

"Oh, and where exactly is that?"

"Alone."

Nico could have sworn he heard Ramsey gasp, but he couldn't be sure. But by the look on her face, she didn't disapprove of his confession. In fact, she swam within inches of him and stared into his eyes.

"When we first got here, I didn't know what you feared." He swallowed audibly, knowing where she was headed and knew he was helpless to stop her. "I dare you to tell me what you fear."

"Why do you want to know?" he asked, a huskiness in his voice. "Because if you just want to use it to make fun of me later -"

"I don't like semi-trucks because as a teenager I was driving down the interstate and watched as a sportscar zipped through traffic and tried to cut a truck off. The truck driver never saw him and..." Ramsey sucked in a breath and Nico wanted to wrap his arms around her for being vulnerable with him. "There wasn't much left of the sportscar or its driver. I had nightmares for months and couldn't even bring myself to get behind the wheel of a car for months. I still have trouble driving to this day and don't do it often. The last time I can remember driving was at least three or four years ago and I had to have Sean take over because I had a panic attack."

Nico tentatively lifted his hand out of the water and cupped her cheek, gently forcing her to meet his gaze. "I am terrified of losing someone I love. Not just because I'd miss them, but without them, I'd no longer be whole. And if I'm being honest, I don't know if I'd be strong enough to continue living."

Ramsey's eyes watered and she pressed her forehead against his, slowly wrapping her arms around his neck and squeezing. "Thank you."

"For what?" He held her tightly, feeling whole for the first time in years.

"Everything," she whispered. She pulled her face back to look at him. His arms were still around her when she slipped both of her hands on either side of his face and leaned down toward his lips. "Nico?" The way she said his name sent a shiver down his back. It could have been due to the chilly water, but something shifted between them, and he wanted to see where this could go.

"Ramsey?" he breathed against her mouth. She hovered above his lips, as if she wanted him to kiss her, but he wanted, needed her to make the next move. His feelings were clear in his mind, it was her feelings that were fuzzy.

Her nails raked through his hair, and she tilted his face toward hers. She was going to kiss him; he could see it in her eyes.

"Ramsey! Nico! Are you two out here?" Cali's high-pitched voice rang out, spurring Ramsey to push herself away from Nico before Cali made it around the bend. "Oh my gosh," her eyes bounced back and forth between them as Sean jogged up behind her. "Did I interrupt something?" When no one said anything, Cali blushed. "I'm so sorry, I just wanted to congratulate you both. I always had a feeling you two would end up together."

Ramsey and Nico exchanged a look before turning their focus to Sean standing behind his fiancée. Wading out of the water and snatching her shirt up from the grass, Ramsey slipped it on and kissed Cali on the cheek.

"Sean didn't tell you yet?" She might have been looking at her future sister-in-law, but the question was for her brother.

Sean handed Nico his shirt when he came up out of the cold ocean water and shook his head. "I haven't had a moment to tell her."

"Tell me what?" Cali's gaze bounced amongst the three of them.

"They're not actually dating," Sean whispered. "They said they were so my mom wouldn't make Ramsey meet some of her friends' sons at our wedding."

Cali blushed and slapped a hand to her cheek. "I'm sorry, I didn't know."

"Why are you sorry?" Ramsey cocked her head to the side, squeezing the water from her hair.

"When I came over here to find you two, I figured – I didn't realize you two were about to... I mean, I..."

Ramsey grabbed Cali's hand, sparing her anymore embarrassment, "It's ok, Cali. Nico and I were just talking. Come on, let's go grab one of these smores I keep smelling." Ushering Cali back up the incline to the fire pit, Ramsey flashed Nico an unreadable look before walking away.

Sean nodded his head for Nico to follow. Neither of them said a word as they joined the rest of the family, but Nico couldn't get Cali's words out of his head. *I always had a feeling you two would end up together.*

Eating smores and cracking jokes with the Price family didn't keep him from dwelling on the interrupted moment between him and Ramsey. The way she'd said his name and ran her fingers through his hair. How she'd lowered her face to his, their lips so close. He could still feel the ghost of her hours later, even when they laid down to sleep.

Ramsey no longer insisted on the pillow mountain between them, but she didn't initiate anything between them, so he turned to his side, facing away from her, and closed his eyes. Sleep didn't come to him easily, but after an hour or so of just listening to her softly breathe, he welcomed the darkness and dreamt of her.

Twenty-Four

RAMSEY

Ramsey's mother had outdone herself with Friday's brunch. Eggs, bacon, sausage, fruit, buttered buns, freshly baked cinnamon rolls, pastries – the list was endless, and Ramsey felt like she was at a buffet, filling her plate to the brim, eager to stuff her face before the family softball game that afternoon.

Making her way to the large dining room with the twenty-foot-long table her dad and brother, Sean, had built together the summer before he left for college, she plopped down next to Nico and quietly began eating.

Things between her and Nico were good, dare she say great, considering the fake dating circumstances. She wasn't sure how much pretending she was doing and how much of her act was based on real feelings. But one thing was for certain, she wasn't going to be the one to bring up their almost kiss in the water the night before, even if she hadn't stopped thinking about his lips, or the fact his fingers dug into her lower back pulling her so close to him, she could feel his heart thrashing in his chest against her own.

Sean and Cali sat across the table from them. She knew by the look on Cali's face that she and her brother had done nothing but talk about her and Nico's arrangement, but Ramsey couldn't shake the feeling of disappointment radiating from her future sister-in-law. She'd been the one to encourage her to give Nico a chance to make her happy because he was a good guy. She wished she could admit Cali was right about Nico, but she knew she couldn't. Despite the few passionate kisses and heartfelt talks, it was still Nico, and by this time next week, they'd be back to their normal lives.

Suddenly, she wasn't as hungry.

Cali smiled at them and whispered, "It's nice seeing you two getting along."

Ramsey felt Nico's shoulders tense. "Yeah," he cleared his throat. "I guess we can play nice when we really want to."

She glanced up and down the table, making sure no one was eavesdropping, before turning her attention to Cali. "At least we haven't killed each other considering we are sleeping in the same bed."

Cali seemed to blush at that, and Sean scratched a finger up and down his cheek. "So," her brother whispered as he bit into his croissant, "you two really aren't -"

"This is your captain speaking," Phineas waltzed into the dining room, holding his fingers to his ear like he was making an announcement on one of his flights, "we are now clear to party."

Ramsey rolled her eyes as the rest of the family greeted the missing brother with smiles, cheers, laughs, and hugs. Even as children she and Phineas seemed to always be at odds, even though he was only a year older than Sean. She also despised the pilot's corny and self-serving sense of humor. But at least he came alone this time. She wouldn't have to deal with that irritating-

"Hellooooooooooo, Price family!"

Melissa Cooper.

Ramsey rejoiced a second too soon and lost her appetite completely. Shoving her plate away from her and throwing her napkin on top, she caught Sean's eye across the table as Melissa continued to greet members of the family in that high-pitched Boston whine of hers.

"Be nice," he mouthed.

She pretended she couldn't understand him, pointing at her ears and pouting. "What was that?" she mouthed back. "Didn't hear you."

Sean attempted to mouth his warning again, but Ramsey slid out of her chair, grabbed her plate, and marched it to the kitchen before he had the chance. She knew Sean would be disappointed with her petty and childlike behavior, but if she didn't leave the room, or at least slam noise cancelling headphones on to block out that banshee's shrill voice, she was more than likely going to spew more than a few hateful comments the blonde stewardess' way.

"Ramsey!"

Oh, dear Lord. The human train-wreck had followed her.

Ramsey dragged her hands off the butcher block island in the middle of the kitchen and turned to meet Melissa's disingenuous smiling face.

"Melissa." Ramsey bobbed her head in acknowledgement.

The flight attendant's heels clicked loudly with each step she took toward Ramsey, dramatically swaying her hips side-to-side, stretching her arms wide for a hug. Before she got too close, Ramsey extended her hand for a shake instead. If Melissa was offended by the deterrent, she didn't show it. She clasped Ramsey's hand and shook it vigorously.

"It's been such a long time!" Melissa cooed like a pageant queen. "We have to get together before the weekend is through and go shopping or get our nails done."

Ramsey would rather peel her own skin off than do either of those activities with his brother's girlfriend.

"Actually, Melissa-"

"How many times do I have to tell you, silly goose," Melissa swatted at Ramsey's arm playfully, "call me Mel. We're practically sisters anyway."

Ramsey grimaced. That would honestly be the worst thing to happen to the Price family since the family of nine all had food poisoning when she was in grade school. Racking her brain, trying to figure out a way to politely tell her to piss off, Nico gallantly, or conveniently, bounded into the kitchen carrying a stack of plates.

"I thought I'd find you in here," he smiled at Ramsey as he dumped the remnants of the plates' contents into the garbage and put the porcelain into the farmhouse sink.

"And who is this?" Melissa's eyes wandered up and down Nico's frame. When she bit her bottom lip and flashed a salacious smile his direction, a rage deep in the pit of Ramsey's stomach began to boil over. Was this... jealousy? Possessiveness? She wasn't quite sure what she was feeling but the urge to mark Nico as off-limits swept over her like a wave crashing against the rocky coastline.

Before she even realized what she was doing, Ramsey crossed the kitchen and planted a kiss on Nico's cheek, before weaving their fingers together. "This is Nico. Sean's best friend and my boyfriend." The words slipped out of her mouth so naturally she almost believed the last part.

Something flashed in Melissa's eyes. Ramsey couldn't tell if it was her lusting after a man she couldn't have or seeing it as a challenge to take him from her, but Melissa looked more like a snake coiled in the grass, waiting to snatch her helpless prey. But Ramsey most certainly was not helpless, nor was she prey. She was a lioness and more than willing, dare she say eager, to tear Melissa apart.

"Mel!" Phineas' voice echoed down the hall. When he poked his head through the archway leading into the kitchen, he flashed a dazzling smile, and joined them. "You alright in here, babe?" He glanced at Ramsey before wrapping his arms around Melissa's waist, hugging her from behind.

Phineas was right to be leery of the women being left alone together. The last time they'd seen one another, Ramsey was calling Melissa out in front of the entire family for flirting with Sean at Christmas, even though they were celebrating Patrick and Quinn's upcoming wedding and Sean and Cali's recent engagement. Sean had to drag Ramsey out of the house when Phineas declared he and Melissa were leaving.

"We're great. I was just meeting your sister's new boyfriend." Melissa's perkiness had a lethal edge to it, but Ramsey wasn't intimidated. If Melissa Cooper wanted to tango, Ramsey would be happy to dance.

"Glad you were able to take time out of your busy schedule to be here for Sean and Cali's wedding, Phineas," Ramsey addressed her brother for the first time in months of them not speaking.

Phineas fingered blonde hair out of his face and smiled. No one could accuse him of being ugly. Irritatingly, he was easily the best looking of the Price boys and the fact he knew it was the worst part. "Glad you were finally able to nail down a date for at least one of our brothers' weddings, Ramsey." He shrugged a lazy shoulder, "Even though it's one of Sean's friends. Guess you couldn't pull a guy on your own, you had to have Sean bail you out again."

Ramsey's face flushed. She was angry and slightly embarrassed by her brother's viciousness. She was about to say, *screw it*, and apologize to Sean later for her royal rumble outburst, when Nico squeezed her hand, drawing her attention. Glancing up into his comforting brown eyes, she felt his warmth flood her and for some reason she no longer had the urge to flay Phineas and Melissa wide open.

"Wow," Phineas chuckled, "Ramsey Price has no comeback. Maybe you are losing your edge."

But then again, she could only be pushed so far.

Ramsey's gaze darted across the room and pierced Phineas' blue eyes. "Make sure to keep an eye on your girlfriend this weekend, Phineas, we wouldn't want her forgetting which brother she came here with again, would we?" Before he or Melissa could retort, Ramsey tugged Nico past them and didn't stop until they'd spilled out onto the back porch and by then her rage had dissipated and she was cackling.

She clutched at her stomach, laughing so hard tears were spilling down her cheeks. "Did you," she wheezed, holding up a hand to a smiling Nico, "did you see the looks on their faces?"

Nico swiped the laugh induced tears from her face and chuckled. "You certainly don't back down from a fight, Price."

"If only I could use my fists instead of my words," she stilled as his thumb brushed her cheek. She cleared her throat and took a step back. "Sean's going to be royally pissed when Phineas goes and cries about me being mean." She rolled her eyes as her butt bumped against the wooden patio railing.

Nico ate the distance between them and planted his hands on either side of the banister behind her, pinning her. Their faces were so close she could see the flecks of green and gold in his eyes. If stardust and magic could be bottled and sold, it would look exactly like Nico's eyes.

"You don't have to worry about marking your territory with me, Price." His raspy whisper knocked the breath out of her.

"What are you talking about?" Ramsey scoffed, trying to hide the fact he was right about what she had been doing in the kitchen. "I wasn't marking my -"

"You were," he interrupted. "Don't pretend you don't know what I'm talking about." Nico's eyes slid from her eyes to her lips. "You don't need to worry about me when it comes to you, Ramsey. Ever."

The scariest thing was that Ramsey actually believed him. There was a truth, a conviction, in his voice that made her knees wobble. What was this man doing to her? When this wedding weekend was over, they'd go back to their normal lives in Philadelphia and their tit-for-tat banter. But a part of her was wondering what would happen if she told him that's not what she wanted. That maybe she wanted them to actually give this relationship a shot.

But what if this was all an illusion? She'd asked him to pretend to be her boyfriend and he was complying. Her resurrected feelings for him might be real, but nothing else was and that's what she had to remember before he shattered her heart again.

"Well don't you two look cozy," Patrick teased, tugging Quinn down the steps leading to the backyard. "If you two are done snuggling up, maybe you can pry your hands off each other and join the softball game."

"Green is not your color, Patrick," Ramsey cooed, straightening from her pinned position.

Patrick furrowed his brow before planting his hands on his hips. "Let's say we make this softball game a little bit more interesting, Ramsey."

"How interesting are we talking?" Ramsey folded her arms over her chest, squaring up to her older brother.

"Patrick," Quinn's voice was strained, but the warning didn't deter her husband.

"Between the two of us," Patrick pointed his index finger between Ramsey and himself, "whoever hits the most home runs, wins."

"What are we playing for?" Ramsey took a step forward. She and her brother both knew she wouldn't back down from any challenge. Now she needed to know what was at stake should she fail to win.

Patrick smirked. "I've booked a private sailboat and romantic dinner for two tonight in Portland. Whoever hits the most homeruns, gets the date, and much needed alone time with their significant other. Loser cleans all the dishes after dinner."

"Patrick, wait," Quinn protested but it was too late.

Ramsey slammed her hand in her brother's outstretched hand. "You've got yourself a deal."

Ramsey hadn't played softball in a while, but the chance to beat her brother and snag a dinner out of the house was worth the risk. Of course, it would be nice to get some alone time with Nico so they could breathe, and not feel like they were in a fishbowl constantly being watched by her family members. But seeing the look on Patrick's face when she rounded the bases, and he was up washing dishes for twenty to thirty people 'til midnight lit a fire in her.

Now, all she had to do was hit more homeruns than Patrick, which would be no easy feat, considering he played baseball in high school.

She dared a glance at Nico who was still standing by her side on the patio. "How mad are you?" she asked him.

Nico rolled his shoulders back, straightening to his full height. "That depends," he smiled. "Is your brother a vengeful person?"

"What?"

"When he loses, is he going to try to blow up the boat we're having dinner on?" Nico wiggled his eyebrows drawing a laugh from her. "If you wanted to be alone with me that bad, Price, that's all you had to say."

Ramsey descended the steps and snatched a baseball mitt out of one of the buckets they kept their softball supplies. "Who said I'd be taking *you* on this romantic dinner for two?"

Nico's eyes darkened, that hunger back with a vengeance. He made his way toward her. His towering frame forced her to look up at him as he whispered, "Maybe I'd make it worth your while."

"How so?" She'd meant to sound confident and in control, but her voice cracked.

"I can't tell you."

She clicked her tongue, shoving a mitt against his chest. "Always the teaser, Giovanni."

As soon as she turned her back to him, she felt his arm slither around her waist and pull her against his chest. Nico dipped his mouth to her ear, his stubble tickling the side of her neck. "If I told you, you wouldn't be able to focus on anything other than us on that boat. I recommend you win this bet with your brother, Price."

Ramsey shuddered as goosebumps rippled over her skin. What was this hold he seemed to have over her? Even just a whispered word had her ready to bend the knee to him.

"Ramsey? Nico?" Patrick waved them forward. "You two coming or do you surrender?"

Nico's low chuckle sent a bolt of electricity through her. "Do you surrender, Ramsey?" Something in Nico's voice made it seem as if that wasn't the same type of surrendering Patrick was referring to.

"That eager to get your ass beat, Pat?" she smirked.

Nico released her from his grasp, and she missed his arm across her belly, finding she enjoyed him being that close to her. "Let's see what you've got, Price."

She flashed him a smile over her shoulder as she jogged down to the make-shift field. "I'm not in the habit of losing."

Twenty-Five

Nico

The family was quickly divided in two teams. Ramsey, Nico, Sean, Cali, Liam, and Collin were on one side and Phineas, Melissa, Patrick, Quinn, Connor, and Connor's wife, Kristen, were on the other. Anne refused to play claiming her knees were acting up again and William, the Price Patriarch, declared himself umpire. Liam's wife, Jen, and Collin's wife, Grace, were more than happy to watch the kids than play softball with their husbands and Nico quickly discovered why.

He knew Sean and Ramsey were a competitive duo but seeing the Price Seven in action was on another level. No wonder their dad wanted to be the umpire. Even with adult kids, he had to keep the peace.

Nico had played some baseball growing up and knew he could hold his own in a friendly game. What he was really interested in seeing was how good Ramsey was. If she played as well as she ran her mouth, she'd be an All-Star.

Sean was up first to bat. As his friend took his stance, his brothers started taunting him, and to Nico's surprise, Sean let loose a few foul words with a smile on his face. Sean didn't like when anyone used curse words, but there he was, swearing like a professional.

"You look surprised, Nicole," Ramsey bumped him with her hip, drawing his attention. "Sean's not as much of a prude as he lets on. Especially when it comes to our brothers."

"This isn't going to end well, is it?"

She cocked her head to the side as they heard Sean's bat crack the ball, sending it flying a good distance, allowing him to easily round to second base. "What do you mean?" she asked.

Nico raked a hand through his hair. "This isn't a friendly family game of softball, is it?" he clarified.

Ramsey grinned and shook her head. "There is no such thing as a friendly game in the Price house."

Liam was up next to bat and secured a single. With Sean now on third, and Liam on first, Ramsey gripped her bat, winked at Nico, and made her way to home plate to bring her brothers home. Nico watched her take her stance and smiled when she seemed to have a ritual in getting ready to swing. She dug her left shoe into the grass, rooting herself, then raised her bat behind her. She stared at Connor, who was pitching, like he was prey, and she was his predator. Connor threw a fastball, but it wasn't fast enough. Ramsey swung and smashed the ball, sending it soaring over Phineas and Patrick's heads.

Sean sprinted home, Liam rounded the bases as quickly as he could, and Ramsey put her daily runs to good use, flying around first, second, third, and then slid home before Kristen, the rival teams' catcher, could tag Ramsey out. William signaled Ramsey was safe and in the blink of an eye, they were up 3-0.

Patrick and Quinn grumbled back and forth mid-field and Nico couldn't help but laugh, feeling a sense of pride that his girlfriend – his fake-girlfriend – was a force to be reckoned with. If Ramsey started the game with a homerun, that romantic sailboat dinner might actually be within their grasp, and he'd give up Chicken Parmesan for the next year if that meant truly being alone with her for the night.

Three hours later, sweaty, dirty, and hungry, the not-so-friendly game was coming to an end. Ramsey had proven herself to be an excellent outfielder, using her speed and sheer determination of will, not to let Patrick hit a homerun. But even with her impressive game, she and Patrick were tied with two homeruns each. It was the bottom of the ninth inning, and Patrick was the last up to bat with Phineas on first base.

The game was 7-6 in favor of Nico's team, but if Patrick could hit one more homerun, he'd not only win the game, but also the bet he'd made with Ramsey, and they'd be on kitchen duty that evening.

Ramsey and Sean readied themselves in the outfield. Liam was flipping the ball around in his hand waiting to pitch the ball, and Cali and Collin were on first and third. Nico got into his crouched catcher's position behind Patrick and waited for the final showdown to begin.

Patrick looked nervous and his hands were twitching holding his bat. Nico overheard Quinn give her husband a tongue lashing about betting their date and said there would be hell to pay if he didn't hit this homerun. So, when Patrick swung and missed the first pitch, he swore and dared a glance back at Quinn who had her arms crossed over her chest, fury written in her features.

For a reason Nico couldn't explain, he felt bad for Patrick. Maybe it was because he knew all too well what sparring with the woman he loved looked like, but he didn't want to see Quinn's night ruined because of a stupid bet.

"Liam is going to pitch a fastball," Nico whispered to Patrick who eyed him suspiciously.

"Why should I believe you?" Patrick snarled, sweat dripping down his nose.

"Do you want to win this bet or not?"

Patrick hesitated a second before he nodded. "A fastball?"

Nico bobbed his head in confirmation.

"Why are you telling me this?" Patrick asked. "Ramsey is going to be angrier than a hornet if she loses."

"You worry about hitting that ball," Nico cracked his neck. "Leave Ramsey to me."

Patrick grinned, "You think you can handle her?"

"No," Nico shook his head and smiled at Ramsey in the outfield. She laughed at something Sean said before taking her stance for Patrick's next bat. "But I think I can make her happy."

Patrick readied up and just like Nico predicted, Liam threw a fastball and Patrick smashed it over Ramsey and Sean's heads and it plopped into the ocean. Rounding the bases, like a hero, Patrick pumped his fist in the air and Quinn greeted him with a kiss at homebase.

Nico knew if Ramsey ever found out that he tipped Patrick off and helped him win the game and the bet, that she would be most unforgiving, but he knew even washing dishes together would be time well spent, because he would be with her.

Ramsey squatted on the ground, took her glove off, and laid in the grass. Once Nico made his way to her, he stood above her until she met his gaze.

"Well, that sucks," she puffed and stood when he extended his hand to her. "Guess I'll be washing dishes all night."

"*We* will be washing dishes all night," Nico corrected and she shook her head.

"You don't have to. This was my bet and I lost." She shrugged her shoulders and bent to snatch her glove off the ground. "Look at his smug face," she rolled her eyes as they marched back to the house. "He'll be gloating about this for years."

"You win some, you lose some." Nico tried to comfort her by throwing his arm across her shoulders and tugging her closer, but he knew she'd be sore about the loss for a while.

"And I'll help you with the dishes. I was willing to share in the winnings, it's only right for me to share in the losses."

Ramsey side-eyed him. "Are you being nice again, Giovanni?"

"Me? Nice?" He placed a hand on his chest. "Never. I just don't want you casting some spell on me while I sleep because I left you hanging."

She laughed but then sobered up as they were passing Patrick, Quinn, Phineas, and Melissa. He knew Melissa and Ramsey had run ins, Sean had told him all about it, but he also noticed how the flight attendant looked at him. That woman was dangerous, and he would keep his distance. Not because he was worried he would succumb to her temptation, but because he was concerned Ramsey would have one of two explosive reactions. She'd either try to fist-fight Melissa or Ramsey would distance herself from Nico for good, and he couldn't live with that option.

"Good game, Ramsey," Patrick stuck his hand out and she shook it, albeit reluctantly.

"Good game, Patrick." Ramsey glanced at a relieved looking Quinn. "I hope you have fun tonight."

Quinn looped her arm in Patrick's and smiled, "I'm sure we will, although you gave him a run for his money. He would have been in the doghouse had he not hit that last homerun."

Nico's fingers twitched. He didn't want them to say anything about him helping Patrick win, so he slipped his hand in hers and pulled her toward the house. "I think your mom wanted some help getting everything ready for dinner."

For once, Ramsey didn't fight him. He'd have to make sure Patrick kept his mouth shut, otherwise, he'd be the one in the doghouse.

"You sure you want to do this?" Ramsey shimmied her sweater off and tossed it on the butcher block island behind her.

Nico nodded with a smile. "For the hundredth time," he unlatched his watch and placed it next to Ramsey's sweater, "I am helping you. You want to wash or dry?"

"I'll wash," she removed her jewelry and watch before filling the sink with soap and warm water. She dunked her hands into the steaming liquid and closed her eyes with a small moan. "I love how hot water feels on my skin."

When she moaned, Nico had to restrain himself from picking her up and pinning her against a kitchen cabinet to kiss her. To distract himself, he snatched a kitchen towel and stood to Ramsey's right, waiting for her to hand him dishes.

He cleared his throat as they started the rhythmic process. She washed the dishes then handed them to him so he could dry them and neatly stack them for tomorrow.

"So..."

Ramsey side-eyed him. "So?"

"You're actually pretty decent at softball."

"Is that a compliment, Giovanni?" she flashed a smile and his heart soared.

He'd done that. He'd been the one to put a smile on her face. It's all he wanted and seeing her glow made all of this waiting worth it.

"You impressed me," he shrugged. He could feel her staring at him, so he turned to look at her.

"You told your sister about me?"

He figured they'd circle back to his sister after ignoring it since they went kayaking. "She knows you're Sean's sister and that you moved to Philadelphia a couple of years ago." Both of those facts were true, but Giulianna was the only one who knew how deeply he felt for Ramsey, how he'd been in love with her since college, but he couldn't tell Ramsey those things. Not yet.

But when? His heart screamed and he knew if he didn't confess to her soon, that he'd miss his chance.

"Is that all you told her?" Ramsey was focused on her task when she asked, but he could tell by her tone that she was hopeful there was more to it.

"I told her..." *I'm in love with you. I've been in love with you for years. I wish you were mine. I dream of you. I see a future with you.* "...how you crumple napkins and leave them strewn around my bar and how you dress like a librarian and a witch had a baby -"

She flicked soap water at him. "Ok, ok. I guess complimenting Ramsey time is over," she snickered.

They continued cleaning in a comfortable silence until Ramsey cleared her throat.

"Can I ask you a question?"

"Anything," he bobbed his head.

She passed him another plate. "In all the time I've lived in Philadelphia, you haven't had a girlfriend. Why?"

Nico quickly met her gaze before refocusing on drying the white porcelain plate. "Just haven't found anyone worth my time."

"That sounds a little conceited," she teased, but when he didn't smirk or playfully retort, she stopped cleaning and squared her shoulders to him. "I was just joking, Nico."

He matched her body language, tossing the towel over his shoulder to stare into her eyes. "I know," he said in a low voice.

"I think you'd make any woman happy," she whispered, a huskiness in her voice that sent a jolt of electricity coursing through his veins.

"What about you?" Nico's fingers twitched, itching to touch her. "Do you think I could make you happy, Ramsey?"

Her eyes darkened; those grey-blue eyes of hers were stormy and if he wasn't careful, he would drown in them. Nico inched closer, slowly raising his hand to brush hair out of her face and rested his palm against her cheek. He felt her plant her hands against his stomach and drag her fingers up to his chest. Her touch was agonizing and heavenly all at once.

"Do you think I could make you happy, Ramsey?" Nico asked again, breathing hard.

"You already do," she said it so softly he almost missed it.

That's all the confirmation he needed.

Nico lifted her up and set her on the white marble countertop. He smashed his mouth against hers and she roughly kissed him back. Slipping his tongue inside her mouth, he earned a delicious moan from her. Nico's heart was beating so fast he thought it just might explode. This kiss was different from the ones they'd shared in her room when she issued her first dare. This kiss was fire and ice. It was passionate and gentle. It was patient and it was rushed. It was the first time they'd kissed because they couldn't deny the attraction anymore. No dares, no fake dating ambushes, no interruptions.

"Nico," she said his name like it was the most sacred word in the English language.

"Ramsey?" he pulled away, but she grabbed the back of his head and forced him to return to her lips. He happily and gratefully obeyed her silent demands.

A loud thud down the hallway caused them to break their embrace. They both glanced at the open doorway but when no one appeared, Nico pressed his forehead against Ramsey's and smiled when she squeezed her thighs around his hips.

"I feel like we're teenagers sneaking around your parents' house," he said softly into her hair.

"One thing is for certain," Ramsey scratched a nail along his stubbled jawline, "if my mother comes down here and sees we haven't finished cleaning her kitchen there will be hell to pay. Especially if she catches us kissing."

Nico laughed and pecked her forehead before gripping her waist and lowering her off the countertops so they could finish the dishes. They were about halfway done. Ramsey wasn't joking before that it would take them all night to finish the task, but he didn't mind. Just being near her, being in her presence, laughing, smiling, and talking with her was all he'd wanted for years. He felt another layer of the stone wall surrounding her heart tumble down and he loved that she was seeing him for who he really was and that she was finally getting a glimpse of how much she meant to him.

Twenty-Six

RAMSEY

The next morning, Ramsey was jolted from sleep when someone knocked on the bedroom door. Nico was curled around her, his arm flapped over her stomach. She gasped softly, wondering how long they'd slept like that, but her thoughts were interrupted when another jarring knock echoed through the room.

Gently removing his arm, she sat up quickly, rubbing the heels of her palms against her tired eyes, and slipped out of bed to answer. Nico was a heavy sleeper because he didn't so much as bat an eye from the pounding. If it was one of her brothers, she would punch whoever it was straight in the throat. She swung the door open, ready to bark out her insults and curses when she stopped dead in her tracks.

"Mom?"

Anne stood in the doorway, dressed to impress. "Good morning, dear. I thought we could get an early start for tonight's rehearsal dinner."

Ramsey glanced at the alarm clock on Nico's nightstand and saw it wasn't even seven in the morning yet. "The rehearsal dinner isn't for another twelve hours."

"Well," her mother puffed, "if you want Sean and Cali's dinner to be left up to chance and last-minute preparations, then by all means, let's wait. Let's see," Anne tapped her chin, ignoring Ramsey rolling her eyes and leaning her weary head against the door. "For us to get the house and backyard cleaned and decorated, make sure dinner is cooked and places set, and we get showered and dressed, that really should only take us a few minutes. Perhaps, we should start prepping thirty minutes before we're supposed to start? Does that seem like enough time, Ramsey?"

"Alright! Alright!" Ramsey held up her hands in surrender. "Let me get dressed and I'll meet you downstairs."

"Meet me at the car. We need to pick up a few things from the store." Satisfied with her daughter's compliance, Anne sauntered down the hall and descended the steps.

Ramsey shut the door, mumbling under her breath. She shuffled to her side of the room, dug through her clothes in the closet and picked out a pair of jeans and v-neck blouse. She should have checked to see if Nico was awake and watching her, but at this point she didn't care if he saw her changing. She was tired, confused as to what was going on between her and Nico, hungry, and her mother was going to fill her day with endless tasks. She'd be lucky if she was able to scarf a morsel of food in between her mom's demands.

"Is everything alright?"

She didn't bother turning around. Sitting on the edge of the bed, she strapped on her sneakers, before hooking her watch around her wrist. "I'll be helping my mom get everything ready for the rehearsal dinner tonight."

"You don't sound too excited."

"Well, I promised her I'd help, so that's what I'll do." Ramsey stood up, grabbed her mascara and eye liner and made her way to the mirror on Nico's side of the room. "I didn't expect to be woken up at the crack of dawn to start, but it is what it is."

"Do you need help?"

Ramsey stared at him in the mirror's reflection. That was a mistake. She'd been avoiding looking at him the entire morning because she knew one look at him, and she'd be thinking about him and those lips on her body the rest of the day.

"Are you trying to tell me that you'll miss me, Naomi?" she winked, doing her best to keep her composure at the sight of his shirtless chest.

Nico sat up and rubbed his hands through his tousled hair. "I thought we'd be past all this by now."

Finishing her mascara application, she asked, "What do you mean? You thought we'd be past what by now?"

"The girl names, the standoffishness, the refusing to let me help you or get close to you." Nico's broken tone forced her to turn around to meet his exhausted gaze. "What will it take for you to let me in, Ramsey? What else do I have to do to show you that I'm not your enemy?"

"I don't know what you thought would happen this weekend, Nico." Ramsey huffed, returning back to her make-up. "Look, I have a lot to do today, and I can't be worried about this."

Nico shot up from the bed and made his way to her. She turned to face him as he planted his hands on either side of the wall, pinning her.

"Ramsey, every night we take a step forward, the next morning you take a huge step back." His eyes met hers and she could sense the frustration, the pain behind them. "I'm trying to be -"

"What?" she snapped, two hand shoving him away from her. "You're trying to be what? Nice? Confusing? Trivial?"

"Damnit, I'm trying to be your friend, Price!"

"My friend?" she scoffed, shaking her head. "Is this one of your games? You get close to me, you befriend me, you make me feel like you're attracted to me, and then when I'm invested, when I've fallen for you, you pull the rug out from under me and laugh as I fall flat on my face."

"You really think that's what I'm doing?" Nico didn't look angry, he looked devastated. "I might be a lot of things, Ramsey Price, but I would never purposely hurt you."

"Oh really, Nico?" She slammed her hands on her hips, feeling the back of her throat tightening, holding back the tears burning to be released.

"Really."

"Then explain college to me." He flinched but she kept going. He opened this can of worms and she would be damned if she waited another eight years before telling him how he crushed her heart and made her feel less than worthy of his affection. "Explain how I tried for an entire semester to be your friend. I invited you out so many times I lost count. Each time I was rejected in new and elaborate ways." She scoffed when he said nothing in response. "I'll give you credit where credit is due though. At least you didn't stand me up like David did. You at least had the decency to crush me from the beginning."

"Ramsey, I -"

"You what? You didn't mean to hurt me? You didn't mean to upset me?" She shook her head, pushing past him to grab her cellphone off her nightstand before making her way back to the bedroom door. "Forgive me if I believe history will repeat itself."

"I'm not the same guy I was in college," he pleaded as she snatched the doorknob.

"You aren't," she conceded, tears filling her eyes, "you're much worse."

"What?"

"Now I've felt the taste of your lips. I've felt your body pressed against mine. I've shared my fears and my desires with you," her bottom lip quivered. If she didn't get out of there immediately, she would come completely undone. "If I let you, you would shatter my still fractured heart into a million pieces and I'm not sure I would be able to put myself back together."

"Rams-"

She didn't give him a chance to respond. She slammed the door behind her and jogged down the stairs, not looking back.

Ramsey's mom didn't ask any questions when she plopped into her mother's two-seater sports car. She didn't ask her any questions as Ramsey moped through the stores picking up various items to decorate the backyard for the rehearsal dinner. She didn't ask her any questions when they picked up groceries or when they spent hours cleaning, cooking, and baking. She didn't even ask her any questions when her sisters-in-law joined their ranks and finished the long list of tasks her mother had.

Ramsey almost made it through the entire day of prepping without having to answer any prodding questions. But just as she was cleared to shower and dress for Cali and Sean's rehearsal dinner, her mother pulled her to the side, out of earshot of the other women, and stared at her intently.

"What is it?" Ramsey asked, a weariness in her tone. She wasn't sure if her exhaustion was due to the hard day's work or if how she snapped at Nico was finally eating away at her bones.

"First fight?" Anne's question took her by surprise, and she wasn't able to mask her reaction in time. "Might I offer you some advice, having been married to your father for forty years?"

"Mom, it's not like that -"

"So, you haven't been sulking and moody all day because of an argument with your boyfriend?" she quirked an eyebrow. Ramsey kept her mouth shut and let her mother continue. "It's healthy to argue once in a while. It shows you care and aren't growing complacent. If at the end of the day, even after trading words, you are happy to be sleeping next to your partner, then remember that this is just a speedbump in a lifetime of happiness. But if when you look at your partner and all you feel is misery, let them go."

"How did you know dad was the one?" Ramsey had never asked her mother that question before, and the thought seeped from her mouth before she could think it through.

Anne smiled and squeezed her daughter's hands. "I knew William was the one when I looked five, ten, twenty, thirty years down the road and realized there wasn't one thing I didn't want to experience with your father."

When Ramsey pictured her future, she thought about furthering her career, buying her first house, walking down the aisle at her own wedding, having her first child. She tried to picture David with her, but his face always faded, and Nico took his place. That both frightened and excited her and she wasn't sure how to juggle her conflicting feelings.

Her mother patted her shoulder, drawing her from her thoughts. "Nico cares for you a great deal. Go shower and get ready for tonight, Ramsey. And talk to him when you're ready."

Ramsey nodded and waited until her mother returned to the kitchen before wandering up the steps to her bedroom. Figuring there was a possibility Nico was on the other side of the door, she took a deep breath and swung the door open, only to find the bed made and room empty. Surprisingly, she was disappointed he wasn't sitting on the bed waiting for her to return, but he was probably with her brothers and grateful to be away from her.

It was an odd thing for her to realize, but her mother was right. She should talk to Nico because when she woke up next to him, she found she was happy and felt safe with him.

Determined that once the rehearsal dinner was over and they could sneak away for a private moment, she would talk to him about how she felt and apologize for snapping at him and running away instead of staying and fighting. He was worth fighting with. He was worth fighting for.

Twenty-Seven

Nico

Nico wanted to chase after Ramsey when she stormed out of the room that morning, but he knew there would be no talking to her when she was on a warpath. He was so confused. The night before, cleaning dishes, they'd been making out, and he even woke up in the middle of the night to see her curled in his arms while they slept. What had happened in a couple of hours to set her off?

After his morning shower, he joined Ramsey's brothers in the backyard where they were drinking coffee before having to set up the ceremony and reception areas for Anne and her team of women to decorate.

"Nico!" William saluted him with a cup of coffee. "Join me, we were just about to start setting everything up before Anne and Ramsey get back from the store."

Nico slipped into the seat next to Ramsey's dad at the patio table and accepted the cup of coffee he was offered.

He'd need it if he was going to get rid of the thundering headache before the day of grueling work.

"Rough night," William asked, his eyes skimming through the morning paper.

"What?" Nico wasn't sure what he was asking.

"You look exhausted," the Price patriarch set the newspaper down. "There were a lot of dishes for you and Ramsey to clean."

"Oh, right," Nico raked fingers through his still drying hair. "Yeah, we were up until nearly midnight cleaning."

"But something is bothering you," he motioned for Nico to speak.

"It's nothing," Nico shrugged a shoulder and took a sip of his coffee, grateful for the caffeine. "We got into an argument this morning and she left before we could talk about it."

William nodded, humming in understanding. "Sometimes its best if she has some space. Take it from me, when women are upset, just leave them alone until they're ready to talk."

"I just don't know what to say or do to make her happy," Nico reclined, rubbing small circles around his temples. "I don't know what to do to fix the situation."

"Do you care about my daughter?" William asked point blank and the question should have scared Nico but surprisingly, it didn't.

"I do," he bobbed his head. "Maybe more than she even realizes."

"Then maybe you should tell her."

Before Nico could respond, someone cleared their throat drawing the men's attention. Sean was standing in the back-door threshold with something clearly on his mind. Since

Ramsey had told her brother about their fake dating situation, Sean hadn't said much to him, but he figured the conversation was coming.

"Everything alright, Sean?" Nico asked, finishing the last of his coffee before setting the mug down.

Sean didn't move. "Can we take a walk?"

That didn't sound like his friend asking him to take a leisurely stroll. That sounded like a brother about to threaten the guy interested in his sister.

Nico exchanged a glance with William before he bobbed his head. "Sure. Anywhere in particular you want to walk?"

Sean shrugged. "I thought we could walk the trail around the water."

Nico stood up and motioned for Sean to move. "Lead the way."

It was a perfect morning for a walk along the gravel, tree lined trail around the bay behind the Price family's house. But Nico and Sean had been walking in silence for far too long and it was starting to give Nico anxiety. He risked a glance over at Sean who had his hands buried deep inside his jean pockets.

"Is everything alright?" Nico finally asked. "Are you nervous about the wedding or something?"

Sean stopped dead in his tracks and turned to face Nico. "This isn't about my wedding."

"Would you care to tell me what this *is* about?"

Sean chewed on his bottom lip before frowning at his friend. "Ramsey told me you two weren't actually dating. That this was all a rouse so my mother wouldn't give her a hard time this weekend."

"That's true."

There was another beat of silence before Sean asked, "Why aren't you really dating my sister?" The question caught Nico off guard.

"Wait," Nico waved a hand in the air, confusion riddling his features. "You're upset I'm *not* dating Ramsey?"

"I figured now that she wasn't dating David anymore that you'd finally ask her out." Sean planted his hands on his hips. "Instead, you're just pretending to date her when everyone knows that you two are perfect for each other."

Nico felt another headache coming and rubbed his fingers over his temples. "Let me get this straight. Sean Price, the guy who threatened all of his friends in college not to even breathe in his sister's direction wants to know why I haven't asked that sister out on a date?"

"I told *Peter* not to ask her out." Sean's eyebrow arched. "I never told *you* not to."

Nico's mouth dropped open. "You mean you wouldn't be upset if I dated your sister?"

"Nico," Sean smacked his friend's shoulder and laughed. "How could I be mad about my best friend being in love with my sister? Honestly, there isn't a man I would trust her with more than you."

Nico raked his hands through his hair and paced back and forth. "Why didn't you say something before?"

"I figured you would ask her when you were ready."

"I wanted to ask her out when she first moved to Philadelphia," Nico sat on the ground and grabbed a smooth stone to skip across the water. "But it seemed like she hated me, and then she met David..." He sighed.

Sean plopped down next to Nico and started skipping stones too. "I'm sorry."

Nico looked at him. "What are you sorry about?"

"All these years you kept your distance from Ramsey because you were afraid of what I would think or say." Sean scratched his chin. "I'm sorry you felt this way for so long."

"You're my best friend," Nico patted Sean's shoulder. "I wouldn't want to do anything if that meant our friendship would be jeopardized. You're like the brother I never had."

"We'll I wouldn't be mad if you and Ramsey were together," Sean reiterated. "You care about her right?"

Nico nodded. "I'm in love with her."

"I know," Sean nodded with a smile. "You should tell her."

"I will once we get back to Philadelphia -"

"No," Sean interrupted him, planting his hand on Nico's shoulder. "You need to go tell her now."

"This is your wedding weekend," Nico protested. "This is about you and Cali."

"If you don't grow a pair and finally tell my sister what everyone already knows, I will find a new best friend." Sean smiled when Nico rolled his eyes. "And let me tell you, I really have no interest in finding another friend who owns a bar. It sounds like way too much work."

"You think she feels the same way?" Nico asked, terrified that she wasn't as invested as he was.

"Do you remember the day in college you came home talking about that incredible girl you had just met and were determined to marry her?"

Nico's eyes widened. "You knew that was Ramsey?"

"She called me after her first class and told me about this guy who'd helped her when she was lost in the quad." Sean laughed as he stood up. "You two idiots were made for each other."

"She didn't tell me she talked to you," Nico hopped up and followed after Sean down the trail.

"I doubt she even remembers. It was her first day of college, she was lost, overwhelmed, and obsessed over the junior who walked her to class." Sean made a gagging noise before laughing and swinging his arm across Nico's shoulders, steering them back toward the house. "Consider this your wedding gift to me and Cali."

"I'm already taking your wedding photos for free," Nico teased and Sean shrugged.

"I think you can afford two gifts. One for me and one for Cali."

Nico pushed his best friend of ten years off of him and laughed. "You got it." Now all he had to do was confess to Ramsey that he loved her and hoped Sean was right that she loved him too.

Nico was slowly dying. He'd wanted to rush to find Ramsey the second he heard she and Anne had returned from the store, but all the women gathered inside and started tackling the cleaning and decorating, robbing him of a moment to pull her to the side.

Since Sean and Cali were getting married in the backyard of his childhood home with the ocean as a backdrop, Nico helped to arrange tables and chairs outside for the ceremony and reception.

As the women began trickling outside to decorate, William told Nico he could go hit the shower before dinner that evening. He looked around for Ramsey but didn't see her anywhere. Talking to her would have to wait and it didn't help that Sean kept looking at him every thirty minutes as if the situation had changed.

Jogging up to the bedroom he was sharing with Ramsey, Nico stripped his shirt off as he opened the door.

"Hey!"

He stopped in the threshold when Ramsey's panicked voice rang out. She was standing in a towel, her hair wet from bathing, and his feet felt like concrete – he couldn't move, couldn't even speak. Nico knew he should say something or at least turn around, but he couldn't bring himself to do either.

"If you're just going to stand there staring, can you at least shut the door?" Ramsey didn't look angry, which should have been a relief, but her expression offered nothing, and that's what made his heart thunder in his chest.

Jarred from his stupor, Nico stepped into the room, shutting the door behind him.

She cleared her throat. "What are you doing?" she asked, her fingers gripping her towel tighter.

"I was about to take a shower, just needed to grab a couple things." He didn't move another inch. Their eyes were fastened on one another and for a second, he forgot how to breathe.

"Well?"

"Well, what?"

She rolled her eyes, "Well I can't get dressed until you get your stuff and leave."

"Right." Nico rushed around his half of the room and picked up his shower items, a change of clothing, and his towel. As he reached for the doorknob, Ramsey's voice stopped him from leaving.

"Nico?"

He turned to face her, his back against the door. "Yes?"

"About earlier," her eyes skimmed the floor before dragging up his body to meet his awaiting gaze, "I'm sorry for everything I said. I shouldn't have snapped at you. I was tired and hungry and-"

"Ramsey, it's ok," he lifted his hands to stop her. "You had every right to be upset with me about the way I treated you in college. I wish I could turn back time and do things differently, take away the pain I inflicted, but I can't." She seemed saddened by that fact. "All I can do is make it up to you now."

"You aren't angry with me?" she cocked her head to the side in curiosity.

Nico shook his head, wishing he could unwrap the towel and show her exactly what he was thinking and feeling, but he maintained his distance. "No, Price, I'm not angry with you. But I am sweaty and should hop in the shower before someone beats me to it."

She nodded in agreement. Was she disappointed he was leaving?

"So, we're ok?" Ramsey asked. "We're friends again?"

The word *friend* coming from her mouth was like a punch to the gut. Of course, for years he'd wanted them to be friends, but he couldn't help the pang in his chest thinking that's all she wanted from him now. He kept his mask firmly in place and bobbed his head with a smile. "We're friends." Before she could say anything else that would sting him, he slipped out of the room and jumped in the shower, letting the hot water beat against his aching back.

He could have told her right then how he felt, but it didn't seem like the appropriate time to ask her out on a proper date while she was standing in nothing but a towel. How he wished he was that towel wrapped around her.

As soon as they were alone tonight, he would confess. If he didn't, he'd likely explode. Or Sean would punch him straight in the nose. Neither were acceptable options.

The rehearsal dinner ran smoothly. Everyone knew their places and Anne had their entrances and exits timed perfectly. She looked like a general mustering her troops. Nico knew Sean would have asked him to be his best man but knowing it would cause conflict amongst the Price brothers, he offered to take Sean and Cali's wedding pictures as his gift to them instead. Sean was disappointed not to have his best friend at his side, but it was better this way. Every Price brother had stood in for another and Nico wasn't going to be the reason the tradition stopped.

Liam took his place at Sean's side. Sean and Cali wanted to keep the wedding affair as small and intimate as possible, so their wedding party consisted of Liam as Best Man and Ramsey as Maid-of-Honor.

Nico sat with the rest of the family in the white wooden chairs they'd set up that afternoon and watched as Sean and Cali went through the motions of becoming man and wife a couple times, until Anne was satisfied they'd met her standards of wedding perfection.

Ramsey stood by Cali's side, but she looked distracted, as if her mind was elsewhere. Nico knew she'd been a part of all her brothers' weddings in one way or another, so she was basically a wedding professional, but this was Sean and Cali's big day, and she wasn't mentally present. He didn't want to assume he was the reason behind her aloofness, but they hadn't gotten a real chance to talk about earlier – about them.

Nico raked his fingers through his hair and was startled when Melissa plopped in the seat next to him, even though there were about fifty empty chairs she could have taken. He quickly glanced around but didn't see Phineas anywhere. When he faced forward toward the mock ceremony, he noticed Ramsey was staring at him. No, not him. She was watching Melissa.

Melissa bumped him with her shoulder and leaned in, so her lips hovered above his ear. "I'm surprised you're not up there as Sean's best man. I bet you'd look great in a tux."

Nico shifted his weight so he put an inch of distance between him and the stewardess. "It's a Price tradition for a brother to be the best man. I'm taking their wedding pictures."

"You're a photographer?" She smiled and fluttered her eyelashes at him. "I've always wanted to take some sexy pictures – like a boudoir shoot. Do you do those kinds of shoots?"

Nico shook his head. "Afraid not. I don't photograph professionally. It's just a hobby of mine." He kept his focus straight ahead on Ramsey, but she wasn't paying him any mind. Her narrow-eyed gaze was still fixed on Melissa; a huntress zeroing in on her prey.

Melissa trailed her fingers up his forearm where his dress sleeves were rolled up to his elbow. "Maybe you can make an exception for me."

Dangerous. This woman was threatening everything between him and Ramsey and he wouldn't risk Ramsey's wrath raining down upon him. He was already needing to speak privately with her about their argument and about how he felt for her – that would be no easy task if she was seeing red.

Nico excused himself, stood up, and scooted out of the row. He felt as if he was able to breathe again. But just as he was about to make his way up to the patio to relax and grab a beer, Anne clapped her hands and directed everyone to take their seats at the long wooden table. It was multiple tables put together, but once it had been decorated, it looked like a fifty-foot custom made dining table.

Anne had gone through great lengths to make place cards with everyone's name neatly written. Nico found his seat next to Ramsey's and he felt a flutter in his stomach. They still wouldn't be able to have the conversation he was itching to initiate, but they'd be next to one another for the first time all day, and that was enough. He would be able to smell her vanilla and jasmine scent and maybe, if she'd let him, hold her hand underneath the table.

Across from him and Ramsey were the bride and groom, and to his relief, Melissa and Phineas were on the opposite side of the dinner table. He wouldn't have to deal with Melissa's flirtation or keep Ramsey from hopping up and knocking the blonde senseless.

"Did everything look alright?" Cali's voice sliced through his thoughts. He hadn't even seen her and Sean sit across from him.

"Everything looked perfect," Nico smiled, sliding his linen napkin across his lap. "I'll be able to take some great pictures of you both."

Cali exhaled a sigh of relief. "That's good to hear. I'm getting a little nervous. I don't like a lot of attention."

"Well, you are stunning," Ramsey slid into her seat next to Nico, "and people won't be able to tear their eyes off of you, Cali."

Nico and Ramsey looked at one another and she offered him a small smile. It was the best he was going to get at the moment, and he would take whatever she was willing to offer him.

"I'm just sad I didn't contribute more," Cali started cutting her chicken, her eyes glued to her cutlery.

Cali was an only child, and her parents were unable to make it to the wedding from South Africa. She'd offered to buy her parents' plane tickets thinking money was the reason they'd have to miss her and Sean's big day, but it was then she found out her mother was quietly battling cancer and was too sick to fly. Nico remembered the night she'd found out. Cali sat at the bar and nursed one glass of wine over several hours and no matter what Sean said or did, she didn't cheer up for weeks. Fortunately, her mother was doing much better and was in remission, but she was still far too weak to travel. Nico promised he would send them all the photos from the wedding and that had eased some of Cali's sadness.

Ramsey reached across the table and snatched Cali's hand. "I am so glad you're going to officially be a part of our family, Cali. And whenever your parents are able to visit, we'll throw another party to celebrate."

Cali's eyes watered and she bobbed her head with a smile, "Thanks, Rams."

"Plus, Sean needed someone to scoop him up before it was too late," Ramsey winked at Sean, "I won't be living with him forever."

Sean pointed his fork at her and chuckled, "Don't think you're getting out of living with me that easily. Cali and I have already told you multiple times you are welcome to stay with us -"

Ramsey waved a dismissive hand in the air. "Yeah, yeah, yeah. No one wants to live with frisky newlyweds," she shuddered making Sean laugh. "I'll start looking for a place when we get back to Philadelphia."

"Rams -" Cali attempted to protest but Ramsey shook her head.

"I told Sean when I first moved in with him it was temporary. It's time."

Nico wanted to blurt out she could move in with him but that would send her running for the hills, so he kept his mouth shut, stuffing more of the roasted potatoes in his mouth.

"What about Nico?" Sean's question caught him off guard and he swallowed a potato slice whole.

Ramsey stiffened beside him. "What about Nico?"

Nico coughed, but before he could say a word, Sean motioned toward his friend and said, "Maybe Nico knows of a place you could move."

She turned her laser gaze toward him, clearly assessing what was going on between him and Sean. "Do you know of a place, Nadine?"

Nico shot a look at Sean, who smirked as he sipped his beer, before turning his sight back to Ramsey. "I can ask around and see what I can find out."

Someone clinked on a glass, drawing everyone's attention, and Nico would have bearhugged whoever was about to make a toast for saving him from the conversation.

William stood at the head of the table, a glass in his hand, and a huge grin on his face. "It is good to have all of my children and their partners together to celebrate Sean and Cali's nuptials." Whoops and claps echoed around the table before the patriarch continued. "When Sean was growing up, he was a handful. Anne and I thought whoever Sean ended up falling in love with would have to be patient, loving, and understanding of his eccentricities."

"Cause you were weird as hell," Patrick spat drawing laughs.

"At least I'm better looking than you, Pat," Sean fired back with a grin.

"Anyway," William's voice boomed, refocusing the group. "Sean surprised us when he graduated college with straight A's and landed an incredible position at his marketing firm. Seeing my son succeed and grow professionally had me bursting in pride. But as happy and proud as I was for Sean's career, it paled in comparison when he brought Cali here to meet us for the first time. Cali," he lifted his glass to her and everyone else followed suit, "you are everything Sean needs in a partner, and we know he will be in safe and loving hands with you as his wife. Welcome to the Price family."

"Welcome!" the Price family said as they took swigs of their drinks.

William walked toward Nico and leaned in when he got close enough. "Could you do me a favor?"

Nico wiped his mouth and nodded. "What do you need?"

"I would ask one of my sons, but I don't want them seeing what I have stashed away in my private collection," William slipped a key out of his pocket and handed it to Nico. "There's a bottle of 1961 scotch in the top right side of the cabinet in my study. Can you bring it to me and make sure the case gets locked up when you're done?"

"No problem," Nico accepted the key and scooted his chair back to leave.

"Good man," he patted Nico on the back.

"I'll be right back," Nico whispered to Ramsey. Her response was nodding to let him know she heard him, but she didn't say anything.

Nico walked through the backyard until he reached the back patio. Slipping through the hallways until he came to William's study, Nico easily found the locked, mahogany liquor cabinet, unlocked it and searched for the scotch the patriarch sent him to find. Once he found it, he grabbed it, and locked the cabinet. As he turned around to head back to the dinner party, he found Melissa standing inside the doorway with the door cracked open behind her.

"Melissa?" Her name left a sour taste in his mouth. "What are you doing in here?"

"Looking for you."

Twenty-Eight

RAMSEY

Nico had been gone longer than she expected him to be considering her dad's study wasn't deep inside the house. Excusing herself from the outdoor dining table, she went looking for him. But as she entered through the back door and rounded the hall, she saw Phineas leaning against the wall outside of their dad's study.

His gaze met hers but before she could ask what he was doing, he put a finger to his lips signaling for her to keep quiet.

She stood on the opposite side of the cracked door and realized she could hear voices. Voices that belonged to Nico and Melissa. Ramsey's eyes darted across to Phineas and he nodded, as if he could read her mind. He was eavesdropping.

Jealousy pooled in the pit of her stomach. She'd watched Melissa cozy up to Nico during the ceremony rehearsal.

She'd wanted to claw the blonde's face up but when Nico got up and walked away, she was put at ease. He didn't fall for the stewardess' salacious ways. But knowing her brother's girlfriend was alone with Nico made her blood boil. She gritted her teeth and took a step toward the door to burst in and find out what exactly was going on, but Phineas' catlike reflexes hindered her.

Despite her best efforts to slither out of her brother's grasp, he tugged her close to him and whispered, "Wait."

Ramsey had the urge to give him a piece of her mind and barge in there anyway. Phineas might not keep tabs on his girlfriend, or believe her when she told him the woman was no good, but she certainly wasn't going to allow Nico...

And then it hit her. Nico wasn't hers. Not really. She had no claim to him and after everything she'd said to him earlier that morning, maybe he decided to move on. She couldn't blame him. She had been vicious because of her insecurities. And worse, she'd done her best to avoid him throughout the day, so she didn't have to admit to him what was really going on in her head and heart. She was coward and she hated it.

"Listen," Phineas instructed, not relinquishing his grip around her waist.

"Come on," Ramsey heard Melissa's voice inside the room and couldn't wait for her brother to release her so she could throttle the blonde. "I know you don't actually care about Ramsey."

Ramsey's stomach churned but she obeyed her brother's plea for her to stay put and just listen.

"That's not true," Nico said calmly.

"Patrick told us what you did," Melissa's heels clicked as she walked around the room.

"I don't know what you're talking about."

"Of course you do, Nico." Melissa's voice was throaty, as if she was trying to cast her spell on him. "You couldn't stand the thought of being alone with Ramsey for that romantic dinner in Portland, so you tipped Patrick off to Liam's fast-ball," the stewardess cooed, and Ramsey's heart sank further. "I know Sean probably pressured you into being with his sister, she does make it hard for men to find her appealing, but I could show you a good time."

"You've got it all wrong -"

"Oh, so you didn't tell Patrick about the fastball so he could win the game and the bet?" she interrupted him with a sweet hiss.

"I tipped Patrick off so Quinn wouldn't have her night spoiled."

"You can tell yourself whatever you want but I know the truth."

"Melissa, stop." Ramsey listened to Nico's feet shuffle and what sounded like a lamp fall over. "I'm with Ramsey. She's who I care about and nothing you say or do will change my feelings for her."

"She doesn't have to know," Melissa pressed.

"I'm sure Phineas would have something to say about that, don't you?" Nico's voice held steady and there was a ferocity in his tone that she hadn't heard before. "Especially if I tell him you tried to get me into bed with you."

Melissa laughed. "Phineas is wrapped around my finger and wouldn't believe a word you said." She was on the other side of the door, blocking Nico from leaving the room. "Ramsey's been trying to tell him for years about me and he doesn't believe her."

"Move out of the way, Melissa," Nico growled. "We can forget this ever happened."

"Look, Nico," the sweetness in Melissa's voice was gone and venom replaced it. "We can have a good time, and no one needs to find out, or I'll tell everyone you tried to take advantage of me. What's it going to be?"

Ramsey glared up at Phineas, who was still holding her back. He met her gaze and shook his head as if to say, *not yet*.

"I'll take my chances," Nico said and Ramsey wanted so desperately to rescue him from Melissa's filthy clutches.

"You think Ramsey is going to believe you? That Phineas or Sean for that matter will believe you over me?"

Her tone was threatening and as upset as Ramsey was with Nico for throwing the game, she was ready to tear Melissa limb from limb. She wiggled out of Phineas' grip, but he'd already swept around her and slammed the door open, startling Nico and Melissa.

Melissa plastered a sweet, innocent smile on her face and reached for Phineas' hand. "Sweetheart, you scared me. What's wrong? You don't look well."

Phineas twisted his hand out of his girlfriend's grasp and though he addressed Nico, his eyes were glued to Melissa. "Nico, I need to speak with Melissa privately."

"Of course," Nico made his way out of the room and found Ramsey with her back against the hallway wall.

"Ramsey?" He was clearly surprised to see her standing there, but when their eyes met, she folded her arms across her chest.

"We need to talk."

Twenty-Nine

Nico

"It's not what it looks like, Ramsey," Nico spat when she ushered him into the library and slammed the door shut behind her.

"What the hell was that?" Ramsey hissed like a wounded animal. "Do you really hate me that much that you would rather help Patrick win a bet than spend one night alone with me?"

"Hate you?" He whipped around to face her, dumbfounded she even thought him capable of feeling that way for her. "You think I hate you?"

"Well, it seems the thought of a romantic dinner repulsed you enough to betray me."

"I don't hate you, Ramsey," his voice cracked as he confessed. "I've never hated you."

"Then why -?"

"I've wanted you since the moment I saw you lost in the quad. As soon as I dropped you off at class, I called Sean and told him all about this beautiful girl I was going to ask out."

She stared at him wide-eyed, looking lost for words. "What?"

"When you showed up for dinner and I realized you were Sean's sister, I ..." He raked a hand through his hair before loosening the top button of his dress shirt, feeling like it was strangling him. "When Sean told me and our friend at the time, Peter, that you were going to be attending school with us, Peter made a comment about asking you out. He meant it as a joke, but Sean got really upset. Told Peter not to even think about asking you out."

She wrapped her arms around herself, "So, you didn't turn me down because you weren't attracted to me?"

"Not a day has gone by that I haven't thought about you. Wished you were mine. Wished I could wake up every single day with you curled in my arms."

"You're that afraid of my brother?"

He shook his head, "I'm not afraid of Sean. I respect him. He's my best friend and at the time, we'd been friends and roommates for two years. If he felt that strongly about his baby sister, I wouldn't ruin our friendship over my desire. What if I had asked you out and it didn't work out? Or worse, I ended up breaking your heart because I was still young and immature? Sean would never have forgiven me."

She took a hesitant step toward him. "And when I came to Philadelphia? Why didn't you ask me then?"

"I planned on it." He sat in one of the two leather armchairs and scratched the back of his neck. "But you were so sharp tongued with me, I figured I needed to give you some time to settle in and show you I wasn't the same guy I was in college. Thought if I spent some time with you, and having known Sean for years, that he'd be alright with us dating. He'd know my feelings for you were serious. But when I mustered up the courage to ask you out, you came into the bar talking to Cali about meeting David and I knew I'd missed my chance. The best I could hope for at that point was us building toward a friendship."

"All this time?" she whispered.

His eyes met hers. "All this time."

"But I've been so mean to you." There was a strain in her voice, as if she was trying to keep herself from crying.

"If that's what you were willing to give me, I was willing to accept it. Even if that meant I never got the chance to have you for myself."

"Nico." The way she said his name spurred him to stand up. "I think you should take your shirt off."

"What?"

"I said," her voice was raspy, " you should take your shirt off."

"Is that a dare?" Nico hoped it wasn't.

"No."

Nico ripped his shirt over his head with his thumb and index finger, tossed it on the ground, and lifted Ramsey into his arms within the same breath. Pinning her back against one of the bookcases, he bit her bottom lip, drawing a gasp from her. One sound from her and he was weak in the knees. He gripped her thighs, and she squeezed them around his torso, stealing a breath from him. Planting an open mouth kiss against her breastbone caused her to quiver in his arms.

Ramsey pulled his hair, forcing him to look up at her. Her blue-grey eyes were glossy, filled with a desire he'd only dreamt of seeing from her. Her lips met his and she cupped his face, her nails scratching his cheeks.

"Ramsey." It was just her name he whispered, but he knew from the tension in her body that she understood what he was asking her for, what he was begging her for.

"Nico," she whispered back, her lips brushing against his ear, sending a shiver down his spine.

"Hold on," he instructed.

She tightened her legs around his torso, her back still pinned. Nico grabbed her wrists and lifted them above her head, nailing them against the mahogany bookshelf.

"I have wanted you for as long as I can remember," he kissed up her neck and along her jaw, enjoying the hitch in her breath.

"I'm yours," Ramsey said softly, letting him take full control over her.

Her words lit a fire inside of him and he was no longer itching to contain it. Releasing her hands, he carried her to the billiards table, laid her down, and hovered over her. Nico let her explore his half-naked body and soaked every inch of her desire for him up like a dog would lap up crumbs from his owner's table. Ramsey was perfect and it seemed like she'd been created just for him.

If she didn't feel the same way, he needed to know now and he would walk away. He could have her for the moment, but he knew it would never satisfy his unquenchable thirst for her.

"I need to know if this is just a one-time thing," he ran his fingers through her long hair, waiting for her to dictate the pace.

"Is that what you want?" she asked.

"Tell me what *you* want." Nico stared into her icy gaze and demanded she make the call. "Tell me and I will obey."

Ramsey opened her mouth to say something but hesitated. For a brief second, he thought she'd rethought their encounter and wanted him to get off of her, but as he inched away from her, she grabbed the back of his neck and pulled him closer. He felt her slither her legs around his, the tips of her high heels poking his calves.

"I want you, Nico Giovanni. I want you in every possible way. I want you now. I want you later. I want *you*." She kissed him before whispering, "I need you. Please."

"You have me," he claimed her lips again, running his hand from her ankle past her knee and up her thigh, tugging her dress up. "You have all of me."

Thirty

RAMSEY

Ramsey's eyes fluttered open, and she stared up at her bedroom ceiling. The events of the night before flooded her mind and she slowly glanced at Nico's side of the bed and found him sleeping peacefully next to her. His arm was draped across her belly and as she tried to sit up, he gently tugged her toward him. She ran her fingers along his arm, loving his possessiveness over her even in his sleep. But according to her phone it was already seven in the morning, and she was late for her morning run.

Gently, she slipped out of bed, put on her work out clothes and running shoes, and quietly left Nico to sleep a little bit longer. She thought about leaving him a note about where she'd gone, but she didn't want to seem too eager for his attention.

She brushed her teeth, jogged down the steps, and made her way out to the back porch where she took a few minutes to stretch and fully wake up. Trotting to the trail behind their house, she put her music on, and felt lighter than she had in years. Could it really be Nico having this effect on her? Was this what it meant to be in a happy and healthy relationship?

But this wasn't a real relationship. At least, it wasn't real yet.

Once she returned to the house, she'd see if her dad was awake and reading in his study before the wedding festivities began. She still hadn't found time to have a one-on-one talk with him and was eager to know his thoughts about Nico and them dating. He had always given her solid and sound advice throughout her life, this time would be no different. She just hoped she liked what he had to say.

After running a mile, she found her way back home, not wanting to overdo it before the long day ahead of her. Ramsey greeted her brothers and their wives on the porch and poked her head into her dad's study to see if he was inside.

"I thought I'd find you in here," Ramsey said, reclined against the doorframe.

"Hello, peanut." William smiled, taking his reading glass off and placing them on his mahogany writing desk. "To what do I owe the pleasure of my favorite daughter visiting me so bright and early?"

Ramsey smiled and walked toward his desk, perching on the edge of it like she used to when she was growing up. "I'm your only daughter."

"And still my favorite," his eyes twinkled as he set his book down. "What's going on? You look like you have something on your mind."

She had a lot on her mind and most of it involved Nico Giovanni. She couldn't tell her dad the truth about their fake dating situation, especially since he seemed so in favor of the relationship, but she had to understand why he felt that way.

"When you found out about Nico and I dating, you seemed excited."

Her dad nodded with a smile. "Of course I'm excited for you two. He's been in love with you for as long as I can remember."

"What do you mean?"

Crossing his arms over his chest and reclining in his high back chair, William said, "For one, the way he would looked at you tipped me off. He would stare at you like you were the answers to all the questions running wild through his head."

"That's it?" That was disappointing. She rubbed the back of her neck as she scanned the pictures on her dad's desk. Pictures of the Price Seven and her mother at different ages. But then her eyes fell on a black and white photograph she'd never seen before. She picked it up and stared at it in disbelief. It was a picture of her

smiling, but she wasn't looking at the camera.

"When did you take this?" she flipped the picture around for her dad to see.

"I didn't take that. Nico did."

"Nico?"

William nodded with a warm smile. "Took that six months ago at Patrick and Quinn's wedding." He scratched at his white stubbled chin. "I saw Nico snapping pictures and when I asked to see some of his work, I found he'd taken quite a few candid shots of you. I picked one out and asked if he'd send me a copy to frame for my study and he happily obliged."

Ramsey sat in stunned silence as she ran the tips of her fingers over the glassed photo. Nico had been taking pictures of her at her happiest. He'd been showing his love for her all this time in secret, and she truly had no idea. Or maybe she just wasn't ready to see.

"Why didn't you tell me?" she looked up at her dad.

"You had to come to the realization on your own, peanut. If I had told you Nico was in love with you, you might not have believed me or worse, you might have run off like a deer in headlights."

She laughed and tapped her foot against her dad's leg. "So, the way he looks at me and his photographs tipped you off?"

"Those were clear indicators the man had feelings for you, but it wasn't until I realized he'd named his bar after you that I knew without a doubt he was helplessly in love with you."

"Dad, he didn't name his bar after me."

William frowned. "You mean to tell me you didn't notice the anagram?"

"What are you talking about?"

He opened his desk drawer, swiped a piece of paper and a fountain pen, and scribbled the letters out. "The *Mythical Sea Breeze*. If you mix those letters up you get," he scratched at the paper like a madman, taking letters from the bar name and reorganizing them until it spelled out, "Ramsey Elizabeth Price."

"Dad, you're missing a couple letters," she tried to still her breath, knowing it was too close to be coincidence.

William rolled his eyes, pinching the bridge of his nose. "Ramsey, you are far too stubborn for your own good. The man named his bar after you and you're more concerned that he couldn't make a couple of letters fit?"

"But he opened his bar six years ago," her eyes bounced from the paper up to meet her father's amused gaze. "He's been in love with me that long?"

"Longer by my estimation, peanut."

"I have to talk to him." She placed the photograph Nico had taken of her back on her dad's desk, scooted off the table, and beelined for the door. Before she left, she turned on her heel, sprinted back to her dad, planted a kiss on his forehead, and then ran out of his office.

She had to talk to Nico before Sean and Cali's wedding started or she'd lose her damn mind. Rushing up the stairs, she burst into the bedroom, but the bed was made, and Nico was nowhere to be found. Thinking he could be sitting on the back porch she hastily made her way back downstairs and out the back door.

"Nico?" But out of all the faces seated under the covered patio, Nico wasn't one of them. "Has anyone seen Nico?"

"I think he and Sean went somewhere together," Jen offered with a smile as she handed Jackson a cracker. "They should be back soon."

"Damn it," she muttered to herself.

"Is everything alright?" Her mother came up from behind her and startled her.

"Yeah, everything is great," she nodded. "Just need to ask Nico a question."

Anne took a sip of her coffee and slipped her arm around Ramsey's. She pulled her back inside the house. "Well, ask him later. It's time for you to help Cali get ready for the wedding."

Ramsey wanted to wiggle out of her mother's grasp, but she had a tight grip and was clearly determined to have Ramsey do what she needed her to do.

"Let me take a shower really quick and I promise I'll help Cali get ready."

Anne nodded, probably because she could smell the woods and sweat wafting up from her daughter. "Make it quick, dear. We have a lot to do before guests arrive."

Ramsey nodded and made her way to the bathroom. If the bride had been anyone other than Cali, she would have fought her mother on forcing her upstairs, but she relented and reluctantly accepted talking to Nico was going to have to wait until later. Hopefully she wouldn't be driven to insanity before they had a chance to talk.

Thirty-One

Nico

When Nico woke up that morning, Ramsey was already gone. He hadn't even heard her leave their room. It made him nervous that she wasn't in the room, but she was an early riser and liked going for jogs. He could only hope that's what she was doing and not trying to avoid him after their encounter.

Their night in the billiards room flooded him and he raked his fingers through his disheveled hair. Eight years. He'd waited eight years and it finally happened. Ramsey fully opened up to him and he relished the fact he smelled of vanilla, just like her.

It was Sean and Cali's wedding day, and he knew he was going to be busy most of the morning and afternoon, so he quickly hopped in the shower before everyone else started to wake up. Once he was back in the room he shared with Ramsey, he put on a pair of denim jeans and slipped a plain white t-shirt on when someone knocked on the door. If it was Ramsey, she would have barreled inside in true Ramsey fashion. He opened the door thinking it might be Sean but was surprised to see Ramsey's mother on the other side.

"Good morning, Nico," Anne smiled, but it didn't stretch far, "I hope I'm not disturbing you."

Nico shook his head, "Not at all, Mrs. Price, what can I do for you?"

"Everyone is busy with getting ready for the wedding and I was hoping you might be able to help me in the kitchen."

"Sure," he followed her out of the room, shutting the door behind him.

They walked silently through the house. Anne was right, everyone was running around trying to get ready for the wedding. Guests would be arriving within the next couple of hours, so he was glad he got up early to get dressed. Once they entered the abandoned kitchen, Nico looked at the counter he'd placed Ramsey to kiss her and smiled. That girl. Would she ever understand the spell she had him under?

Anne cleared her throat drawing his attention.

"What did you need help -"

"What are your intentions with my daughter?" Anne interrupted him, standing on the opposite end of the butcher block island.

Nico straightened to his full height and said, "I love your daughter, Mrs. Price. I have loved her for a very long time, and I intend to do everything I can to make her happy."

Anne stared at him skeptically. What was she thinking? Now he knew where Ramsey got that expressionless glare from. It was nerve-wracking when Ramsey did it. But Anne was terrifying. Did she not believe him? Maybe she suspected they weren't a real couple and was waiting to lower the boom on him.

"My daughter isn't one to show a lot of emotion," Anne interrupted his thoughts and her gaze softened. "She was raised to be tough and I'm glad she's independent and has a no-nonsense attitude, but sometimes I can't help but feel like my husband and I didn't let her explore her emotions enough. That she felt to be a Price, she had to be like one of her brothers. I worried for years that she would never find a husband, not because she isn't worthy, but because she was not your typical female prospect. I pushed Ramsey to find a partner because I wanted to make sure if something happened to me or her father, she wouldn't be alone."

Anne poured herself a cup of coffee and offered Nico a mug. He gratefully accepted it and sipped the steaming beverage as she continued.

"I have been hard on her. I know I have. But all of her brothers have someone," Anne puffed a breath out and rolled her eyes. "Well, I suppose not Phineas. Thank God he sent that bimbo home."

Nico spit his coffee out and laughed.

"What?"

"I just haven't heard you call anyone outside their name before." He smiled.

Anne chuckled; a small smirk snaked across her face. "She wasn't good enough for my Phineas. I'm glad she's gone."

"Why are you telling me all this?" Nico met her gaze and her typically icy grey eyes were a vibrant blue.

"I think you are the perfect match for Ramsey. You challenge her, you push her to express herself, and I know for certain you make her happy." She rounded the island and rested her hand on Nico's shoulder. "I hope one day soon we'll be officially welcoming you to the Price family, Nico." Kissing his cheek, Anne left the kitchen with her coffee in hand. Nico could hear her ordering a few of her sons around, making sure everything was perfect for the ceremony, and he laughed as he caught a glimpse of what Ramsey would be like in the future.

Thirty-Two

RAMSEY

"You look stunning," Ramsey took a step back from Cali and admired the bridal ensemble. She'd been there the day Cali picked everything out and thought she couldn't look any better, but her future sister-in-law once again surprised her with her beauty.

"You think so?" Cali slowly turned around with a smile. The strapless sweetheart gown boasted a tulle A-line skirt and had lace and beaded applique from the waist up. Her long veil and beaded headband framed her face and looked perfect over her curled brown hair.

"Sean might faint when he sees you," Ramsey teased which drew a laugh from Cali. She could tell the bride was nervous and the best way to ease Cali's anxiety was to make her smile. She took Cali's hand in hers and squeezed.

"You don't hate me for making you wear blue?" Cali asked with a sheepish grin.

Ramsey ran a hand down the chiffon, floor-length dress and smiled. Even though she never would have looked twice at the off-the-shoulder gown, it was a beautiful ocean blue and complimented both Ramsey's complexion and her eyes perfectly, so she really couldn't complain. Plus, if anyone was going to convince her to stray from her typical black, grey, white, and occasional red color pallet, it would be Cali.

"I could never hate you, Cali," Ramsey wrapped her arms around her future sister-in-law and tugged her close.

A knock on the door jarred them both; the voice on the other side belonged to one of Ramsey's favorite people and brought a smile to her face.

"It's me, may I come in?" William was there to walk Cali down the aisle since her parents were unable to make it. When Ramsey opened the door and he caught sight of the bride he put a hand to his chest, a tear in his eye. "Cali, you look beautiful."

Cali's bottom lip quivered, and Ramsey handed her a tissue to pat around her makeup. "Thank you, Mr. Price."

"It's William." He offered his arm and she accepted.

Ramsey took a deep breath before the string quartet began to play, signaling the ceremony had begun. She was going to walk down the petaled aisle and wait for Cali at the floral archway just like they'd rehearsed the night before. Once the music started, she stepped out on the back patio and all eyes turned toward her. Her gaze found her brother, Sean, and he was beaming. She wasn't a romantic by nature, but she knew Cali made him happy and seeing her older brother, her best friend, find his other half made her heart leap. He was so deserving of happiness, and she was grateful to be there to witness them vow to love one another for the rest of their days.

A click of a camera snapped her from her thoughts, and she saw Nico at the end of the aisle, crouched in front of Sean. He took a few more pictures of her before meeting her gaze. His smile melted her insides and she wished she could run to him and whisper she loved him too. But he slipped out of the aisle to make way for her and continued snapping photos of guests and the ceremony. She made fun of him before about loving photography but having seen the one photo he'd taken of her that was proudly displayed on her dad's desk, she realized he actually had talent. She couldn't wait to see the film from today's festivities.

As Cali walked down the aisle, arm wrapped around William's, Ramsey couldn't help but notice how fearless the bride looked. She never liked all eyes on her, but Cali wasn't looking at anyone but Sean. When she glanced at her brother, she saw him mouth, "You look beautiful."

What was happening to her? Ramsey swiped a tear that slipped down her cheek. Ramsey Price never cried at weddings. She hardly cried period. A week ago, Nico would have joked that the Grinch must have had a heart after all, but when she searched for him amongst the guests, she saw he was already watching her with a smile on his face. *That man.* He had broken down her walls brick by brick and all she could think about was feeling his arms wrap around her waist and nuzzling her face in the crook of his neck.

The traditional vows were exchanged and just like that, the ceremony was over, and the reception was beginning. Guests carried their chairs to the family style table and took turns visiting the impressive buffet spread; buttered lobster tails, glistening oysters, garlic seasoned fish, salad, freshly baked rolls, desserts galore. Anne had truly outdone herself in picking out the catered food.

Nico spent most of the reception snapping photos of the bride and groom along with their guests and she couldn't help but smile anytime he noticed her and winked at her from across the yard.

Ramsey filled a plate with all the seafood delicacies and turned to find a spot to sit when she spied her brother, Phineas, seated at one end of the table by himself, nursing his beer. He looked miserable; his tie was loosened, and his suit jacket was thrown haphazardly behind the back of his seat. There was a fifty-fifty shot if she went and sat next to him, he'd tell her to piss off, but despite their constant bickering, and long stretches of not speaking, she loved her brother and wanted him to be happy. She was willing to risk his wrath if it meant having the chance to talk with him privately.

Weaving through the sea of smiling faces, Ramsey slowly approached the table. Taking the unoccupied seat next to him, Phineas didn't even bat an eye or give any indication he'd noticed her. After a minute of silence, she cleared her throat to grab his attention and thankfully it worked. He glanced over at her and nodded his head in greeting.

"You alright?" she asked, taking a sip of her beer.

Phineas leaned back in his seat, tapping his left foot. "I've been better."

"Look, about Melissa -"

He waved a hand stopping her from finishing that sentence. "I should have listened to you before. It's my fault."

"No, it's *her* fault, Phin." She snatched his hand in hers and squeezed. "You're a great guy and she doesn't deserve you."

He met her gaze and huffed. "You tried to warn me months ago and I didn't listen." He shrugged taking another swig of his drink and snatched the roll off her plate. "I know we had our problems, but I guess I put up with her because I didn't want to be alone. How pathetic is that?"

Ramsey shook her head, taking a bite of her fish, "Not pathetic at all."

Phineas scanned family and friends dancing and pointed at their parents swaying back and forth. "I would kill to have what mom and dad have. What Sean and Cali have. Hell, even what you and Nico already seem to have."

"What's that?"

"Love." His answer takes her by surprise.

"Phineas -"

"When I see the way you and Nico look at each other..." He squared his shoulders to her, and she froze, her fork midway to her mouth. "I'm happy you two have each other."

"Phin -"

"I mean it, Rams. I wish Melissa looked at me the way Nico looks at you. Or how mom looks at dad." He twiddled his fingers between his knees.

"You'll find her one day," Ramsey said.

"I've been in relationships since I was fifteen years old. The longest period of time I've gone being single has been maybe a couple of months tops." Phineas rolled his shoulders back, sitting up straighter. "I think this will be good for me. Maybe the next woman I date will end up being the right one."

They sat quietly for another minute. She allowed him to swipe the lobster tail from her plate and they ate in silence, watching their parents dance and listening to Cali laugh at something Sean whispered in her ear.

"I know we've had our differences in the past," Ramsey turned toward her brother and smiled, "but I hope we can be friends."

"Rams, we've always been friends. You're my annoying little sister." Phineas smirked, "And even if I wanted to, I couldn't get rid of you. You're far too stubborn to let that happen."

She swatted his arm and laughed. She couldn't remember the last time she and Phineas had just sat and talked or joked with one another. With Melissa gone, maybe they could rekindle their lost friendship and that made her happier than she thought it would.

Ramsey stood up and extended her hand to him. "How about you dance with your annoying little sister?"

"I would," he grimaced, standing up and towering over her, "but I think someone else would enjoy that more."

She folded her arms across her chest. "Phineas Cornelius Price, dance with me."

Phineas wiggled his eyebrows, staring at someone behind her. When she turned around, Nico was standing there, hands buried in his pockets, sleeves rolled up to his forearms, with a smile on his face. "Are you sure you're prepared to deal with Ramsey's bossy ass for the rest of your life?" Phineas teased Nico and Ramsey smacked his chest.

Nico's eyes were still on Ramsey when he nodded and said, "I think I can handle her." He stretched his hand out to her and she happily accepted it as he led her to the dance floor.

She'd been wanting to talk to him all day about what she and her dad had discussed that morning. How he'd named his bar after her, how he'd been taking candid photographs of her, how he'd been showing her how much he loved her for years and she never noticed. But as soon as he wrapped his arms around her and pulled her to his chest to sway to the slow music everything she'd rehearsed to say vanished. It felt right to be in his arms, to have his stubbled chin pressed against her temple. Silently, they danced together, soaking each other in. She loved the smell of his cologne and the hint of whiskey on his breath.

Oh, she was so far past the point of no return. She was in love. Crazy in love. And with Nico Giovanni, the man she thought hated her, or barely tolerated her, was the one she'd been waiting for her entire life.

"What are you thinking about right now?" he whispered.

Ramsey pulled back to look into his eyes and smiled. "How happy I am."

"For Sean and Cali?"

"Yes, but I meant, how happy I am with you."

Nico stilled, his hand resting on the small of her back twitched. "You mean that?"

She nodded. "Nico, there's something I've been wanting to ask you all day."

"You can ask me anything."

Mustering up the courage, ignoring all the butterflies in her stomach, she smiled up at him and asked, "Nico, did you name -"

"Ramsey?" The familiar cheerful voice sent a shiver up her spine.

Looking into Nico's surprised and worried gaze, she knew exactly who was standing behind her. It seemed as if the entire jovial party stopped, like no one wanted to miss the soap opera about to take place.

"David?" She turned around, meeting her ex-boyfriend's eyes. He flashed a dazzling, perfect smile as he approached her on the dance floor, snatching her hand in his and kissing her cheek.

"Surprised?" he asked.

"What are you doing here?" she said in a low voice, glancing around at everyone watching them.

"Ramsey?" Anne walked toward them, eyeing the newcomer suspiciously. "Who is this?"

David extended his hand to her, "I'm sorry for my tardiness, Mrs. Price. I'm David, Ramsey's boyfriend."

Ramsey wanted to run when she heard the gasps and whispers wash over the guests, but her feet refused to move. She reached her hand behind her to see if Nico was still standing there but didn't feel him, nor did he take her hand in his. She felt the panic creeping up her chest to her throat but if she dropped to the ground now, she'd be the talk of the town and the highlight of family newsletters for years.

"Ramsey?" Anne turned to her daughter, shocked but doing her best to still her features. "I thought you broke up with him. You're dating Nico."

"Nico?" It was David's turn to look surprised.

Even though they were outside, somehow Ramsey was feeling claustrophobic. She tried once more to reach for Nico, but when she risked a quick glance behind her, he wasn't there.

"David, can we -"

"Ramsey," David interrupted with a confident air about him, drawing the attention of the gossiping guests, "I've done a lot of thinking the week we've been apart and realized you were right to threaten to break up with me. I thought I needed to wait until I was forty before proposing, but I know now that I want you in my life. I need you in my life. You helped me become the man I am, and I think I'm ready to officially make you mine."

"David, wait -" Her pleas were ignored again as her ex-boyfriend got down on one knee and smiled up at her.

"Ramsey Elizabeth Price," he said her name like it was a reverent prayer. "Would you make me the happiest man in the world and marry me?" Ohs and ahs catapulted around the reception and Ramsey once again searched the crowd for Nico. Her eyes met Sean's and there was a sadness in them that made her want to sob.

Nico left. Why had he left? She was just about to ask him about his bar, about the pictures, about how he felt about her and confess her love for him.

"Ramsey?" David drew her back to him kneeling, flashing an enormous solitaire diamond in a Tiffany's box, and the reason for Nico's disappearance smacked her in the face.

He left because he thought that's what she wanted. Because she was going to get the diamond engagement ring from the man she'd been planning to spend her life with for last two years. But everything had changed that week. Nico happened and there was no going back to the woman she used to be. The woman she pretended to be. Only when she was faced with the choice of the perfect man or the perfect man for her, did she finally understand those men weren't the same.

"David, can we talk in private?" she tugged at her ear as she whispered her request.

"Um, yeah," he stuttered, and it made her heart ache. "Sure." He snapped the ring box shut and stood, quickly following her up the back porch steps and disappearing into the house.

Thirty-Three

RAMSEY

To escape the prying eyes and ears from the wedding guests, Ramsey ushered David into the first available room that would give them privacy. Her heart was racing in her chest. She still couldn't believe David crashed her brother's wedding to propose to her. The pain that flickered in Nico's face when he saw David standing on the dance floor nearly ripped her heart out of her chest.

"Everyone seems really surprised to see me," David started the conversation as Ramsey shut the door to the library.

She turned around, pressing her back against the door coming face to face with the billiards table where she and Nico made love the night before. The room screamed of Nico, and it seemed wrong to be standing in here with her ex-boyfriend instead of him. Like this was now their sacred place and it was tainted with the most recent ghost of her past.

"David," she whispered, unsure of what to say. For years she'd wanted David to propose to her, hell, she'd even given him an ultimatum. She'd wanted to be Ramsey Miller so badly but after the last few days she realized he wasn't the right person for her.

"What was all that commotion about you having a boyfriend named Nico?" he asked, his eyes searching her face for answers. His normally jovial face was sullen, so she took a step toward him.

"Nico is my brother's best friend." Ramsey admitted, he deserved an explanation. "When we got here, my mother was asking about you and I panicked at the thought of her trying to set me up all weekend, so I lied and said I was dating Nico. He agreed to pretend to be my boyfriend for the wedding, but..."

"You fell in love with him."

Ramsey nodded and wrapped her arms around herself. "David, if we hadn't broken up, I probably would have said yes to your proposal."

"But?"

"But we would have been miserable together."

David looked wounded and she clarified, "You are a wonderful man, just not the right man for me. I'm sorry you came all this way to hear that."

He clicked his tongue, staring off into space. "So, this is what this feels like?"

"What feels like?"

His blue eyes met hers and he offered a weak smile. "Rejection."

"I'm sorry, David."

Running his thumb over the ring box, he shrugged. "You see spending the rest of your life with this Nico?"

With tears filling her eyes, Ramsey nodded. "I do."

"Well," David approached her, sticking the engagement ring in his pocket, "I hope he makes you happy. You deserve that, Ramsey."

She wrapped her arms around his neck and kissed his cheek. "You do too, David," she whispered. "I hope you find her one day."

He squeezed her and sighed. "Please offer your brother and his wife my congratulations and apologize to your parents for my intrusion."

"You're welcome to stay -"

David shook his head and kissed her forehead. "I have a plane to catch."

Ramsey stepped out of his way and let him open the door to walk out of not only her childhood home, but out of her life.

"Ramsey?"

She faced him, "Yeah?"

"Make sure you remind him every day how lucky he is to have you. Take it from the guy who took you for granted and lost you." Without waiting for her to respond, David slipped out of the library, and she didn't move until she heard the front door open and click closed.

A part of her would always miss David. After all, she intended to spend the rest of her life with the man. But once her eyes were opened to what true love and affection felt like, once she experienced being at the forefront of a man's thoughts and motivations, she was ruined from going back to the life she thought she wanted.

Once she took a few minutes to collect herself, Ramsey rejoined the reception festivities in her parents' backyard, but as she scanned the guests dancing, eating, and laughing, she still didn't see the one face she was dying to find.

"He's gone," Anne said, standing next to her.

"Who?"

"Your boyfriend, or should I say, your fake-boyfriend." Her mother met her nervous gaze but instead of disappointment she saw sadness. "I'm sorry, dear."

"I'm the one who should be apologizing to you." Ramsey squared her shoulders to her mother's. "I'm the one who lied to you about Nico. This is all my fault," she rubbed her palm against her forehead. Nico was gone. Her mother had said so. He must have thought she'd choose David over him and left so it wouldn't be awkward for her. Damn that man.

Anne snatched her daughter's hands in hers and squeezed until Ramsey looked at her. "If I hadn't pushed you so hard to find someone to spend your life with, you wouldn't have felt it necessary to lie to me about your dating life. I'm sorry, Ramsey. I was just so worried about what would happen to you if you never found someone that I ruined our relation-ship."

Ramsey slipped her arms around her mother's neck and pulled her close. She couldn't remember the last time she initiated hugging her mother, and it brought tears to her eyes. "Mom, is it too late for us to start over?"

Anne pulled her back and smiled as Ramsey swiped a tear from her face. "It's never too late, my darling girl. But we'll start over tomorrow. Tonight, you need to go after Nico."

"But you said he left."

"Don't tell me that will stop you from bringing him home." Anne pursed her lips and arched an eyebrow. "The Ramsey Price I raised wouldn't back down from a challenge." Her mother dangled her car keys in front of Ramsey's face and with a determined smile, she snatched them and ran to the garage.

Ramsey tried calling Nico's phone, but it went straight to voicemail. He was either ignoring her calls or his phone was dead. Hesitation and doubt creeped in her mind, wondering if she'd already lost him by not rejecting David publicly. Maybe he didn't want to see her again. Maybe she should let him go if that's what he really wanted.

No.

She rattled those thoughts free and stabbed the key into the ignition of her mother's sports car. She stopped. Flashes of the semi-truck smashing the sports car years ago crippled her. She couldn't do this. She couldn't drive this car. Stepping out of her mother's vehicle and slamming the door shut, she thought about dragging Sean or Phineas out to the garage and pleading with them to help.

You're the strongest person I know. Nico's words echoed in her mind, and she wanted so desperately to be the person he believed her to be.

Taking a deep, steadying breath, she once again started the car, and zipped down the driveway.

If she hurried, she'd be able to catch him before he hit the interstate. There was something she needed to say to him, and no fear would keep her from doing it.

Thirty-Four

Nico

Nico couldn't bring himself to watch the woman he loved accept a proposal from another man. He should have told her how he felt before it was too late. But he was more concerned on what she would think or if she would reject his advances that he froze when it came time to confess. At least he could take solace in the fact he tried his best to show her what he was willing to offer her.

A piece of him knew David wouldn't give her up that easily. Ramsey was incredible and she should be happy, even if she chose another man over him in the end. It didn't hurt less to know that she was most likely showing everyone the dazzling engagement ring that adorned her left hand and embracing her future husband. What had happened between them in the billiards room, what had happened between them in Maine in general, would be memories he'd cherish for the rest of his life, but he'd lost, and he'd have to live with that.

He would apologize to Sean when his friend came back to Philadelphia after his honeymoon with Cali about slipping out without saying goodbye, and by then, he would have figured out a way to move on from what could have been.

Nico had a general idea of how to get back to the interstate to head back to Philadelphia but weaving down the two-lane back roads had him second guessing himself. Maybe he'd missed a turn somewhere and was headed toward New Hampshire instead of in the right direction. He'd left in such a hurry, he hadn't realized he'd left his phone on silent from the wedding ceremony and when he tapped the screen to get directions, he saw he had four missed calls from Ramsey. It pained him to press the redial button, wondering what type of apology or excuse she was going to give him about choosing David over him, but he did it anyway. He couldn't help himself. It was Ramsey after all.

It only rang once before she picked up. "Nico?" Her voice was breathy, like she'd been running a marathon and was gasping for air.

"Is everything alright?" Nico asked, trying to keep his voice steady, though the lump in his throat burned. "I saw you called. I didn't realize my phone was still on silent from the ceremony."

"Where are you?" she asked, brushing over his explanation as if it didn't matter.

"I'm headed back to Philadelphia -"

"I know that," she interrupted him, panic rising in her voice. "Where are you on the road? How far from the house are you?"

Nico glanced around his whereabouts and noticed he was passing where they had a flat tire. "Remember where I had to change the tire? I just passed it."

"Pull over," she demanded.

"Rams -"

"Damn it, Nico, pull your truck over!"

Nico obeyed, pulling to the shoulder lane. "Ramsey, what is going on? Are you alright?"

Before she answered, he looked in his rearview mirror at a sports car screeching up behind him. The question of who the crazy driver was was answered a heartbeat later when Ramsey hopped out of the driver's side like she was on fire. Nico opened his door and stepped out, walking toward the bed of his truck.

"What the hell, Price?" He rested his arm against his vehicle when she stopped at the front end of her car. "You must have been driving like a maniac to catch up to me. You could have gotten hurt -"

"The Mythical Sea Breeze," she stood a few feet away from him, her hair loose and wild from her convertible ride. "It's an anagram for Ramsey Elizabeth Price, isn't it?"

Nico's eyes widened. "How did you...?

"Yes or no."

The way she looked at him sent a warmth surging through his entire body. She discovered his secret somehow. He thought he'd been rather clever when thinking of what to name his bar. His friends and even his family members couldn't understand why he'd chosen such a random name, seeing as they lived nowhere near the sea, but when he was doodling in a notebook, trying to figure out what to call it he thought of her. Of course, he couldn't outright name his bar after her without scaring her so he mixed up the letters and, although he couldn't use a couple letters, the *Mythical Sea Breeze* was born, and he never looked back.

"How long have you been in love with me, Nico?"

"Eight years, two months, and three days."

Ramsey stared at him, not at all surprised by his confession, as if she already knew the answer and just wanted to hear him admit it out loud.

"I turned him down," she said as a car zipped by them, wafting her hair and dress in the wind.

It took Nico a second longer than he would have liked to admit to realize what she was trying to tell him. "You turned down his proposal? Why?"

Ramsey smirked, tears filling her blue-grey eyes. "You're too smart to say something that stupid." He'd said the same thing to her when they were in her bedroom deciding if they should go through with her crazy plan of pretending to date. "I have one dare left," her voice sliced through the memory, and he met her hopeful gaze.

Nico smiled. "What's your dare, Price?"

"I dare you to stay." With those five words, Ramsey Price had torn down her walls and finally let him in. He gripped the railing of his truck bed, steadying his weakening knees. "Let's do this for real, Nico."

Nico found his bearings and took a few steps forward. "Is that what you want?" He smirked as she met him between their cars. "This girl I know has told me multiple times that I'm a pain in her ass."

"And you are," she rested her hands on his chest. "But I love you anyway."

If his heart had feet, the organ would have leapt for joy hearing those words come from her mouth. "You love me, Price?" He slithered his arms around her waist and pulled her close to him.

"Almost as much as I love American History," she wiggled her eyebrows, making him laugh.

"I love you too, Ramsey," he leaned down and kissed her softly. "You know what would make this moment perfect?" he asked as he pulled an inch away from her.

She brushed strands of hair from his face, "What?"

"If you'd sing the National Anthem for me," he flashed an impish grin and she swatted at his chest.

"You brute," she cooed. "If you think I'm going to let you get away with that just because I told you I loved you, you have another thing coming, Nico Giovanni -"

Nico kissed her again, swallowing any further insults she was set to spew. He smiled against her lips.

It had taken eight years, two months, and three days, but Ramsey Price was finally his and he wasn't letting her go.

Epilogue

Nico woke up early February 22nd, not just because it was his and Ramsey's six-month anniversary, but because it was also Ramsey's birthday, and he had a special day planned for them. He'd convinced her, by the grace of God and by sheer stubbornness, for her to take the day off so he could do something nice for her. She wasn't one to celebrate her birthday, but in Nico's family, birthdays were a big deal and should be celebrated.

He kissed her gently on the forehead, turned her alarm off so she could sleep in a few extra minutes, slipped out of his room, and went to work making her favorite breakfast: Belgian waffles, sliced strawberries, and coffee with hazelnut creamer.

Ramsey begged him to tell her what he had planned, but he refused to tell her. Nico was stubborn, but Ramsey was relentless, so he finally broke down the night before and told her he planned for them to do a Tourist Day around

Philadelphia. This was the city where he was born and raised and knew it like the back of his hand, especially since he did all the tourist activities during field trip days at school. Ramsey wasn't a local, and she happened to be the biggest history lover he knew, so he figured taking her to all the historical sites, eating Philly cheesesteaks from a street vendor, walking through the parks, and riding the trolly would put a huge smile on her face and score him endless points as the best boyfriend.

As he was plating their breakfast and pouring creamer in their cups of coffee, Ramsey shuffled out wearing just his shirt. He was reminded of the first time she'd spent the night at his apartment, and he smiled knowing she was now his.

"Happy birthday!" Nico rounded the kitchen counter, wrapped his arms around her, and kissed the tip of her nose. "I made your favorite."

Ramsey grinned, squeezing her arms around his neck. "You're the best, Nico Giovanni."

Reluctantly releasing her from his embrace, he ushered her to the four-seat dining table and pulled out her chair. She protested, saying she could help him set the table, but he shook his head and insisted she let him spoil her. Once she conceded and slipped into her seat, Nico grabbed everything from the kitchen and placed it in front of the birthday girl.

Her eyes rolled back as she sniffed his birthday breakfast offering. "It smells so good!"

"Let's hope it tastes as good as it smells," he wiggled his eyebrows as he sat across the table from her.

Nico watched as she dug into the meal he'd prepared for her and couldn't help but feel grateful that the stars had aligned, and she'd agreed to date him. Sometimes he had to pinch himself to make sure he wasn't stuck in one of his dreams and was thrilled each time he felt the surge of pain zip through his body, reminding him that this was all real.

She must have felt his eyes on her because she looked up at him through her lashes and smiled. "So, what exactly do you have planned for me today?"

He shrugged a shoulder and took a sip of his warm coffee. "You'll have to wait and see. I've already told you too much."

"You told me it's a Tourist Day," she huffed with a small laugh, shoving another bite of waffle into her mouth. "I need to know what to wear."

"Something warm and something comfortable to walk in." Nico chose his words carefully, he still wanted some of their activities to be a surprise.

"Alright, Giovanni, you win this one." She lifted her mug and blew the steam off the top, "When do I need to be ready?"

"As soon as you finish breakfast and get dressed, we can go."

Ramsey got ready faster than he'd ever seen her get ready before. She was acting like a kid on Christmas morning and his heart was bursting in pride. He only hoped she enjoyed being a tourist with him as a tour guide.

She tugged her black peacoat tighter, sinching the belt around her waist. Plopping her Phillies baseball hat on, slipping on her sneakers, and making sure she didn't leave the apartment without her favorite watch, the two of them set off.

They spent the next several hours exploring the Independence National Historic Park, the Reading Terminal Market, Independence Hall, and they even made it through the Philadelphia Museum of Art, racing up the seventy-two "Rocky Steps". Ramsey beat him fair and square, but he claimed he let her win because it was her birthday and knew that would get a reaction out of her.

During their outing, he kept snapping candid photos of her because she had always been his secret muse and now, he could freely photograph her happiest moments and be one of the reasons she smiled.

"Are you going to be taking pictures of me all day, Nico?" She giggled when he laid on the sidewalk to snap her walking with her hands buried in her coat pockets.

"I've been taking your picture for years, babe." He stood up and winked. "Now I don't have to be secretive."

"That's creepy, Giovanni." She slithered her arm in his when he offered it.

"You still chose to date me," he teased.

"I did."

"Any regrets?" he asked, and she shook her head.

"None," Ramsey smiled. "I'm happy."

And Nico was happy too. "We're almost finished with our tour. There's just a couple things left that I want to show you."

"Lead away, Giovanni."

After eating their deliciously cheesy Philly Cheesesteaks, they made their way to the one place Nico was anxious to take Ramsey: The Liberty Bell.

Ramsey stood quietly observing the cracked bell until she finally read aloud the inscription. "Proclaim LIBERTY Throughout all the Land unto all the Inhabitants Thereof." She glanced at Nico and smiled. "Thank you for bringing me here. I've always wanted to see it for myself but never made the time."

He returned her grin and exhaled a nervous breath. Reaching for her hand, they walked through the rest of the museum until they were standing in front of the Love sign in Love Park. He bumped her hip with his, drawing her attention.

"You know I have one dare left," he chuckled when she rolled her eyes in response.

"No way. You used all your dares already."

Nico shook his head and ticked his fingers as he rattled his list off. "I dared you to sing in front of your family, I dared you to swim with me, and I dared you to race me to shore when we were kayaking. I didn't use my fourth one and I want to cash it in today."

"Oh, here we go." She rubbed her hand down her face, looking around the park to see if anyone else was around. "What's it going to be, Giovanni? You want me to streak? Or throw my hat on the ground and perform for pennies? Or maybe even -"

"I dare you to marry me," he blurted before he lost the nerve. Lowering himself to one knee, he slid the rose gold engagement ring out of his pocket and offered it up to her with a smile.

"Nico, are you serious?" Her eyes were wide, and she covered her mouth with her mittened hands.

"If you will let me," he said softly, "I swear I'll keep life interesting, and I promise to do my best to make you happy for the rest of our days."

Ramsey quirked an eyebrow, her eyes watering, "And I can crumple napkins and leave them around the bar whenever I want?"

Nico grimaced drawing a laugh out of her. "If that's what will make you happy, then yes, Price, you can leave a trail of napkins around the bar."

Ramsey knelt in front of him, slipping her hands around his face. "You won't be able to call me Price anymore."

"Does that mean you'll marry me?" he whispered.

"Yes, Giovanni," she nodded with a smile, leaning toward him. "I'll marry you."

Nico kissed her, slipped the mitten off her left hand, and slid the ring on her finger. "It was my grandmother's. I hope you like it."

Ramsey admired the Art Deco Marquise diamond and smiled. "It's beautiful."

"Did she say yes?" a voice cried out from around the corner followed by, "He hasn't given us the signal yet."

Ramsey glanced over Nico's shoulder, and he rolled his eyes. "I wanted it to be a surprise," Nico raised his voice so the hidden observers could reveal themselves, "but someone just couldn't help themselves."

"So, does that mean we can come out now?" a sheepish voice asked and realization of who it was hit Ramsey and she kissed Nico's cheek.

"You can come out now, Patrick," Ramsey said.

But it wasn't just Patrick who Nico had invited. The entire Price family, Poppy, and even members of the Giovanni family emerged from bushes and from behind trees, bundled up in their winter finest, and congratulated the newly engaged couple. Nico knew how important family was to both of them and thought it only fitting for them to be a part of celebrating Ramsey's twenty-seventh birthday as well as their engagement.

"Thank you," Ramsey kissed Nico's cheek, squeezing her hand in his. "This has been the best day of my life."

"This is just the beginning," he smiled.

Acknowledgments

First and foremost, I want to thank God. Without Him, I would be lost. I truly cannot believe this is my fourth book! Since I was a kid, I'd always dreamed of publishing my stories and I am so proud of everything I have accomplished, and I look forward to what's coming next!

To my husband and best friend, Brad. Thank you for every bit of encouragement, support, and love you send my way. Without you, I would have given up on my dream years ago.

To my daughter, Remi, thank you for telling me how much you love me. You will never know how much that means to me.

To my son, Archer, thank you for your hugs throughout the day. They are my favorite interruptions.

To my daughter, Roux, thank you for bringing all the sass and smiles. It fueled me.

To my Mom and Dad, for all your love and support. Thank you for encouraging me to read and write from such an early age.

To my friends Pier, Gabbie, and Hazel. Thank you for reading bits and pieces of this book in its raw form and for hyping me up! I appreciate your friendship and encouragement and I am so happy you loved The Maine Attraction (especially Nico)!

To everyone reading this. I appreciate YOU! Thank you for your support and for reading (and hopefully loving) my work.

For my Fantasy fans, *The Raven and the Wolf* (the third and final book in the *Mark of the Hunter Trilogy*) is coming out April of 2023.

For my Contemporary Romance fans, keep your eyes peeled for news regarding the second book in *The Philadelphia Chronicles Trilogy*, featuring Poppy and her quest for finding Mr. Right!

ALSO BY MORGAN

Fantasy

Wolves of Adalore (2021)

The Red Maiden (2022)

The Raven and the Wolf (2023)

Contemporary Romance

Aloha, Seattle (2021)

The Maine Attraction (2022)

About Author

Morgan Gauthier lives in East Tennessee with her husband and best friend, Brad, and their three children, Remi, Archer, and Roux (who are 5 years old and younger!). If five people wreaking havoc in the same house wasn't enough, Morgan also has three dogs, Potter, Skye, and Bubba.

In addition to contemporary romance, Morgan also writes Fantasy, and you can read her YA Epic Fantasy: *The Mark of the Hunter Trilogy* now!

If Morgan isn't writing or reading, she can be found binge watching Netflix shows, attempting to cook like Gordon Ramsay (not even close to his level), and practicing archery.

You can follow her on:

Instagram: @authormorgangauthier
Facebook: @authormorgangauthier
Pinterest: @authormorgangauthier
TikTok: @authormorgangauthier
Goodreads/Amazon: Morgan Gauthier

CPSIA information can be obtained
at www.ICGtesting.com
Printed in the USA
BVHW051458111022
649158BV00006B/812

9 781736 828298